So why was someone phoning her in the middle of the night? She grabbed the handset, Robin's dying eyes still in front of her. She was shaking so much she could hardly speak.

'Kate? Kate? It's Zenia here. Zenia from next door.'

She must have managed some sort of reply.

'Are you all right, girl? Only we heard this screaming – wondered if you needed any help?'

'Oh. Oh, Zenia. I'm so sorry. I must have yelled in my sleep. I was having this dreadful dream ... Did I wake everyone? Oh, I'm so sorry.'

'Well, I'll tell my Joesph he doesn't have to break in and rescue you. You're sure you don't want me to come round, now, love?'

'Sure. Yes, quite sure. I'll go and get some hot milk or something. Then I shall be all right.'

She would. But Robin was gone, dead and gone as poor Edward Read.

Power Games

Judith Cutler

NEW ENGLISH LIBRARY
Hodder & Stoughton

Copyright © 2000 by Judith Cutler

The right of Judith Cutler to be identified as the Author of the
Work has been asserted by her in accordance with the Copyright,
Designs and Patents Act 1988.

First published in Great Britain in 2000 by Hodder and Stoughton
First published in paperback in 2001 by Hodder and Stoughton
A division of Hodder Headline

A NEL Paperback

10 9 8 7 6 5 4 3 2 1

A CIP catalogue record for this title is available from the
British Library.

ISBN 0 340 76824 X

Typeset by Palimpsest Book Production Limited,
Polmont, Stirlingshire
Printed and bound in Great Britain by
Clays Ltd, St Ives plc.

Hodder and Stoughton
A division of Hodder Headline
338 Euston Road
London NW1 3BH

To a man with hwyl

ACKNOWLEDGEMENTS

This novel could not have been written without the assistance of Andrew Howell, Graham Townshend, Nick Keane, Peter Leather, Ursula Pearce, Ann Levitt, Anna Meredith and David Symons who kindly shared with me their various areas of expertise.

I'd like to give especial thanks to Stephen Hayward, a wonderful coach who has been endlessly patient and encouraging on the courts of Billesley Indoor Tennis Centre, Birmingham. Apart from his hard work and commitment, he bears no resemblance to his fictional opposite number at Brayfield. Neither do any of the Billesley Centre staff.

Thank you all for your contributions, great or small.

Chapter One

—◆◆◆—

'Backhand: start low, end high. Backhand: start low, end high.' Kate's new mantra – if she were ever to get that ball over that net. More often than at present, at least. She continued to mutter it as she unlocked the car, slinging her kit on to the back seat. 'Backhand: start low, end high.' The tennis centre's car park was virtually empty. Well, it would be at eight in the morning.

Kate had started to play tennis again with two new police friends from her nick. Play again? Where were the skills she'd had at school? So here she was, just finishing her weekly seven o'clock session with a coach. And then straight to work.

If her car resented a sweaty driver, that was its problem, she told it as she tried to pull into the main road. Shower in a horribly communal area? With water as cold as it often was this early? No, she'd wait till she got to work, where serious trainers and a tracksuit that meant business wouldn't exactly lose brownie points.

By now her usual route into the centre of Birmingham would already be clogged up. So she took to the side roads – sorry, she didn't approve of rat-runs but there you are – tacking from one to another like a small boat against the wind. If it was slow going, at least she was moving. Next left up that steep hill. Then she came to a dead stop. A traffic jam *here*? And what were those people doing in the road? Abandoning the Fiesta with two wheels on the pavement, she hauled herself out. Hell, the joints were stiffening already! Grabbing her waterproof and bag from the back of the car, she ran to the source of the problem.

Not the predictable car-to-car clip. No, this was a big bang. A very big one. A lorry stuck cab-deep in a small cottage. No sign of fire service or ambulance yet. Kate radioed. And for good measure phoned to tell the boss she'd be late. Just in case.

A couple of men were already trying to reach the driver. An old couple in night clothes wrung their hands as they looked at the remains of their home. Not hurt by the look of it, but certainly shocked. And hanging round on a cold March morning would do them no good at all.

Kate grabbed a gawping neighbour, flashed her ID. 'Get them indoors if you can. Blankets, hot sweet tea.'

'Their budgie's still in there. They won't come in till it's all right.'

Jesus! 'Tell them it'll be the first thing I get, soon as I know the building's safe.'

The neighbour nodded. 'I'm at number fifty-three. We always knew something like this would happen. Letting big lorries loose on quiet residential roads like these ...'

'Quite—'

'They're from that big development up the road – they come tearing down the hill. We've always said there'd be an accident like this.'

'We'll talk about it in a minute. Meanwhile, please – just get them inside, Mrs—?'

'Hurst. Linda Hurst. Number fifty-three.'

'Thanks. See you later.'

Meanwhile back to the driver. Out of the tail of her eye, Kate saw the old couple being steered gently across the road. Good. And the familiar sirens were getting nearer.

The lorry driver was now on terra firma. 'It was the other side took it,' he was saying. 'The on-side, see. Or I'd be cold meat. Cold meat.'

He might have jumped down himself, but he couldn't shift from the spot. He stood pointing. 'Cold meat. Just cold meat.'

'Come on, sir,' Kate said. 'Let's get you away from here.

The brickwork's a bit dodgy. Come on. Over here.' She took his elbow, and drew him towards the ambulance now slewing to a halt. Right. All she had to worry about now was the budgie. First she'd better talk to Uniform. Who were here, two car-loads of them, hot on the tail of a fire appliance.

The first man out of the car was Guljar, a sergeant she'd met and liked her first week in the city.

'What are you stirring up this time, Kate?' he shouted. Then, as he took in the extent of the damage, he whistled. 'Bloody hell, what if there'd been a car in the way? Anyone in there?'

'Just a budgie. Which,' she added dryly, 'I've promised to get out.'

'Not yet you won't,' said a fire officer. 'No one goes in there till we know it's safe. You know: structure. Gas. Whatever.'

'I'll get someone to talk to the driver – soon as the paramedics say we can,' Guljar said.

'He doesn't seem badly hurt – he got himself out, at least,' Kate said. 'As did the old couple who live here – they're at number fifty-three. With a Mrs Linda Hurst. And no budgie.'

'We'll go take a look round the back,' Guljar said. 'I take it some of your lads are round there already?'

The fireman nodded. But then looked up sharply. 'No one goes into the building. Right?'

'Right,' Guljar agreed, taking Kate by the arm and leading her down the side path. 'Wow, how about this for a garden! How long d'you reckon it is?'

'Fifty yards at least,' Kate said. 'It's perfect, isn't it?' That little greenhouse, all those fruit trees – they'd even got some espaliered on the end wall. 'God, what I'd give for something like this.'

'That lot there must drive them wild,' Guljar said, pointing at a patch of waste land next to their fence, big enough for three or four cottages. 'All those weeds coming through. I wonder why no one's ever built on it?'

One of the fire fighters overheard. 'Bomb damage, according to my dad. Took out two or three houses this size. And no one's ever done anything about it all these years.' He wandered over and pressed a boot into the earth. 'The ground's very wet, of course – maybe there are springs or something that would make it expensive to build on. Ted Roberts,' he added, addressing himself to Guljar and the stripes on Guljar's sleeve.

'Guljar Singh Grewal. And this is Kate Power – a DS, for all she looks like a refugee from a health farm.'

Roberts looked her up and down without obvious enthusiasm.

'Been playing tennis,' she said by way of an explanation. 'What do you reckon about this lot?'

They made their way to the back door. It was still ajar. On the gas stove, a kettle steamed beside a jet still going at full blast; on another jet porridge was burning. Kate could hear the budgie chuntering to itself, though there was no sign of it in the kitchen. No chance of a quick dash, then.

'Seems as if the gas main's OK,' she said.

'Pity we can't say the same for the structure,' Ted said, pointing.

The rectangle of the door-frame was now a parallelogram.

'When that lorry comes out – rumble, rumble, splat,' he added.

'What about hydraulic lifts? Come on, it's someone's home,' Kate said.

'Rebuilding would cost an absolute bomb. And is it insured? You know what old people are like, thinking they can't afford insurance.'

'The lorry driver must be insured. His firm, at least,' Guljar said. 'And I shall want to have a word about the amount of rubble in the truck. A little trip to a weighbridge, I should think. And I'd like a look at his brakes. He must have come down the hill like an aries.' He gave it three syllables.

'Eh?' Kate and Ted gaped.

'Sorry. My A level Latin will keep rearing its ugly head. It means sheep.'

'Ah!' said Kate, clutching her forehead. 'As in Aries, the birth sign?'

'Right. An aries was a Roman battering ram. Ram, ram
– geddit?'

They groaned.

'He's lucky to be alive,' Ted agreed. 'Like you, come
to think of it, if you make jokes like that very often.'

The budgie embarked on 'Frère Jacques'.

Ted looked hard at Kate. 'I'll just go and tell the gaffer
about the gas stove.'

The moment he was out of sight, Kate stripped off
her jacket.

Guljar looked hard at Kate. 'You can't: not for one sodding cage-bird. Wait till they've got the hydraulics in.'

'Budgies don't like noise. It can give them strokes
and kill them. That guy Ted – he left us on our own
deliberately.'

'Come on, Kate – think about it. Putting your life at
risk for a bird.'

'Trouble is, Guljar, if I think about it I won't be able
to do it.'

Kate sidled in, praying she didn't have to push on any
internal doors. If she did, she'd turn back, she promised
herself. The door from the kitchen to the hall was open.
She slid through, ending up a foot from the truck's front
bumper, which was blocking the stairs. As she paused,
plaster fell on her hair.

To her left, another door. The lintel looked sound. She
risked a gentle push. And waited. No, no movement. She

darted in. The cage was on a stand next to a Victorian upright piano, over by the back window. The piano was a forest of photos in frames. She grabbed a cushion, shook the cover off, and stowed as many photos inside as she could carry. In an ashtray on the grate glittered an engagement ring with a trio of pitifully small diamonds. She slipped it into a jacket pocket.

Plaster pattered in the hall. The patter turned into a rush.

She stood stock still.

'Give us a kiss! Come on, give us a kiss!'

She grabbed the cage, slung a crocheted shawl over it. Better keep the little thing warm. Back the way she'd come, then. No, not with the lintel creaking like that. The back window, then. That frame was creaking, too, but it still held. She shouldered it open – someone should have a word with the old couple about window locks – and passed Guljar the cage. There was a dreadful judder. The doorway to the hall was a giant rhombus.

She pulled herself through the frame. Guljar jumped her down and settled her on her feet. The plaster was falling quite briskly now. Time for her other booty? Just. If only her arm were longer!

Guljar flung her aside and grabbed the cushion cover. As he straightened, the glass in the adjoining window cracked and broke.

The frame still held – just.

He peered into the cushion cover. 'Fucking hell, Kate! All that for a few photos!'

'Mad, aren't I? Except that those few photos and that bloody bird are all they'll have to show for a whole lifetime. Come on, you'd better distract the firecrew and I'll sprint across the road. Come on, Joey.'

'Give us a kiss,' Joey suggested.

Mrs Hurst greeted Kate with a mouthed warning that Mr and Mrs Sargent were being difficult. She gestured her into the living room, hung with framed tapestries. It was immaculate apart from a ring of fur on the hearth rug. Mr and Mrs Sargent sat rigidly side by side on a sofa, their bare legs mottled with blue as they disappeared into slippers. A paramedic was literally on his knees, presumably trying to make them go for a check-up. A clutter of empty tea cups on a tray suggested that Mrs Hurst had at least persuaded them to have a drink. Tea was just what Kate needed at the moment, and she said so, loudly and brightly.

The Sargents looked up as one. And got to their feet as one.

Joey, unwrapped, bobbed at a mirror. 'Give us a kiss. What about a nice fly around?'

'You stay where you are, young Joey,' Kate said. 'I fancy Mrs Hurst has a cat.'

'I'll lock him in the conservatory,' she promised. 'And bring a clean cup.'

The bird still in its cage on Mrs Sargent's lap, the old people sat down again. 'He's Billy, dear,' she said. 'Billy, not Joey.'

'Sorry, Billy. Well, there's no kind way to say this, I'm afraid: the house is in a pretty bad way,' Kate said, sitting down. 'One of my colleagues will be round in a few minutes — they'll tell you more then. But when I was collecting Joey — *Billy* — I got these, too.' She opened the cushion cover. In their haste, either she or Guljar had cracked some of the glass.

Mrs Sargent looked at her husband. 'There used to be this radio programme. After the war. Wilfred Pickles. You remember, dear.'

'*Have a Go*, that's what it was called. He used to ask people what they'd save if their house was burning down. I always said if they ever asked me I'd say the family photos.'

Taking her hand from the cage, Mrs Sargent laid it on his. 'He was making me a cup of tea, dear, and starting the porridge. And I said he was taking all day and I came downstairs— And then, and then ...' She couldn't go on.

Kate drew Mrs Hurst quietly out. The paramedic followed. 'Best leave them on their own a few moments,' he said unnecessarily.

Mrs Hurst led the way into the kitchen. 'Poor things. Now, I've managed to get in touch with the daughter. She's got to come all the way up from Truro. So I'll keep them here, overnight if needs be.'

'Surely Social Services—'

'No. I'm not having them shoved into some sort of emergency accommodation. I don't know what it would be like and I don't want to find out. Old folk like that, who've always kept themselves to themselves. The very idea. And my Andrew – he's in insurance, so he'll be able to help sort out their claim.'

'Thanks: you're being more than kind. Look, I have to go off to work, now. Here's my card – if anything crops up during the day, give me a buzz. Otherwise I'll pop back this evening, if that's convenient, just to see they're still OK.'

Chapter Two

Kate was trying to persuade her legs, now embarrassingly stiff, to take her up the stairs two at a time when she heard someone running lightly down. Thank God – an excuse to wait a moment. Time to catch her breath after the sprint from the car park.

And to snap to something like attention. Not that Rod Neville ever demanded such behaviour in his office, but – in public at least – detective superintendents should be treated with visible respect.

'Goodness, Kate,' he said, coming to a swift halt, 'what on earth have you been doing? Rehearsing for the lead role in *The Snowman*?'

She rubbed her hand over her head. Plaster flakes. 'An RTA out my way, sir.'

He shook his head, as well he might. 'CID involved in

an RTA?' He leaned forward to pick another flake from her hair.

'Only till Uniform arrived, Gaffer.' She grinned. 'So long as not a word of this reaches our friends in the Fire Service — a lorry smashed into a house and I needed to effect a rescue.'

He frowned. 'I'd have thought a fire-fighter better equipped—'

'But their chief had forbidden entry — and there was this lone budgie . . .'

He shook his head and threw up his hands to silence her. 'No more, thanks. Or I shall have to bollock you for risking your life — for a budgie? Oh, Kate!' So it was more in sorrow than in anger.

She grinned, allowing, on this occasion, her dimples to show. 'All's well that ends well, Gaffer. But seriously I don't think the house will survive the removal of the lorry — this old couple, losing everything except each other—' She saw those mottled blue legs, those reddened hands.

'And their budgie. Well done. Now—' He flicked a glance at his watch.

She grinned again, sketched a salute, and set off up the stairs.

Hair still damp from the shower, and now in her usual self-imposed uniform of dark trouser suit, Kate gestured with the kettle. 'Tea or coffee, Colin? How did Rowley take my being late?'

'Tea. No problems: you had a pretty good excuse. Everyone safe?'

'Fine. But the local people will go over that lorry with the proverbial fine-toothed comb. How no one was hurt ... Both the old folk were in the kitchen. If they'd been in the hall—' She stopped, shuddering. 'And the truck driver was pretty lucky. He says he lost his steering and his brakes. But he ended up completely unscathed.'

'Lucky bugger. And lucky everyone else in his path!'

'Quite. Guljar Singh Grewal—'

'That handsome sergeant from Kings Heath?'

'The same. He'd love to do them for unsafe loads and overloading, because there's been a stream of complaints from the residents. There's a big building development – very posh houses – at the top of the hill that the lorry came down. Next to the cottages, now there's quite a big piece of ground. Lovely site for houses.'

'Do I sense a disenchantment with your own place? Oh, Kate, not after all the work you've put into it!'

'You should see their garden, the old folks', that is. And you should see mine. When it rains, it's beginning to remind me of the pictures you see of the Somme.'

'The *Somme*?'

'Big pits where they've dug out the sycamore roots,

the odd strand of barbed wire from an old fence, all that mud—'

'Why on earth didn't your aunt do something about the trees? She's no fool. She must have known where the roots would get.'

Kate shrugged. 'Goodness knows. And why did she let the house itself go so badly? She must have been so intent on stashing everything away for her old age she lost sight of the present.'

Colin shook his head. '*Carpe diem*, that's my motto. Enjoy today and let the pension look after tomorrow.'

'But if you didn't have much of a pension and your chief source of income was your married lover? Anyway, there she is, sitting on piles of money in that retirement oasis, and here I am, living in a house so changed she'd hardly recognise it, poor old dear.'

'And a garden that's a tip.'

'Well, if I survived the house being a tip, I can cope with the garden for a bit. Or so I tell myself.' She straightened. 'And the design your friend's suggested looks lovely.'

'I'm sure it will be. As will my coffee if you ever stop staring at that kettle.'

She flicked the switch to bring it to the boil again. 'Sorry. Anyway, I'd better let Rowley know I'm in.'

'She said to take your time.'

'Can you imagine the late but unlamented Detective Inspector Cope saying anything like that? You know, it's a real insult to people who've spent all their careers in uniform to have him punished by being put back into uniform.'

'Hmm. Must make them feel second rate. Trouble is, what could they have done with him? Apart from reducing his rank – which they've done anyway. He was a good cop in many ways.'

'And a nasty human being in many others.'

There was no doubt that life was better without Cope. For her, for Colin, and for Fatima, the young Asian DC. She herself would have survived. But Colin had always lived on eggshells: being a gay policeman was no one's idea of an easy life and Cope would almost certainly have made his life hell if the rumour had ever got that far. And his treatment of Fatima had been brutal. Almost as brutal as Selby's had been.

Cope had taken his punishment, but Selby had so far escaped. His sick leave had been extended twice already. Sick! The man might be sick in the head, but he was a vicious, idle bastard, for whom the words sexist and racist might have been invented. The thought of him sitting around unpunished, leaving the squad short-handed while drawing a detective constable's pay made her grind her teeth in rage.

'Thanks.' Colin took the mug but pulled a face. 'Is that all the milk there is?'

'Whose turn is it to bring it in?' She ran a finger down

the rota. 'Oh dear: Roper, C. Shall I cadge a cup from the canteen? I've got to grab a bite before I start.'

'Bananas, that's what you need. I've seen those blokes at Wimbledon stuffing the things.'

'And not amiss in a place like this monkey-house anyway,' came a voice from the door. 'Morning, Sergeant. It was cold, first thing.' Sue Rowley, the new DI, was a kindly-looking woman in her forties. Her sarcasm was far too mild to be threatening

'Morning, Gaffer. My tennis lesson. And then this RTA.'

'Sure. Everyone all right? Good.' DI Rowley nodded amiably enough. 'How's that dodgy knee coping with the tennis?'

'It likes it better than jogging, ma'am.'

'The medics said it would.' Rowley pulled her reading glasses further down her nose and peered at Kate's feet. 'You've got the right sports shoes?'

Kate nodded. Her stomach rumbled.

Rowley laughed. 'Go and get those bananas, then, Kate. And an apple for me, if you wouldn't mind. Oh, and while you're about it, better bring up some milk – seems the cow's on strike. Either that or young Roper here didn't notice he was rostered for this week.'

Colin flushed. 'Sorry, ma'am.'

'When you're fed and watered, I'd like to talk to you both. Ten-thirty?'

'Ten-thirty it is, Gaffer,' Kate said, grabbing her purse and heading downstairs.

Fatima was deep in conversation with Colin when she returned. She turned to Kate. 'Heard the news?'

'What's up?' Kate put the cup of milk with the rest of the tea things. 'Hang on: I'd better deliver this first.'

'Apple for teacher time.' Colin explained. 'The gaffer.'

Fatima stared at the apple. 'Ah! Currying favour!'

'God, that's awful!' Kate groaned.

Fatima stuck out her tongue.

Kate dodged out to Rowley's office. Seeing that Rowley was busy on the phone, she popped the apple on her desk, and withdrew.

'So have you heard this?' Colin resumed, as soon as she returned.

'The rumour is, changes,' Fatima said. 'In the squad.'

'More changes? I mean, we needed those we've had. But more?'

'At the top. Not us,' Fatima said.

'The top? You mean—'

'Graham Harvey. That's what the rumour is,' Fatima said.

'Not the sort of DCI that grows on trees,' Colin said.

'Absolutely,' Kate agreed tamely. She wasn't about to tell them that her stomach clenched tight at the thought of Graham's removal. He and Colin had made life bearable for her when she'd arrived in the autumn. Like Colin,

Graham had become a friend. But not the sort of friend that Colin was. No. 'So where's he off to?' Yes, her voice was perfectly level.

'To head up some new initiative or other,' Colin said, who would have told her later if it hadn't been.

'MITs,' Fatima said. 'That's the current term, isn't it? Major Incident Teams.'

'But they'll be called something else next week,' Colin said. 'I wonder if there's a Booker Prize for acronyms.'

'The idea is,' Fatima said, drawing herself up and speaking in a pseudo-official voice, 'that there'll be a full-time team of experienced officers, led by a senior officer, on stand-by to deal with any serious crime as and when the need arises. And,' she added, apparently getting bored with the lingo, 'they'll pull in anyone else to help if they want them. What happens to the work *they're* supposed to be doing . . .' She broke off to answer the phone.

'That'll get spread out amongst the plebs like me,' Colin said. He waited until Fatima was engrossed in the call to whisper, 'Well, Kate, this is your job: go and tackle Graham. Find out the truth.'

Refusing, in public at least, to rise to the bait, she smiled, tapping her watch. 'We'd better go and see what Rowley's got to say, hadn't we, Colin?' She flapped a hand at Fatima as they left.

All that remained of Rowley's apple was the stalk, apart

from the bits of skin stuck between her front teeth. What she needed was a toothpick, even a pin. As it was, she punctuated her sentences the whole meeting with irritated little sucks.

'Any news on that warehouse fire yet?' she asked, her lips undulating with the efforts of her tongue to shift the peel.

'Not yet, ma'am,' Kate replied. 'There's a meeting set up with the Fire Service and the insurance people for three this afternoon. I'll be able to report back to you after that.'

'That's official news. Anything from the streets?'

'It'd be nice if we could make my *Big Issue* seller into an official informant, wouldn't it?' she said. 'After that beating he took last year for talking to us, it's the least we can do for him. He'll get precious little from the Criminal Injuries Board.'

'He'd do better to sue the scrotes that did it,' Colin observed. 'He'll get Legal Aid, surely.'

'A little help now wouldn't come amiss, would it?' Kate pursued.

Rowley nodded. 'Put it on paper, Kate. But don't call him an informant. It's sarbut up here. And I tell you, though I hate to admit it, we don't often get women managing sarbuts.' She looked at Kate doubtfully.

'"Sarbut"?' Kate repeated.

'Brummie for informant,' Rowley grinned. 'Forgot you were a foreigner!'

Kate grinned to acknowledge the dig.

'I see him regularly anyway, ma'am. Every time I go to Sainsbury's, as it happens. He's got into a hostel in Moseley. It's easier for him to get to the Kings Heath pitch.' This was nothing like as lucrative as the Selly Oak Sainsbury's. It was a much smaller branch, for one thing, and the shoppers less affluent.

Rowley nodded as she made notes. 'I'll talk to them upstairs. But he'd have to come up with hard news, mind – not just bits of gossip from his mates. Being an informant isn't meant to be a thank-you for being good in the past, either,' she said, looking over her glasses with a frown. She gathered her papers. 'Right. And I suppose you two have heard the rumour, eh?'

'About DCI Harvey?'

'Who else? But as far as I know, it's no more than a rumour. Just a question of watch this space.'

Kate waited a second before she said, 'It'll put a lot more on you, ma'am, if they take away a DCI.'

'Well, that's the pattern, these days, isn't it? And not just on me – on you, too, Kate. Until you go flitting off somewhere on this accelerated promotion scheme you're on.'

Kate's turn to suck her teeth. 'Between the three of us, I'm having doubts about that.'

Sue Rowley looked at her shrewdly. 'Don't like the idea of fourteen-hour days, seven days a week?'

'I get enough of that anyway, don't I? And I'm studying for the next lot of exams, just in case I change my mind. But it's not the work that worries me. It's the nature of the work.'

'You prefer to lead from the front, not from behind a desk, don't you? Well, don't decide anything in a hurry, Kate. There's a lot to be said for catching all the experience you can get.'

'And for picking up the pay to match,' Colin said.

'As to that, the rate she's going, she'll make it to inspector soon enough. Time I was reaching for my slippers and my knitting,' Rowley sighed. 'Be off with you then. Time to fight a bit of this crime we're always hearing about. But don't fall over my Zimmer on the way out.'

Chapter Three

Kate was forcing those stiff joints and muscles to walk briskly back from the Fire Station when her mobile tweeted.

'That you, Kate? Alf here. I was wondering, could you get yourself back here before it gets dark tonight? Only I've found something in your garden you ought to see.'

She hunched into a doorway to cut the traffic noise.

'What sort of something?' she asked.

'Remains, like.'

'Remains! *Human* remains?'

'Not as such. Not a body, like. But it's something you should see before I clear the rest of this shed.'

'I'll try and be there by six,' she promised.

'See you at seven — that's what you mean, isn't it! No,

don't wait till it gets too dark. Go and tell your gaffer you're pursuing your inquiries or something.'

'Something nasty in the woodshed, Kate? How wonderful!' Graham passed her a mug of Darjeeling. 'Diamonds under your bedroom floor and now something nasty in the woodshed. I wonder what lies concealed in the other houses in Worksop Road ... Now – you don't have a house name, do you?'

She shook her head. He knew that as well as she did. She braced herself for the sort of laboured joke he made when he looked as tired as this.

'Well then, you could set a trend. Cold Comfort House.' He drifted over to the window.

She laughed obligingly. Should she risk a joke about finding a handsome, sexy Seth? No, perhaps not.

'So what do you reckon it is in your woodshed?' He turned to face her.

'So long as whatever it is doesn't involve coroner's officers and inquests, I don't care.'

'Well, you must care enough to get back in time to talk to Alf about it. Remember me to him, by the way. He did a grand job doing up my mother-in-law's house.'

Mrs Nelmes had sold up and moved into the same retirement home as Aunt Cassie, providing Cassie with an endless source of vindictive amusement. Especially now she'd discovered Graham's wife was burdened with the name of Flavia.

Kate nodded. 'He's a good man. Honest as the day is long.'

'All the more reason not to keep him waiting. You put in enough hours here not to worry about slipping off – provided, of course, that Sue Rowley's happy about it,' he added, smiling straight into her eyes. He poked a geranium cutting that had dried out too much. Wasn't it time they were planted up now?

'Thanks. The Fire Service people' – after all, this was what they were supposed to be talking about – 'are pretty well convinced there's an arsonist about, by the way. You remember that spate of school fires they had in the Black Country? We've got warehouse ones on our patch. Yesterday morning's was the third.'

'Any connections?'

Kate shook her head. 'Nothing in common apart from the fact that they're warehouses. One practically in West Bromwich, one in Selly Oak, one closer to home – Perry Barr, near the University of Central England. Chemicals – nothing toxic; fabric – that went up like the clappers; and household goods. Same modus operandi in each case – getting up on to the roof, prising open a roof-light, sprinkling petrol on to the floor below, and a rapid exit.'

'Bloody risky. In an explosion, the roof could go—' He gestured. 'Any theories?'

'Crazy kids playing chicken. But why are the sites so far apart? Highly mobile kids, if they are kids. And there's no car thefts to tie in with the arson. So how are they getting there? Taking a can of petrol on an all-night bus?'

'Or older kids with their own car? Are the warehouses all covered by the same insurance company?'

'Three different ones. Three different firms – no connection that we can see.'

How could she bring the conversation round to his departure? He was already looking at his watch. He drained his mug in one go.

'Come on, Kate – time you weren't here.'

'But it's only just after five and I can't see my desk for—'

'Come in early tomorrow. Stay late tomorrow. Only now,' he grinned, 'vamoose!'

It seemed as though all Birmingham were leaving work early to see what was under a garden shed. Plus every set of lights was at red, every yellow line had a parked car. But she got home at ten to six – nowhere to park nearby, of course, as she could have predicted. When at last she scooted up her entry she found several panels of the fence removed and an ominous blue plastic sheet where her shed had been.

Alf greeted her with a flap of the hand. 'Glad you got

back, Kate. Only I've never seen anything like this before. And I thought you, being in the police, ought to. You might know what to do. Oh, don't worry about those panels – it was just that it was easier for us to barrow out the last of the trees, see. Come on, aren't you going to have a look? I mean, there's nothing to be afraid of, not that you policewomen don't see nasty sights every day, of course.'

Despite herself, her hand was shaking as she lifted a corner of the heavy plastic. Fear of creepy-crawlies, she told herself, was a thing of the past, conquered by all that therapy. So it couldn't be that. Would it be something human so decayed that Alf could no longer identify it? No. There was no smell to alert him or her.

A burst of evening sun spotlit the ground. Amid the splintered wood – the ex-shed – were some bricks and some greenish discs.

Dropping to one knee, she touched one of the discs. 'Coins?'

'That's what I thought. I've got my heart set on a spot of treasure trove for you. But you have a closer look. They can't be English ones – all these funny patterns.'

Kate picked one up from the extreme edge of what she was already calling a site. Scrubbing it clean, she inspected more closely. 'Well, it's metal, all right ... No, it can't be gold ...? Coin of the realm it isn't. Wasn't.' She scraped a bit more soil free. 'But there is a crown! Look!'

'What about these, then?' Alf held out a smaller disc, quite plain.

Kate took it, turning it carefully. 'Hey, that's a shank.'

'And if you fit this to that – if you pressed this spare metal round here—'

'You have a button,' Kate concluded. 'Well, I'm blessed.'

'Some bone ones – here.' Alf dug in his overall pocket and held out three or four.

'You're right. Now, why should anyone want to leave all those buttons under my shed?'

Alf shrugged. 'Ask me another. You could do with getting that *Time Team* in.'

'Be nice to be on telly, wouldn't it? But they'd take months to get here, even if we could interest them in the first place.'

'Do you want me just to dig everything up so I can get on with the rest of the job? I've got the hard-core coming at the end of the week. For your path. And don't forget that friend of your mate's wants to be planting as soon as possible – and we're into April tomorrow.'

If only she could have said yes. What was she letting herself in for? Endless phone calls to try and find an expert; time-juggling to fix an appointment for whoever to come out; endless delays to the garden if the site were interesting.

He took her silence as the negative it was. 'So you'd

rather I got on with the other things? I mean, I've still got those two stumps to get out.' He pointed. 'And I suppose I could fix the toilet roof. Yes, I'll tell my mate to hold the hard-core another couple of days. Your word is my command,' he added, with a flourish.

Or her silence. Time to say something. And not to correct his idiom.

'Yes. You're right. I've got to get someone to check it out, haven't I? Well, maybe we should look on the bright side. It may turn out to be something to tell your grandchildren about.'

'Or a damp squib.' He looked at one of the buttons. 'Doesn't look much ...'

'It's just that there are so many of them, isn't it? I don't sound very grateful, do I, Alf? But I am. Any other bloke would have just dug the whole patch over without even a second thought. How about a cuppa to celebrate your find?'

As she fished it from her sports bag, her tracksuit reminded her it needed washing. She might as well put a load in while she prepared and ate her supper. And better check all the pockets, in case she'd left in a tissue and everything ended up covered with shredded paper. No. None in her tracksuit pocket. Nor anywhere else. But – yelping, she was up and across the kitchen, grabbing her waterproof and fumbling in the pocket.

Her hand came up triumphant. My God, fancy forgetting the old woman's ring! Supper had better wait. Except – she twirled the ring gently – it wouldn't hurt it to be cleaned in some of the stuff she occasionally used herself. Any more than it would hurt her to grab – if not the chicken risotto she'd promised Lorraine she'd try to cook – a chicken sandwich.

'I never know where I've put it,' Mrs Sargent said, pushing her ring on to her finger. It looked very bright, very new, against the deeply weathered skin. 'So I couldn't ask anyone to look for it. But it's as precious to me as those old photos are to Len.'

The Sargents were side by side on Mrs Hurst's sofa. A BMW parked in the road outside suggested that their daughter might have arrived.

Kate smiled, embarrassed. 'And how's Billy Budgie?'

'He's fine, bless you. Mrs Hurst went and got him some of his favourite seed and he's perfectly happy. I don't know how he'll like the trip down to Cornwall.'

'You're off to your daughter's, then?'

'She's got a granny flat all ready for us. She's always wanted us to move down there but we've never quite got round to it. Not with the garden.'

'Round tuits are much in evidence in Cornwall,' announced a strong female voice. 'You can get earthenware and pottery round tuits in all the gift shops. Meg Hutchings, Sergeant.' The card she flipped to Kate announced she was an LLB and Barrister-at-Law. With a presence like that she could have been a Law Lord.

Pocketing it, Kate suppressed a smile. At last the Sargents' legal problems were in formidable hands.

Kate didn't stay long. It was obvious from the savoury smells that Mrs Hurst was taking her duties as hostess seriously and was producing a good meal, and under Meg Hutchings' steely gaze Kate didn't find herself equal to the very dry sherry on offer. Hutchings asked for – and got – Kate's card.

'I shall be in touch, Sergeant. Your conduct was entirely commendable today.'

'Far from it, Mrs Hutchings. In official eyes I was foolish to the point of a disciplinary. And then the ring—' Kate shook her head.

'No one would have known if you'd pocketed it.'

Kate flushed. 'I would.' No need to point out it wasn't worth stealing anyway.

From one powerful presence to another. Great Aunt Cassie was ensconced, not in bed, but in her armchair. After pouring her the obligatory stiff gin, Kate sat down on the day bed opposite her.

'They're still working, these new pills,' Cassie informed her, proving it by holding out one hand only for the tumbler. 'And you've no idea how much better they suit my insides. The diarrhoea's much better. And the doctor thinks he'll try some new tablets next time I have my water-works troubles.'

'Perhaps you won't have any more trouble if you carry on with your daily cranberry juice,' Kate said, deciding that the general tenor of the conversation could be improved.

'Nasty bitter stuff. And have you seen the amount of sugar they put in it to make it palatable? What's that you've got there?'

Kate laid the button on her aunt's outstretched palm. The skin was so dry. She'd better buy the old lady some rich hand-cream – always assuming she'd use it, of course. She was just as likely to give it to one of the carers. Cassie was like that. She had not only given Kate the house, she'd lent her a great deal of money to repair and decorate it. Now the London house was sold, Kate had paid her back, only to have the old woman refusing a penny in interest.

'I think it's a button,' Kate said. 'It's from your back garden. Alf – the workman, do you remember him? – found a hoard. So now we've got to decide what to do with them. And with the site.'

Cassie snorted and held her hand out for Kate to retrieve the button from where she'd placed it. 'Nothing but rubbish. You get on with your garden. That's what matters. You're paying that man good money to dig the place over – let him dig it. No need to worry about this muck. Chuck it in the bin. Forget about it.'

'Oh,' came a quiet voice from the door. 'I don't think she could do that, do you?'

Graham!

Who came in and, taking Cassie by the other hand, kissed her cheek, something Kate rarely dared to do. And the old dear obviously loved it – well, why not? A good-looking man must be a rare enough occurrence in her world.

Straightening, Graham held out his hand for Cassie to tip the button into it and turned to Kate. He was still smiling, but a quirk of his mouth might have suggested embarrassment, too. As for Kate, she didn't know what she felt. How could a man who could be hard to the point of unforgiving at work find time to be kind to an old lady who'd perfected ungraciousness to an art form? Cassie's oft-repeated explanation was that he couldn't stand his mother-in-law and regularly slipped in for five minutes while he waited for his wife to escape Mrs Nelmes' clutches. So it was nothing unusual for him to be here. But for them both to be here, out of their usual context, disturbed Kate – and, she suspected, him too. If she couldn't forget what had passed between them, she was sure he couldn't.

Hesitating a moment, Graham sat down beside her. He held out the button on his outstretched hand, just as Cassie had done.

'It was this that was under your woodshed?'

'And lots more. And' – she dug in her pocket – 'some bone ones, too. Too many to be ignored, really.'

'I don't know what you're making such a fuss about,' Cassie put in, holding out her glass. 'And more to the point, why you want to pull that shed down.'

Kate got up to refill the glass. She gestured with a spare glass to Graham, who blinked with amusement as she sliced lemon and clinked ice, and shook his head. She fixed herself a very small one, too. It was strange to sit down beside Graham again. Goodness knew how many meetings they'd sat side by side; but this was more shoulder to shoulder, thigh to thigh, than she was used to. And he was still holding the buttons.

She knew how well-shaped his hands were, and that the left was weighed down with a particularly heavy wedding ring. But she'd never had to touch one before. He could simply have scooped the buttons up and passed them to her, couldn't he? But they lay over whatever destinies the lines on his palm were supposed to promise, waiting for her to gather them.

'The wood was beginning to go rotten,' Kate said,

reaching for the buttons as gently and unobtrusively as she could. She turned to flick a smile at him.

For a crazy moment she thought he was closing his fist around both the buttons and her fingers. If he was, he thought better of it.

'You could have repaired it,' Cassie grumbled. 'Where will you keep your garden tools? Your lawn-mower?'

'In the coal-shed!' She didn't think it wise to tell her at this point that she wouldn't need a lawn-mower as she wasn't going to have a lawn. 'Alf's going to clean it out and put a proper floor in. And then replace the corrugated iron roof with a polycarbonate one – you know, strong transparent plastic. So it'll almost be a potting shed. And the outside lavatory – I'll put some shelves in to overwinter any plants I manage to grow.'

'And I thought you'd got green fingers,' Graham put in.

She spread her hand for him to inspect them. 'I'm afraid that they look pretty ordinary pink ones to me.' Why on earth had she done that? And risked glancing sideways up at him, to find his eyes fixed on her face? It was so dangerous.

'She kills house plants, I can tell you that. When she was a little girl and she used to stay with me – I'd give her cuttings to take back home and they'd always die. Wouldn't they?'

'That might have been something to do with that cat – the one that used to pee on them.'

'Our cat does that,' Graham said. 'Wretched creature — I can't think why my wife keeps it.' His face closed. And suddenly he was on his feet and halfway to the door. 'See you soon, Aunt Cassie. Kate.' He nodded formally and was gone.

'Well, you know your own mind best. But where'll you keep your coal?' Cassie demanded, without pausing to do more than nod goodbye.

Probably he wouldn't have noticed, any more than he'd noticed Kate's wave.

Kate rallied. 'Come on, when did you last have a coal fire? You don't need it with central heating.'

'I always had some standing by. Just in case. Power cuts and three-day weeks. You need a stand-by. Now, you were saying you'd started to play tennis. Don't you go getting a new racquet, spending your money where you don't need to. There's a perfectly good one in the loft.'

Not quite the ultra-light graphite one Kate had treated herself to.

'Behind the chimney, I think it is. Me and my Arthur used to like a good game. Always took our racquets on holiday. I had this lovely dress—'

'What was it like?'

'Oh, quite daring it was for those days . . .'

Well, she reflected in bed later, she'd escaped a cross-questioning for that evening. Tales of Cassie's tennis and her clothes had kept them going till Kate could decently go home. But she had a nasty suspicion her great aunt had missed not one blink of the interplay between her and Graham. That tension. Then he'd mentioned his wife, and the very thought of her had driven him to his incontinent escape.

Oh God! Cassie's bladder, Graham's cat — and at last the word she'd been trying to avoid all evening! But for all her chuckles, she couldn't keep at bay the memory of those half-touches, and the intensity of Graham's gaze.

Chapter Four

Kate had thrown up twice already. Her stomach was warning her it could do it again, any moment now. She must get the smell out of her nose. Mints might help. One in her mouth, one in a tissue pressed to her nose. But nothing could disguise the smell. Nothing could disguise the fact: this charred mess had been a human being.

'Smoke inhalation would get him first, of course,' Kevin Masters, one of the fire officers, was saying. 'So it wouldn't be like one of your martyrs, burnt at the stake. Though I believe they strangled them first, didn't they?'

'Only if they were bribed to,' Kate said. If showing off his general knowledge helped him deal with the death, why should she discourage him? It certainly made a change from the ghoulish humour that was her squad's usual defence mechanism. In any case, Rowley and the SOCO and the rest of the team were all busy, and a bit of bridge-building between services never came amiss. Especially when you had a bit of a conscience about a budgie. 'And wasn't there,' she continued, trying to smile, 'some guy who held his right hand into the flames, because it had signed papers which betrayed his cause?'

Masters, a spare man in his early forties, scratched his chin. 'Would that be Sir Thomas More? Or Saint Thomas More, depending on your persuasion.'

She shook her head doubtfully. 'Or maybe it was Cranmer? He had quite a lot to recant, after all. I rather think More had a nice swift death – off with his head. This poor bugger here didn't, though,' she said. 'What did he do? Get so drunk swigging meths he spilt some, and then – when he lit a fag – whoosh?'

'Could have. But I wouldn't like to pass an opinion till the FIT people have had a thorough look.'

'FIT as in our MIT – Major Incident Team?'

'FIT as in Fire Investigation Team. They do the same sort of job as your SOCOs – searching for needles in haystacks to make sense of everything. It'll be very interesting to see how the two teams work together,' he added darkly.

'But where will they start?' Kate looked helplessly at what was left of the warehouse. 'I mean, this was once a three-dimensional structure – now you've got all the walls, all the ceilings, turned into one soggy mess. Who's to know whether that girder there was part of the wall or part of the roof?'

Masters laughed. 'Training. Experience. Instinct. The same sort of things you people bring to a murder case.' He looked sideways at her. 'Which you may have here, of course.'

'If the poor sod didn't set fire to himself.'

'Or herself. Would you take bets on whether it was male or female?'

She forced herself to look again at the charred flesh, the teeth bared in a manic final grimace. She swung away, holding back bile.

A stir of activity distracted her.

'Ah! That'll be the experts. The big, tall chap with glasses – he's the Forensic Science Agency fire expert. The short one with hairy legs – that's the other expert.'

Kate opened her eyes in a cynical stare. A dog?

'No, I reckon the canine expert's as important as the human one. In his own way. He's trained to sniff petrol, you see. To pick up the fumes.'

'Like other dogs sniff cannabis or dead bodies?'

'That's right. So if he has a good nose round and comes up with the smell of petrol, it'll blow our theory of the drunk meths-swilling tramp out of the water, won't it? Anyway, let's see what Star comes up with.'

Star, a black Labrador, stood patiently to be fitted with little leather boots.

'You see,' Masters said, 'they're to protect his feet from broken glass. Off he goes.'

Dog and handler started, appropriately enough, she supposed, where the corpse had been found. But Star gave no reaction. As he ranged over the rubble, however, he started to get a lot more interested. Then excited. Finally very excited, in a doggy sort of way. And certainly his handler looked pleased.

'Petrol?' Kate asked.

Masters nodded. 'Looks like it. Now, didn't those other fires start with someone pouring petrol through skylights? Well, believe it or not, Kate, that is almost exactly where a skylight would have been.'

Sue Rowley came towards her with SOCO and the taller of the experts. 'Come on,' she said, 'let's get out of here. All the smells,' she continued, stumbling over a twisted girder, 'of a fire like this. Wood; paint; chemicals. And now – a human.'

Masters nodded. 'It drives me crazy, people saying how they enjoy their garden bonfire. I tell you, some days I can't face a barbecue. There. That's better, isn't it?'

Kate returned his smile, sniffing. 'Lovely fresh rush-hour air! You're right. Even the smell of all those buses is sweet.' She found she was shivering.

So was Sue Rowley. 'What puzzles me is how some people manage to turn their stomachs off – I mean, those forensic teams in Yugoslavia, as was, and pathologists, going in real close—' Shaking her head, she closed her eyes. 'A day like this, I can't wait to have a shower and get into some clean clothes.'

Kate nodded. That was exactly what she had in mind.

'Now, Kate,' Sue continued, 'fancy coming back to the Fire Station? I think we both deserve a cup of tea and a bit of breakfast and it'll do no harm to chew things over with the others.'

'I'd love to, Gaffer. But I've got to be in court in an hour's time, remember.'

'That's a shame,' Masters said. 'It'd be nice to have an attractive young lady gracing our canteen.'

Putting her hand on Masters' arm, Rowley winked at Kate. 'You pop off, Kate, and I'll give our friend here a bit of equal opps. training over the bacon butties.'

Kate and Graham almost collided on the steps to the police station's main entrance as she ran the last few yards from the car park.

Before he spoke, he looked at his watch. There was no indication in his face that only twelve hours ago they'd sat side by side examining buttons. Perhaps she was grateful. All she had on her mind at the moment was showering away the fire smells and getting on with routine. Anything to keep at bay the memory of those teeth grinning at her from between the blackened lips.

'The second morning you've been late,' he said. 'And you're due in court in forty minutes, for goodness' sake.'

If she didn't want tenderness, she didn't want this crap, either. Hadn't he eyes to see, a nose to smell, where she'd been? 'Major fire, sir. This time there was a victim. I've only come away because of the court case.'

He flinched, half lifted a hand. 'You're all right?'

She nodded, but wouldn't respond to the concern in his voice. 'I can shower off and change in ten minutes flat. I won't be late.'

He nodded. 'I'll see you there, then.'

He was waiting outside the Law Courts clutching a take-away coffee and something in a paper bag.

'In case you'd lost your breakfast,' he said, smiling.

'I did. Twice. Thanks.' The coffee was cool and weak, almost unpalatably sweet; the little bag contained a Danish and a smoked salmon bagel. 'It's just—'

'No time to talk. Just get it down you. We don't want you fainting in court.'

Kate didn't faint in court. She didn't do anything in court, and neither did Graham. The whole day was filled – wasted, in their terms – by legal wrangling that could have taken place before the trial started. At least they'd been set free early. Would Graham assume they were going back to do a couple of hours' work – which she needed to do? Or would he suggest a delicate bit of bunking off?

His behaviour all day had given no clue. He, like her, had taken advantage of the wait to attack piles of portable paperwork, and their lunch-sandwich conversation had been about the frustrations of waiting and details of the fire. Should anyone have bothered to try to overhear what they'd been talking about, they'd have been impressed by their professionalism.

In the watery sun that greeted them as they emerged into Corporation Street, he turned. 'I wonder what time the museum closes? You haven't talked to an archaeologist yet, have you?'

It sounded almost like an accusation, which was rich since he knew exactly what she'd been doing all day. But his face implied no criticism.

'Not yet,' she said mildly. 'I'll phone them from the office, as soon as I get in.'

'Why not pop up now?'

Now that was an interesting suggestion from a man who'd bollocked her for bad time-keeping less than eight hours ago.

'Paperwork, Gaffer, that's why. And then filing said paperwork. Plus, if the truth be told,' she added, allowing a dimple to show, 'I'll bet the place would be closed by the time I get there — closed to casual visitors, at any rate. And it looks as if it's about to rain.'

So they walked back briskly together, in a peaceable silence.

Was it coincidence that they left their offices for home at almost the same instant? Possibly. It was on her part at least. At any rate, they fell into step.

'Did you get your filing done?'

'All of it. And I got through to the museum. They've got someone called an Assistant Keeper for Archaeology.'

'Have they indeed?'

'I presume they've got a keeper for him to be Assistant to. But my buttons aren't grand enough for him. Anyway, I've arranged to take a couple round tomorrow lunchtime, other things being equal.'

'Meanwhile, they just lie there?'

'Well, they've lain there happily for the last hundred or so years. And Alf's covered the site as tenderly as if it were a baby.'

'All the same ...' He held the door open for her. 'Actually, Kate — I wonder if I might ask you a favour. My car's in for a service, today — would you mind dropping me on the bus route?'

She pointed to the rain swirling across the street. 'I'll

drop you at home – or wherever it is you're heading,' she said. So it hadn't been coincidence. But why hadn't he asked earlier? Because, no doubt, his wife would expect him to go by bus; whatever the weather, she wouldn't approve of the current arrangement.

'Thanks. I see you're not taking any time off for the Easter break.'

'No. It always rains, and you only end up in miserable traffic jams. But I am off to watch the tennis on Sunday at the National Indoor Arena.'

'You're getting very keen, aren't you?' He sounded amused.

Squad gossip occupied the rest of the journey. And Graham started new topics whenever one ran dry. But he kept off the one thing she wanted to know – had almost been briefed to find out.

At last, just as she was to turn into his road, she asked, point blank. 'So are the rumours true, Gaffer? That you'll be leaving us for fresh fields?'

'It's actually, "Fresh woods and pastures new",' he said mock-pedantically. 'And – just over there, on the right. By the pillar box.'

'And will you?' She turned and slowed, looking for his house.

'Just drop me here. This is fine.'

Though she could have sworn there was a good hundred yards to go. Still, if he preferred a soaking to a door-to-door delivery, who was she to argue? Particularly as they both knew who would be waiting behind the door.

She pulled into the kerb, and cut her lights and the ignition.

'Thanks.' He reached for the door handle.

'Just one thing, Gaffer, before you go.'

'I'm very late, Kate,' he said, suddenly severe. 'I promised my wife I wouldn't keep supper waiting.'

'Won't take a second. Yes or no to the rumours?' He couldn't get out anyway – she always kept the doors on central locking when she was driving through town.

It was too dark to see the look he gave her, but his voice mixed exasperation with something else. It didn't seem to be amusement.

'As it happens, the rumours are wrong. Now, I must go. Thanks for the lift.'

She released the lock before he touched the handle – perhaps he wouldn't realise he'd been locked in.

'That's OK, Gaffer – no problem. All you have to do is ask. Just one thing!' she added, as he got out and turned to slam the door. 'Your case – it's on the back seat.'

Chapter Five

———◦◦◦◦◦———

Easter Saturday afternoon saw Kate not sitting in the rain in an enormous traffic jam but squatting in the sun in her back garden.

'Button-making was a home industry, you see, like nail-making or chain-making in the Black Country. I'd say this brickwork –' Stephen Abbott, the man from the museum, brushed away earth from a section which had lain under her shed – 'was the foundations of a late eighteenth-early nineteenth-century workshop.'

She pounced, excited. 'What if *Worksop* Road were a corruption of "workshop"?'

'Hmm. Could well be.' He sounded doubtful. But surely an archaeologist would know that sort of thing. 'Monday, I'll nip into the Reference Library and check on documentation there – old maps, trade directories, that sort of thing. What I'd guess is that when they built your row of houses, they just flattened this. Now I'd say this could be an important site – of its type. Which is, I'm afraid, not in itself as important as – say – a Bronze Age kiln we found in someone's garden a few years back. So I can't see you getting a huge grant to preserve it. On the other hand, I'd quite like to spend a little time looking at it, and recording it, before it disappears under your garden pond, or whatever. Look,' he said, holding a button between finger and thumb, 'at this one – you can see the pressing marks. Excellent. And aren't they in good condition? Why they should make bone buttons too I've no idea. I'd need to check the archival material for that, too.' He stood up. Stereotypical grey-haired, stoop-shouldered archaeologist Stephen Abbott was not. Nothing dry-as-dust about him. Apart from his job title, of course. He was probably no older than Kate, and not a lot taller. He had exactly the right sort of bum for jeans. Broad shoulders. Under his sweat-shirt there seemed to be muscles to die for. The whole lot was topped off by a nicely-shaped head, under a mop of blond curls, now glinting in the sun. And the face – well, Kate had always considered herself proof against a pretty face, but now she found that she might not be.

'I suppose the spring isn't the worst time to be working outdoors,' she said tentatively. Despite the sun, there was a cold wind, and she wished that vanity hadn't meant she'd left her fleece indoors.

'Not bad at all. The days are getting longer, for one thing. And I may have to make this a private project, working in my own time, so it could take – well, several weekends. Are you sure you're prepared to put up with that sort of inconvenience?'

Put up with several weekends of Stephen? Not half! Despite the fact that the garden designer wanted to plant the shrubs and roses in early May at the latest.

'If it's covered with garden path, it's gone forever, hasn't it?' she said, reflectively.

'It depends on the path. In one sense, a few inches of solid concrete are a very good way of preserving your site. Think about all those city-centre sites that are preserved under tower blocks.'

'But people can't see them. Not,' she added hastily, 'that I'm thinking of opening my place to the public. But I wouldn't be putting concrete on this – blocks on top of hard-core. No?' She too stood up as gracefully as the knee would let her: certainly not as elegantly as Stephen. 'Then it seems to me I've no option, morally at least. Your show must go on!' She made a grand gesture.

He nodded briefly. 'OK.'

She was taken aback by his lack of enthusiasm. 'Cup of tea?' she asked at last. She had, after all, added goodies to her Friday evening's Sainsbury's trolley in the hope that Stephen – whom she'd met briefly at the museum in her Friday lunch break – would stay. Her social life might be improving, but it currently didn't include attractive male company – not heterosexual male company, at least. Colin was the most delightful friend, and she was more than happy to be his beard. Potential lover he was not, however. And her last relationship had shrivelled on the vine. As for Graham . . .

'Why not?' he said. He stopped. 'I ought to tell you you won't be able to claim treasure trove or anything.'

'I wasn't expecting to. Isn't there some new legislation . . . ?' Interesting it might be, but it wasn't at the core of every officer's knowledge.

'That's right. A new Treasure Act. There's a portable antiquities recording scheme.'

'Is there indeed!'

'Hmm. Run by the Department of Culture, Media and Sport,' he said. 'Known in the trade as "duckmess",' he added, with a grin that lit up his whole face.

But the transformation was short-lived.

They trudged down her building site garden towards the kitchen door.

'What are you having done, precisely?' Stephen asked, staring at the holes, still awash with water after Thursday's downpour.

'Having tree stumps removed. The trees – three or four sycamores – were towering over the house. And my neighbours' houses.'

'Nasty things, sycamore roots. And then? I mean, there's not much you can do with a patch this size.'

She bridled. 'Oh, I don't know. OK, it'll never be Chatsworth, but with a bit of clever planting, a bit of trompe l'oeil, it could be quite attractive.'

Hands on hips, he looked around. 'You'll still be overlooked by all those houses. That's the trouble with terraced houses. I prefer a bit of space.'

'So do I, but beggars can't be choosers.'

He stared at her. 'Come on, you're in the police, aren't you? You're not on local government rates.'

She stopped by the back door to pull off her shoes. Mud and gravel and new kitchen floors didn't mix. He scraped perfunctorily at his boots, but seemed inclined to keep them on.

'Would you mind going stocking-footed? Otherwise I shall have to be like my mum, and lay down newspaper wherever you're likely to walk.'

'I can't think why you didn't have quarry tiles – they'd have been more appropriate for a house this age.'

'Two factors. Money – sorry, but even police officers have cash-flow problems. And the fact that things like plates don't bounce on quarry tiles.'

The prospect of his company every weekend was beginning to lose its attraction.

'True.' He pulled his boots off.

She gestured to a seat at her kitchen table. Muddy jeans

wouldn't mix with her new three-piece suite, courtesy of the January sales. And the kitchen, with its new paint and bright prints, was very pleasant, with the mid-afternoon sun warming the light maple of her units.

'Tea or coffee?'

'Coffee, thanks.'

'Cafetiere or espresso?'

'Instant decaff. If you've got such a low form of refreshment.'

'Oh, even highly-paid police officers sink to instant occasionally,' she grinned. 'Come on, Stephen, don't you ever get presents? Or do you still have to drink out of a jam-jar?'

He had the grace to look sheepish.

'And, if you like, I could offer you a dry crust, while I sit and stuff amaretti biscuits? Or there's a treacle tart?'

She made tea for herself, coffee for him, plonking milk still in its carton in front of him. Yes, she'd produce plates, too – no point in getting crumbs everywhere. And then she sat, knife poised over the treacle tart, looking at him ironically.

'I suppose if I asked for sugar,' he said, grinning, 'you could offer me white or golden granulated sugar lumps, or demerara, or muscavado—'

She laughed. 'No, this is the only stuff to help the medicine go down.' She passed the sugar basin, full of ordinary Silver Spoon. She slapped a hand to the side of her head. 'D'you know, I do have some sweeteners, too.'

Straight-faced, he declared, 'I never accept sweeteners.'

'So I truly don't know what to make of him,' she told Midge, as they took their places in the National Indoor Arena.

Midge – and her colleague Lorraine – were the officers who'd promised to improve Kate's social life. Apart from encouraging her to play tennis, they'd now brought her to watch it.

'My life seems full of moody men at the moment,' Kate continued.

'Don't give him a thought. Just think about mean men instead. Golly, doesn't Henman look young!' Midge exclaimed, as the entire auditorium rose to its feet to cheer him and the rest of the Davis Cup players on to court. 'Except that you haven't had much luck with men recently, have you? I mean, we hoped you'd hit it off with Cary Grant, and then there was Pat the Path – weren't you two an item for a bit?'

'It just – sort of fizzled out,' Kate said. There was no way she would reveal even to friends exactly how. 'God, look at those quadriceps . . .' What wouldn't her bad knee give for them?

'And then,' Lorraine put in, 'there was a very strong rumour that Someone Senior was after you.'

Kate hoped her face was entirely blank. It was inevitable that she and Graham should have become objects of gossip, but she thought she'd scotched any rumours months ago. 'Not that I ever noticed. Who – come on, you can't leave me hanging in mid-air like that!'

'Why, young Rodney, of course. Superintendent Smarm. Ah! Go on, Tim! Go on!'

And they were only knocking up, so far. What sort of volume would the crowd produce when Henman actually won points?

So it wasn't Graham who'd got the job: it was Rodney Neville. So how would Graham feel about that?

But now the match was starting in good earnest – with Courier looking in ominously good form – she would postpone thinking about it. And concentrate on willing Henman through.

If only . . .

Bank Holiday Monday morning was living up to its reputation, weatherwise at least. There was a bitter wind confronting a rainy sky. The bonus was that the traffic was light. She'd worked steadily through the piles of paperwork avalanching over her desk when the phone rang. Another person working over the holiday: Patrick

Duncan. He was in strictly professional mode — no one could have guessed he was a fizzled-out ex.

'You're still on that warehouse fire case?' he asked, with no preamble.

'"Still"? Is there any reason why I shouldn't be?'

'Come on, Kate, you know what rumours are like in this business ... Anyway, if you are, I thought you'd like to know your stiff was a woman.'

'Jesus Christ.' That the blackened flesh — once a woman like her.

'Are you still there? ... It's the pelvis that gave it away, of course.'

She must pull herself together. 'Of course. Anything else about — about her?'

'I'd say not young. And the teeth were in pretty poor nick. Fits in with the Fire Service view that she was a dosser. Bag-woman. Meths drinker. Whatever. Kate — are you OK?'

She tried for a laugh. 'It's just that even in this job you get an attack of "but for the grace of God".'

'You mean your drinking? Kate, you're over that now,' he said forcefully. 'You can even drink socially.'

'I know. It's just that—' She pulled herself together. No point in saying she'd really seen herself simply as a woman, like the corpse. She and Patrick weren't yet back on those terms. 'Well, at least we've something more to go on, now. Colin won't just be asking vague questions about missing men of the road – he can be much more specific.'

'Is he getting any co-operation?'

'Not a lot. If you give up society I suppose the last person you want to talk to is a copper.'

'Find someone who doesn't look like a copper, then.'

'Funny you should say that, Patrick – I might just have someone in mind.'

Chapter Six

Sue Rowley was working at her desk when Kate popped in to see her. She looked up, interested, like a bird, brown head on one side, ready to dart at any crumb of the arson case that Kate might have missed. 'What do you think about fraud as a motive?'

She flicked a glance at her watch as she spoke. Like Kate, Sue'd opted to work on the Bank Holiday, and seemed, like Kate, to be regretting it.

Kate couldn't very well match the gesture, but knew it must be some time after six. 'Claiming for contents they don't have? None of the firms I've spoken to had their goods over-insured. Not according to the assessors, anyway. And we've got different insurers for each of the firms that have been torched. All of them tell me that the claim seems entirely reasonable given the nature of the business. Businesses, that is – they're all in different lines of country. No individual assessor smells any sort of rat.'

Sue made a note. 'What about the premises? Were they over-insured?'

'On the contrary. One firm, in fact – the one involved in the most recent blaze – is likely to lose a lot of money. They can't afford to pull down the wreckage and rebuild on the same site. They'd have to go somewhere cheaper, if they can find anywhere, that is.'

'Oh, there are plenty of vacant warehouses around. More's the pity,' Rowley reflected.

'The Selly Oak firm – now they admit they were paying an extraordinarily low rent – old, rather tatty premises, they were. I want to get on to the Health and Safety people about them – just in case they'd been warned to make expensive improvements and had chickened out. But that wouldn't apply to the other premises. The trouble is, Gaffer, there's nothing consistent in any of the premises – except the modus operandi. This silly business of someone scrambling on a possibly fragile and treacherous roof, pouring petrol through a skylight and scarpering, just in time.'

'You're sure it's always been just in time? I'd check out the A. and E. departments. There aren't many hospitals these days doing that sort of stuff – it shouldn't take you long.'

Kate nodded. 'It's already down as Fatima's first job when she comes in tomorrow, Gaffer.'

Sue snorted with laughter. 'Trump me, will you? OK, that's what you're paid to do, and that's why they've fast-tracked you. Any more thoughts about that yet, Kate?'

She shook her head. 'Been a bit busy, what with one thing and another.'

'So I should hope! After all, Kate, we are into a murder inquiry, now. And I'd like to get as much done as we can before an MIT swoops in.'

'Ah, the Fifth Cavalry! And they'll no doubt spot there's one thing we haven't checked out yet – who owned the land on which those premises were built. I'll get Colin on to that first thing tomorrow.'

'Good thinking. Now, are you off home or are you and the lads going for a quick jar?'

'Not a lot of lads around.'

'Ah, of course. Bank Holiday. You know,' Rowley continued as she cleared a neat spot in the middle of her desk, 'the culture's changed so much. When I was your age it was assumed we'd be off, boozing and bonding – not that we even knew the word, mind – till we were half-pissed and nowhere fit to drive. Especially us women, if we wanted to get on. Now, they know we've got homes, families, even.' She touched a framed photo on her desk. 'What about you?'

'I've got this great aunt,' she said. 'But she doesn't worry if I have half a snifter after work. So long as I have a peppermint afterwards and she can't smell the beer on my breath.'

Aunt Cassie was so full of news she might not even have complained if Kate had rolled up drunk, provided she'd sat and listened without interrupting. In fact, she could scarcely wait for her first glass of gin to impart it all.

'Mrs Nelmes tells me that son-in-law of hers is in the soup,' she said gleefully. 'You know, young Eyore. Oh, he's not as bad as that, but he always looks fed up. Graham, that's it. The fair Flavia's husband.' The Harveys, man and wife.

Kate sipped her tonic and sat down to wait. Acquiescence was usually the best policy where Cassie was concerned. Moreover, if she tried to stop a flow of gossip, the old lady, balked, would turn to other prey. Kate herself, most likely. And in particular her unmarried state. And maybe Cassie would connect Kate's unmarried state with Graham's married one. No. Let Cassie have her head.

'Apparently he was very late home the other night. Very late. They nearly missed some special do at that church of theirs. And though he was supposed to have been on the bus — and it's a fair walk, according to Mrs Nelmes, for the bus — he was scarcely damp, despite the downpour. Well, that's what Mrs Nelmes said. So what do you make of that?'

'Why was he on the bus?' Kate asked, straight-faced.

'Oh, there was something the matter with the car.'

'I wonder why Mrs Harvey didn't pick him up. She's got a car of her own, hasn't she?'

'Doesn't like town traffic or some such. Especially in the rain. So what d'you reckon?'

Kate wouldn't bite. It was bad enough listening, wasn't it? 'What do *you* reckon?' She asked at last, taking the old woman's glass and refilling it.

'I reckon the obvious thing. That someone gave him a lift. Or he might just have taken a taxi. But apparently he didn't want to talk about it. Told her he was back in time for that do and that was that. Told? Well, he shouted, according to Mrs Nelmes.'

Good for him! But Kate said nothing.

But Cassie needed no encouragement. 'Of course, I don't see what the problem is, and so I told Mrs Nelmes. A man does a long day's work, gets a lift from a friend, gets to this God-bothering in time – no wonder he gets cross when his wife starts cross-questioning him. After a day like that, he should get a nice warm welcome, no questions asked. That's what my Arthur expected. And got,' she added with satisfaction, swigging the gin in one.

Kate reflected silently on the difference between a wife and a mistress.

'So I told her,' Cassie continued, 'I wasn't surprised the worm had turned. Only it seems that Flavia is the only one entitled to call the poor lad a worm, so Mrs Nelmes is no longer speaking to yours truly. So there you are. So I think I'll have another – just a finger – to celebrate. What about you?'

'Why not?' She helped herself to another tonic. So what was Cassie celebrating? Her spat with Mrs Nelmes or a marriage with a problem?

'You don't call that a drink?'

'I do at this time of night when I've got to be up at six tomorrow.'

Cassie cackled. 'Oh, aye. Got yourself a breakfast date, have you? Oh, not with the worm?'

'No. With a very attractive young man called Jason. My tennis coach. And we start hitting little yellow balls at seven prompt.'

'Start low, that's it, and end high. Let me see the side of that racquet. That's it. What a shot! Now – just to show it wasn't a fluke – another backhand.' Jason sent down another ball. She might be hot enough to have shed her tracksuit and to have started to swig from her water bottle, but he – all six foot one of him – was still cool, not a drop of sweat glistening in his curly black hair.

They were in the tennis centre. The centre – which

held eight courts — was divided in two by a high-level walkway, designed to stop people straying on to others' courts while they were in use. Heavy canvas curtains at the end of each court reduced the echo and deadened the flight of the balls. The other side of the walkway was completely unoccupied and in darkness. Only their court and the next one had lights on. Not that anyone was on the next court. No, as far as Kate knew, she and Jason were the only people in the whole complex, apart from the receptionist, still bug-eyed with sleep, and a cleaner, the only evidence of whose existence was a trolley half-way out of a door marked PLANT.

They'd spent ten minutes or so knocking up, to get the eye in and the joints moving, and had then collected up the tennis balls. Jason somehow transformed the ball basket into a ball-gatherer. Kate simply gathered as many as her racquet would carry.

'You'd think in a place like this people would dispose of their litter more thoughtfully,' Jason said, slinging a couple of plastic ball-tubes and a bottle into the bin beside the net. 'Ugh.' The bottle was obviously sticky.

Kate was fossicking behind a curtain: five or six balls were lurking behind it. And a couple of empty bottles. She kicked them free. As soon as she'd deposited the balls in Jason's basket, she went back, and slung the bottles with unnecessary force into the bin.

'It's as bad as the bloody High Street,' she said. 'Some

days you see whole families coming out of McDonald's and dropping litter. Why can't they use bins?'

'Because they don't want to draw attention to themselves by being different,' Jason suggested, finding a chocolate wrapper and binning it. 'Right. Ready to work on your forehand?'

She nodded, heading for the far end of the court.

'Ready position. Knees bent, remember, take the racquet head down really low – that's it! How's that knee?'

'Protesting a bit. But it might as well shut up because – yes!' She was getting more and more accurate.

Now all that could be heard, above the constant hum of the extractor fans chilling the place unbearably, was the plop of the balls that Jason fed to her, the clip as she struck them, and then a more distant thud as they bounced off the far end of the court.

So when a woman screamed there was no doubt about what it was. A serious, terrified scream.

Kate hurtled through the door. The cleaner – a redhead in her forties whose skin was so white she might disappear if she got any paler – was yelling at the receptionist, and sobbing. She was pointing, it seemed, at the women's changing room. Kate pushed her way in. No, nothing in the lavatory area. She checked the individual cubicles. Nothing. So into the changing room itself. No. Nothing. Until, that is, when she ducked round to the shower area.

On the tiled floor, just by one of the drains, lay a woman's body. Naked.

'We'll have to stop meeting like this,' Guljar said, pushing through the centre's front doors. 'What's up, eh, Kate? Has that budgie of yours started playing tennis?'

The thin constable behind him grinned nervously.

'I wish. No, a body in the women's showers. A middle-aged woman, fifty, fifty-five, possibly. Judging by her face, that is. No immediate sign of foul play.' A woman she wouldn't mind looking like in twenty-five years' time. Oh, the flesh wasn't as firm as hers, but there were no varicose veins, no pads of fat. The hair had been high-lighted — where it had fallen forward Kate had seen more grey than the woman would have wanted made public. Whoever it was had cared for herself.

'Natural causes? Too much running about — a woman her age, you know.'

'No, I don't. I know lots of women aged fifty-five who could run me off the court without raising a sweat. But let's wait to see what the police surgeon has to say. I've just preserved the scene, that's all. On a temporary basis, of course. I wouldn't want to offend you Uniform types.'

'I should hope not.' There was a flicker of irritation, all the same. Then he grinned, sardonically. 'I mean, it's bloody typical, isn't it, CID muscling in on the only two interesting incidents in this patch this month. Come on, just to show there's no ill-feeling, show us this corpse, then.'

'You're sure? I could just finish my lesson and pop into work?'

'Another pair of eyes never hurts. Come on, I'll get young Des here to log us in – just in case we do have a crime on our hands.'

The thin constable swallowed hard and produced his notebook.

The police surgeon, Nesta Holt, was a spruce young woman a couple of years older than Kate. She straightened and shook her head, addressing herself to Guljar. 'Well, she's dead, all right. Classic heart failure, I'd have said. But—'

'"But"?' Kate put in, looking down at the dead woman, resisting the urge to wipe a trace of saliva from the corner of the slack mouth.

'Well, it must have had a very sudden onset. I mean, physically she looks fine. Look at the muscles in her arms and legs. I wish a lot of the kids I see exercised as well as this. And no, none of the warning signs of long-term heart failure. No sign of high colour in her cheeks which might have suggested blood-pressure problems. Nothing unnatural here. As for time of death – how long have those heaters been on?'

'Heaters?' Kate looked round. The low roar she hadn't originally registered came from the hair-dryers, both of which had been kept on with, now she looked more closely, Blu-tack between the dab-button and the body of the machine. She pointed. Guljar whistled and made a note. 'The place was like an ice-box when I was in here last,' she said.

'Well, it isn't cold now! So I'd say – and remember, time of death's notoriously hard to pinpoint – between twelve and eight hours ago.'

'Between eight and midnight, then,' Guljar said.

'Something like that.'

'Would they still be playing at that time?'

Kate nodded. 'Until ten, at least. Then there's time to shower and have a drink and so on.'

Guljar looked at her under his eyebrows and made another note.

'Right, that's that, then,' Nesta said. 'I've got a surgery to go to. And I bet it'll be full – all these people with their tennis elbows and their swollen knees. It only takes a couple of hours of tennis on TV to bring them out of the woodwork.' She turned to Guljar. 'You'll do the necessary with Coroner's Officers and so on?'

'Sure. See you around, Nesta. And thanks for coming out so fast.'

'It's just I'm dying to see all those knees.' Nesta looked at Kate's shirt and shorts. 'If you've been playing, you ought to get changed – you don't want to chill too quickly – not that there's much danger of that in here, I suppose. But that foyer's pretty cold.'

Kate nodded. She held the door for her, then ducked back to the changing area. She pointed to the sports bag, in splendid isolation on a bench. 'Any sign of any ID?'

Guljar looked once again as if he might bridle. Then he shook his head. 'No ID at all. And it's expensive gear.'

'What about house keys, car keys?'

He shook his head. 'You know, Kate, I have to admit it's weird. How did she get here? And how was she going to let herself in when she got home?'

Kate leant against a wall, hands in the pockets of her top. 'It can't be unknown for a kind hubby to bring the little wife and collect her. But – and it's a big but––'

'Why didn't he kick up a fuss when she didn't come out? Come charging in here, or something?'

'Quite. And why did none of the players notice she hadn't left the building with them – you don't play tennis on your own, do you? There must have been someone the other side of the net for at least an hour.'

'Maybe whoever it was was in a rush,' he suggested, sitting down on the bench.

'Or they'd had a disagreement about a line call or something?' she said, straight-faced, sitting beside him.

'Quite. You obviously play here. What's the system for recording players?'

'Everything's on computer. Whether it's a private game or a coaching session. You can phone in and book by credit card. Or you can do it in person. As far as I know, you only need give *your* name if you're booking in advance.'

'So even if four people were playing you'd only get one name. Well, player number one would presumably be able to identify the other three. Will you hang on here while I talk to the woman on Reception?'

OK. It was his patch, not hers. But she wished he'd said, *Let's go and talk to the woman on Reception*. Guljar was a smashing bloke, and a bright one too, to make it to sergeant so quickly. No assistance from the accelerated promotion scheme, either. But – no, he wasn't her, and she liked doing that sort of thing herself.

He was soon back. 'The funny thing is, the computer went down last night.'

'So there's no record of any of the players?'

'Funny little coincidence, isn't it?'

She nodded. 'Like those hair-dryers being jammed on. It's usually like a bloody morgue in here. Looks as if someone might have wanted to muddy the time-of-death business.'

'Which brings us to the question of a p.m. Costs more to have a full forensic p.m., doesn't it? A lot more. He's always on about his budget, our DI Crowther,' Guljar said.

She looked up sharply. Some needle there between the two men? But she simply asked, 'Isn't everyone budget-crazy these days? It wouldn't hurt to preserve the scene, would it, while he thought about it? I mean, a place like this – you can see how immaculate it is – must be cleaned every day. All the litter disposed of. All the evidence – if evidence there is – would be completely lost. We can't afford that.'

She was rewarded by a grin. 'All the bloody paperwork – if it proves a false alarm, you can bloody come and do it, your next day off.'

'What's one of those? OK, you're on. If we're wrong, I'll type up the whole caboodle for you.'

'What are we waiting for, then? I'll call our CID and their SOCO friends, and make sure nothing is disturbed, nothing thrown away. That'll really make the tennis-playing public happy, I don't think.'

'To say nothing of the coaches like Jason, who don't earn if they don't work,' she added.

'Tell you what, Kate,' he said, pulling himself to his feet, 'I could wish it had been Josephine Public, not you, who'd found her. The next few days would have been a lot easier.'

'But – if we're right – the ensuing ones would be a hell of a lot worse.'

*   *   *

At last, leaving him to radio back to his colleagues in Kings Heath, she went out into the foyer, where Jason was still waiting. He'd brought out her tennis bag, the tracksuit tucked into the handles. Kate dug in her bag for her purse and the lesson fee. When he demurred, she said flatly, 'You managed to get here at seven. Don't tell me you don't deserve the lesson fee for that alone!'

'Well ...' He took the money, obviously embarrassed. 'What if you just booked another lesson for later this week ...'

'No: I'd better stick to the usual Tuesday date. I've got a nasty suspicion this is going to be a heavy week,' she said. 'For me; for you; and for everyone at the Centre. Once the Press get hold of the fact that a corpse lay undiscovered at Brayfield Centre overnight, they're going to want to talk to a lot of people. And my colleagues over there just might, too.' She nodded at the influx of police personnel. 'Just to kick off, though, Jason. Were you here last night?'

He shook his head. 'I was coaching over in Handsworth.'

'So you've got a nice lot of witnesses?'

'About twenty – it was a very busy night. Everyone thinking they should be playing Davis Cup tennis! You should see the courts in Wimbledon fortnight!' He smiled shyly: 'Look, I've organised a cup of hot chocolate for you.'

Not from the machine, either.

'I got them to put in extra sugar. Shock,' he explained, as she raised startled eyes. 'You know, the body.'

She swallowed her remarks about seeing worse sights every day with the first mouthful of chocolate. It was good, and there was no point in offending the person who'd procured it. In fact, it made a nice change to be treated as a human, who could feel frail in the face of such events.

Time to go into work. The full back-up team was now on the scene. There was nothing to do except drink her chocolate and go. It was all in other people's hands. Nonetheless, as she left the building she spoke to the woman on Reception: Sylvie, her badge said. 'Was it busy here last night?'

Sylvie shook her head. 'I wouldn't know.'

'Don't you get to know the regulars?'

'Yes, but it was the relief manager on last night. The regular manager's off sick.'

'So when will the relief manager be back in?'

'In about three weeks! He's going to fly straight off to see his mum in Jamaica. His flight left — what, half an hour ago.'

Kate leaned her head against the car roof. She didn't want to go, didn't want to leave a case like this. But she had no option. She let herself in slowly. She'd not been to see Simon for a bit. What about a nice quiet chat with him while the traffic eased?

He was just opening his *Big Issue* bag when Kate reached Sainsbury's. She grinned at him, but didn't stop to talk. She'd whiz round while it was relatively quiet. He knew, of course, that whatever she shoved in her basket would include stuff for him, but he always seemed pleased to see her for her own sake. At least, that was what she told herself, as she picked up high-protein snacks and the milk chocolate he loved.

As she bought her *Big Issue*, she handed him a couple of folded notes. 'I'm after a favour. And it may involve you lubricating a few throats,' she explained as he stared at them. 'Not necessarily the cleanest or the youngest throats.'

'Go on.'

'These warehouse fires – you know we found a body last week.'

'Poor bastard.'

'Quite. Except it was a woman. And we can't get a handle on her. Any chance you could ask the odd question at the hostel?'

He nodded. 'I hate it, Kate. I'd rather be back in my little squat. The coughing. Other folks' nightmares. I like a bit of privacy.' He smiled, his face suddenly transfigured. 'But I'm still alive. Thanks to you. And you never know – things might look up.'

If only she could make him a firm offer, hard news for hard cash. 'I'm sure they will. Just hang on in there, Simon. Just hang on in there.'

Chapter Seven

Rowley pushed her sandwiches aside and looked quizzically at Kate: 'No, don't apologise. At least, not to me. It seems you've ruffled the odd feather down at Kings Heath nick. Or at least, one Guljar Singh Grewal has. Acting, I'd say, with a bit of a push from you.' She gestured Kate to a seat.

'Me, Gaffer?' Kate personified wide-eyed innocence. 'No, all I did was find this woman's body in the showers. And notice that someone – possibly, just possibly with the intention of making it hard to pinpoint the time of death – had Blu-tack'd the hair-dryers on. So it was nice and cosy in a room Scott of the Antarctic might normally have shivered in. It was actually Guljar who noticed that the centre's computers were down. And he who checked that no one had got round to reporting the woman missing. It just seemed a bit funny to us, that's all.'

'Funny enough to warrant a top-price autopsy instead of a bog-standard one? It's upset my opposite number, Kate, that's the problem. And he wants me to give you a flea in your ear.' She leant forward, arms on desk, more like a headmistress about to give careers advice than a DI about to give a bollocking.

'And are you going to, Gaffer?'

'Well, I asked him a question or two, as it happens. Like had they found out who the lady in question was. And they'd got no idea. I take it you didn't check her sports bag.'

'I didn't want to tread on anyone's toes, Gaffer,' Kate said virtuously. Then she grinned. 'But Guljar did, of course.'

'Fair enough. What would you have looked for if you had?'

'Car keys with a helpful fob. House keys ditto. After all, I didn't see a handbag, and she was a bit grown up for a name-tape in her coat.'

'Anything else?'

'Anything to give us an idea who she was.'

'And there was nothing?' Rowley shook her head.

'Not even a bus pass!' Why was Rowley banging on about elementary police work? And now she was waving a half-eaten sandwich to prompt Kate to continue.

Which she did. 'So we have an anonymous woman who hides her identity and walked to Brayfield Centre. Or paid cash on a bus. And had no money to buy a drink or get home.'

'Yes, we're on the same wavelength. And so, by the time I'd asked the same questions of our young colleague in Kings Heath, was he. Not that he liked having to accept advice from a woman he clearly sees as in her dotage,' Sue said grimly. 'Anyway, I think we might get our forensic post mortem. Want to be there?' she asked, ultra-casually.

Since Christmas, every time there'd been a stiff, someone had wanted to know if Kate wanted to watch Patrick Duncan cut it up. The news had evidently got round very quickly that Kate and he were no longer an item. The joke was wearing distinctly thin but Kate would not bite.

'Not our stiff,' she said, equally casually.

'True. OK, off you go. Just one thing, Kate,' she added mock-wistfully, 'you couldn't change your tennis lesson to another day? Only Kings Heath seems to like its crime on Tuesdays.'

Kate got to her feet, grinning at the pallid joke.

Sue shrugged. 'Which reminds me – any news of the old dears and their budgie?'

'I'll have to ask Guljar for an up-date on the lorry business. But I'm sure they'll get a tidy sum from the driver's insurance. Well, his or his employer's. The daughter's a barrister: I wouldn't like her on my trail! Anyway, her parents — and Billy the budgie — have settled in OK: I had a postcard yesterday morning. They tell me they're going to take their daughter's garden in hand.' And Kate was pretty sure that she would have a round tuit, whatever that might turn out to be, ready and waiting for them.

'A charity! All that land owned by a charity! The *same* charity!' Kate must have sounded as incredulous as she felt. She pulled up a chair to Colin's desk and waited for more.

Colin nodded. 'Yes. A charity. An old and respectable one, too. You've heard of Anna Seward?'

'No,' Kate said blankly. 'Should I have done?'

Colin flung his hands in the air, presumably to catch his eyebrows. 'Goodness me! Never heard of the Swan of Lichfield? Well, I suppose you southerners are a pretty ignorant tribe.'

'OK.' Kate was going to have to indulge him, wasn't she, if she wanted to get at the kernel. 'Who was she?'

'She was a poet. Born that place in Derbyshire where they had the plague. You know, "Ring a ring o'roses".'

'You're losing me, Colin.'

'OK. She lived most of her life in Lichfield. Doctor Johnson was a fan. You've heard of him?'

'Might just have done.'

'And Sir Walter Scott published all her poems post-humously.'

'Good for him. Though personally I'd rather have my five minutes of fame while I'm alive.'

'And she had a sister, who died young. Sarah.'

'Have you been mugging all this up for *Mastermind*?'

'Did a project on her at school. Now, Sarah was very bright, and Anna herself a bit of a blue-stocking. So when Sarah dropped off her perch, Anna decided the most appropriate memorial was a school for young women. A good one. So she set up this charitable foundation to fund it. And several other schools. There are Seward Academies – nothing as vulgar as a school, you'll notice – in several towns round here. Walsall, Wolverhampton, Lichfield itself, of course, Tamworth.'

'What about Birmingham?'

'Oddly enough, no. They own a lot of land in the area, but no schools.'

'Why "oddly"?'

'Because education in Brum's always been dominated by boys' grammar schools. Until they spotted the implications of equal opportunities legislation, there were about ten boys' places to every one girl's. So you'd have thought a chain of private grammar schools would have been the answer to a whole lot of maidens' prayers.'

'"Maidens' prayers"?'

'Just a Black Country expression.'

Kate nodded absently. It was either that or yell. Finally she settled for a bit of irritation. 'Colin: where's all this going? So why do they own land, not just schools? And why in Brum?'

'Not much of a capitalist, are you? They need property and investments — I bet they've got land all over the country, not just here — to bring in income in ground rents to fund the trust. They've got to maintain the schools and pay the teachers.'

'So the girls don't have to pay?'

Colin roared with laughter. 'Not much, they don't! Only about two thousand a term, give or take the odd hundred.'

'Jesus! Where did you find that out?'

'Saw an ad in the *Evening Mail* the other night.'

'Well, we know there's money in education. So I suppose these are particularly high-class establishments with state-of-the-art everything. And what the fees don't cover, the ground rents do. Any idea what else they own?'

'What sort of else?'

Kate pulled a face. 'No idea. What do organisations like that usually own? Buildings? Pictures? You wouldn't care to find out, would you? Just so we know where we are when we start talking to them.'

'Talking to them?'

God, where was he today? 'Well,' she said with irony, 'all these embarrassing fires are on their land. They might just have a view. Hi, Fatima! Come and join us! Colin's just about to put the kettle on.'

Colin pulled a face, and himself to his feet. 'Yes, boss. Tea or coffee, Fatima?'

'Tea, please.' She bowled a lemon at him, overarm. It spun in the air. 'Black, with a slice of this, please.'

'You're not slimming or anything, are you?' Kate demanded.

'No. Just that the milk supply's been a bit irregular and the shop down the road's open all hours.'

'Like Ronnie Barker's?' Colin asked.

'No, like Safeway. OK, Gaffer,' Fatima continued, 'I've checked the A. and E. department at all the hospitals within the West Midlands. There are no young people with burns or possible explosion-related injuries.'

Kate looked at her. 'No young people. What about older ones?'

Fatima blinked. 'I didn't know you wanted to know that.' My God! First Colin and now Fatima! 'But,' she continued triumphantly, 'before you hit the roof, I did ask, just in case. And there was one, in the Burns Unit in Selly Oak. A middle-aged guy. Art-dealer.'

'And why did he end up there?'

'He was trying to light his bonfire.'

Kate raised an eyebrow. 'Did you believe him?'

'He wasn't in a position to talk to me. Very bad

facial and chest burns. Admitted early last week. Still seriously ill.'

'Did you get an actual time and date of admission?'

Fatima shook her head, biting her lip.

'I know the theory was that our arsonist's likely to be a teenage hell-raiser! But get on to the blower to them – I like dotting i's and crossing t's.'

'Or drinking them.' Colin placed a mug on her desk. 'There you are, Kate. And Fatima.'

'Thanks, Colin. Thanks both of you. Not that it gets us any further forward, not yet—'

The phones, which had been unnaturally quiet for some time, now rang, one on Colin's desk, another on Kate's.

'Kate?'

She half-recognised the voice, but it was a very poor line. 'Oh! Stephen! Have you got news about my buttons?'

'Yes. I've been checking with some of my colleagues. One's a real expert on buttons. D'you fancy dropping round to here in your lunch hour? I'll stand you a sarnie in the Edwardian Tea Rooms.'

Lunch hour? Now that was a nice civilised concept. She looked at her watch. Didn't time fly when you were enjoying yourself! 'Sounds good. In about half an hour?'

She was just leaving the building when she heard Graham's voice behind her. Turning, she stopped to wait for him.

He looked very tired, very grey. But his face lit up in an answering smile and he took the last four or five steps at a run. 'Any news of your buttons?'

'I'm just on my way to find out. Stephen Abbott – he's in charge of finds like mine – phoned me a few minutes ago. It concentrates the mind on the paperwork, taking a lunch break. How are you?' She hoped she didn't sound as concerned as she felt. To cover, she asked, 'How was your weekend? Did you get away from Birmingham?'

'Fine. Yes, fine. This gathering tomorrow night—'

'Gaffer?'

'Ah, you probably don't know. There'll be a note on everyone's desk by two. Rod Neville's just heard he's going to head up one of these MITs. He's inviting everyone to a jar or two after work.'

'That'll be good,' she said, without emphasis. 'Will you be going?'

He pulled a face. 'Oh, I don't know. I've really got such a lot on—'

'Graham: you should be there. You really should. Or people will say it's sour grapes because you didn't get it.' OK, sergeant talking to DCI this wasn't. More friend to friend. Which they were. But it wasn't always a good idea to speak so bluntly.

He stared. 'It was always going to be just a sideways move for someone.'

'You might know that. He might know that. But you know the smart money was on you.'

'So whoever put it on lost it. Well, we'll see about tomorrow night,' he said at last. 'I take it you'll be going?' He turned towards Colmore Row. 'You know, Neville thinks a great deal of you. As a police officer.'

Kate fell into step with him. Shoving her hands deep into her pockets – the wind was cold despite the bright sun – she grunted non-committally. It was interesting that Graham should need to qualify such an apparently innocent remark. She wouldn't mention – not to him, not to anyone – that she suspected Neville found her attractive. It was bad enough that being on the accelerated promotion scheme gave her a reputation as a Butterfly, a PC Curriculum Vitae, without giving anyone cause to suspect she might fancy sleeping her way to the top. Goodness knew there were enough rumours about her and Graham. And she couldn't, after that strange moment in Aunt Cassie's room, deny the tension between the two of them. It might ebb and flow. But it was always there. Even when, maybe especially when, he was angry with her. And if his anger was unjustified, as it often was, what was the cause of it?

'And' – the sound of his voice made her jump – 'as a woman. I rather think.'

She wouldn't bite. 'You know they call him Superintendent Smarm?'

He managed a laugh. 'He's a good officer,' he conceded. 'Good to work under.'

She might just risk it. 'Don't you think, Gaffer, that that could have been better expressed?'

Chapter Eight

━━━◦◦◦◦━━━

Stephen unlocked another door deep in the entrails of the museum, ushering her through into a vast but dingy corridor. He gestured. 'I suppose if you go backstage anywhere – even somewhere as prestigious as Symphony Hall – you get the same difference between front of house and backstage areas.'

'Like in a stately home—'

'That's right. Magnificent one side of the green baize door, Spartan the other. What about at your place?'

'Pretty much the same throughout. Executive design it isn't. But maybe we wouldn't want that. So long as it's clean and decent, we'd rather the money were spent on other things.'

'How very noble and self-sacrificing!'

'Oh, there's still a bit of Dixon of Dock Green in most

of us,' Kate said. 'Most of us joined to help people, one way or another.'

His grunt suggested he wasn't convinced. She didn't persist: she wasn't here to score points but to get information. If it was to come to her for some reason best known to Stephen not in the civilised surroundings of the Edwardian Tea Room but in his office, so be it. Part of her rather hankered for gentle conversation with a pianist strumming familiar tunes as a background. As it was, lunch would be a sandwich across a desk, a familiar enough scenario. The desk was familiar enough too – a toppling set of filing trays and piles of folders. There were a couple of obligatory photographs.

She moved them aside so her sandwiches wouldn't mess them. 'Interesting,' she said neutrally, adding, with a grin, 'When we have photos they're usually of scenes or victims of crime.' These were of an old building.

'You wouldn't be far out, there,' he said grimly, sitting the far side of the desk, and leaving her to drag up an old dining chair abandoned near a cupboard to sit opposite him.

'Really!'

'It depends on your definition of crime, I suppose,' he conceded.

She waited, head on one side.

'I mean, fancy not preserving a place like that. Nineteenth-century. Might even have been designed by Thomas

Telford.' He paused. 'Though I must admit that's open to discussion.'

'It looks a bit like a toll-house,' she suggested.

'How do you know about toll-houses?'

He sounded as suspicious as Graham on a bad day.

'We went on a canal holiday once when I was a kid. I think I had an *I-Spy* book of things to look out for.'

He nodded curtly. 'There are quite a number of similarities between this and the toll-houses Telford designed for the Holyhead Road – no, not the city one, the one in Wales. But they are usually single-storied – this has two floors, see? And they're much smaller than the Lodge.'

'The Lodge?'

'That's what it's always been called. Out by the reservoir—' He broke off as one of his colleagues backed in, carrying a plate in one hand and a bottle of water in the other. 'I suppose there's still no sign of Rosemary, Sarah? It's not like her to miss a meeting. We've had a Lodge Preservation Society sub-committee group here this morning.'

Sarah, a handsome woman in her forties, shook her head. 'She didn't leave a message with anyone that I've met.' She sat at her desk, reached for a periodical, and settled to her salad.

'Rosemary Parsons,' he said parenthetically to Kate. 'A stalwart of our committee. Nice woman. Lives not far from you. She'd give her back teeth to have had a button workshop in her garden.'

'She could have mine?' A couple of prawns slid out of the baguette. She retrieved them.

'She could certainly fit it in. Between the fountain and the tennis court. It probably wouldn't even be seen from the conservatory. Authentic Victorian, none of your nasty modern UVPC.'

What was this man's problem with money? Him and his insistence on the worst coffee and all that crap. She fielded another prawn. 'She can't live very close to me.'

'Oh, out on the Kings Heath–Moseley border, anyway. She's really great. Her husband's an academic – spends a lot of time abroad. Since academics aren't usually swimming in money, I presume they've inherited a load. One of them. Some of which she spends on trying to preserve the Lodge. She's organised fund-raising dinners, called in favours from her blue-rinse friends – and she must spend a fortune on paper and phone calls but she never asks for a penny expenses. Not a penny. Oh, by the way, this is my colleague Sarah: she can tell you all about your buttons—'

Rod Neville, taking the stairs down with more speed than sense, had to grab Kate to steady them both. Was it imagination, or did his hands linger longer than necessary on her shoulders?

He flashed his most brilliant smile before becoming

almost stern. 'Kate — this tennis club death out in Kings Heath. The place you play, according to Sue Rowley. Do you know the woman involved?'

'If I did, I'd have been able to ID her, sir. And it's not actually a club. It's just a tennis centre, without a membership fee, so anyone can turn up and play. Even a rabbit like me.'

'Anyone?'

'That's what their charter says. Anyone. Regardless of ability. They don't even have a dress code.'

'So you don't know *any* of the individuals who might be involved?'

'Only my coach. And he tells me he was teaching at a centre in Handsworth last night.'

A glimmer of amusement flickered across his face. 'I thought you might have asked. Will you be joining us at the pub tomorrow?' he added.

'Everyone will, I should think, Gaffer.'

'Glad to be rid of me, eh?'

It wasn't quite a joke, was it? 'No one likes losing a good gaffer, Sir. And you've steered us through some very tricky times. Yes, you'll be missed.'

There was a pause. Perhaps he'd hoped for a different answer.

'See you tomorrow, then, Kate.' He ran lightly down the rest of the stairs and out of the building.

Fatima was on the phone when Kate reached the office.

Kate flapped a hand at her, and another at Colin, who flapped a hand back. She headed over.

'There's a meeting about your sarbut at four, Graham's office. OK?'

'OK.'

'And Guljar from Kings Heath was on the blower. Do you want to go to your tennis-player's post mortem?'

'Funny thing, Rowley's already asked me. I said no.'

'And someone else on the blower, too. Pat the Path himself. Would you like to go to your tennis-player's post mortem?'

'Shit! No, I would not! Damn it, it's not like going to someone's wedding, or even their funeral. It's to see them bloody cut up! It was bad enough seeing her huddled on the floor of the shower – she was dribbling, as if she were asleep.'

'Come on, I don't buy that corpses look as if they're asleep nonsense!'

'Neither do I. Not when the body's two shades of blue, as they are after that time.'

'Very Picasso,' he said.

Which reminded her of her lunchtime conversation: 'Colin, you're au fait with all things Brummie—'

'No, I'm bloody not. I'm Black Country and proud of it.'

'OK. Spare me your regional geography lecture. Do you know anything about the Lodge at the reservoir?'

'The rezza? Out by the ballroom? I know I was conceived out there—' His voice was suspiciously light.

'You what?'

'Oh, part of my dad's man-to-man talk about birds and bees. How, despite the myths, a girl can conceive standing up. A matter of some moment to me, as you can imagine,' he added in his campest voice.

But it would be a matter of importance, if not as a fact of life, to any child. What sort of man told his son he was an accident? 'I was a mistake, too,' she said. 'My mum thought she was past it. I proved the hard way she wasn't. Anyway, do you know anything else?'

'Lovely spot. Sailing on the rezza itself. You can walk all the way round. Plenty of space for the kids. Interesting views from the top of the reservoir wall. There was talk of having some Rosie and Jim theme park or something near there.'

'Rosie and Jim?'

'Characters from some kids' TV programme. Not on the site itself, but on an arm of the canal nearby. I've got an idea the land round the rezza is some sort of nature reserve.'

She asked off-hand, 'Any idea who owns it?'

'Could be British Waterways, I suppose. It supplies water for canals, not for the city. Or it could be the city. I take it you'd like me to find out?'

'Yes, please – no! Don't bother! It's not police business

after all. That guy Stephen Abbott must know. No point in reinventing wheels. I'll get on the blower to him. When I've dealt with this lot, that is,' she added, patting a toppling heap of paperwork.

So the powers that be didn't think they could get enough mileage out of Simon to make him an informant. Sarbut! Not formally. Not yet. Fuming, but knowing deep down that the decision made sense, Kate stomped back into the office, to find a note waiting on her desk. Guljar had phoned, suggesting half a pint at the Station, just opposite Kings Heath nick. Why not? She owed him if the CID boss was hassling him. She phoned to agree, then made another call, this time to Stephen Abbott. She got not him, but his answerphone, telling her to catch him on his mobile if the matter were urgent. She jotted down the number, but decided not to bother. It could wait till tomorrow, which the paperwork couldn't.

'Busy?' Graham was smiling down at her, for all the world as if an hour ago they hadn't had the gloves on over Simon.

She steadied a file and grabbed a Biro going roll-about. 'Average.'

'Equals busy.' He smiled again. 'I just wondered what

you'd learned about those buttons.' He perched on the edge of her desk, his thigh three or four inches from her hand.

'Military. Early Victorian, they think, though the design was still in use up to eighteen seventy-one. Made for the – let me get this right – the Twenty-fourth (Second Warwickshire) Regiment of Foot. Mine would be for officers. The other ranks got pewter instead.' And now she was sounding like Stephen.

'So someone wearing buttons made in your garden could have worn them – where?'

'Probably in the UK suppressing incipient trades union-ism or crushing goings on in far flung bits of the Empire. Wasn't the Indian Mutiny some time in the fifties? And then the Boer Wars? And would the Twenty-fourth Regiment of Foot have been involved in that?' She bit her lip. 'God, I'm so ignorant.'

'Aren't we all? And the more you know, the more you realise how much there is to know. And how much you want to know it.' He looked her straight in the eye. But he had slipped from the desk and left the office before she could register the meaning of his words. Or the gaze that accompanied them.

'This is such a luxury,' she said, drawing on the half of mild which Guljar assured her was a Midlands speciality and wasn't too bad at all, 'drinking without having to worry about the limit. Nice pub, too.'

'Parked at home, are you?'

She nodded. 'I've even got myself a parking space near to my house!'

'So you can drink the bar dry.'

'Quite. And on the way back home, I can pop in to Safeway, to see if they've anything on their shelves which Sainsbury's lack.'

'You might make all sorts of interesting choices with a skinful inside you,' Guljar said. 'God, what a day!' He stretched: she could hear a crunch as he eased his upper back.

She frowned: it must take a good deal of tension to make joints as stiff as that. 'Your DI being a problem?'

'You can say that again. That's why I suggested a drink here, not the canteen. You convinced me there's a rat to smell. But the more he talks to me, the less I can smell it.'

'Why should he be hassling you? It's CID's business now, whether he likes it or not.'

'Which he doesn't. I gather they've spent all day pestering the folk at the Tennis Centre, but they've still not got an ID. Their computer's well and truly sick; the manager's flat on his back with a slipped disc; the reception staff are down with a gastric flu bug, so they've brought in relief people from other centres.'

'None of the players any help?'

'None. But I gather it's a different clientele in the evening. We're going to have to do some sort of reconstruction, I suppose. We've got a big item on the regional TV news – both channels – so that should produce some results. "Do you know this woman?" That sort of thing. There's a team lined up to take the calls. In the meantime, I wondered if we could have a quiet brainstorm.' He produced a notepad.

Kate blinked. Unorthodox or what? 'OK. So what do we know about her?'

'Fifty-five-ish. Healthy – until she croaked, that is. Exercised regularly. Married – well, wears a ring, anyway.' He checked the facts on his fingers.

'So why hasn't her husband reported her missing?'

'Hasn't noticed?'

She pulled a face. 'So maybe separated or divorced but still wearing a ring for social protection … Possible, I suppose. Just. She took care of her skin – not a lot of wrinkles for her age. And dyed her hair. No, probably had it done professionally – it looked pretty well-cut.'

'Her tennis kit was expensive. Racquet's the make Tim Henman uses, apparently.'

She snorted. 'Not that his did him a lot of good this weekend.'

'Stylish gear. Good quality towel. Epitomised the well-off Moseley-ite. What's the matter? Something bad in the beer? Told you not to drink mild.'

She burrowed for her mobile. And for the line in her diary with Stephen Abbott's number. 'I've just got this weirdest suspicion,' she said.

Chapter Nine

'My God, poor Rosemary,' Stephen said, biting the back of his index finger. 'And to think I was cursing her for not turning up this morning. My God, if only I'd known.'

'You couldn't have known,' Kate said, steering him to a seat in the morgue foyer. He hadn't thrown up, but looked very close to tears.

She was followed by Nigel Crowther, Guljar's *bête noir*, and a sergeant in his forties she thought was called Tony.

DI Crowther said sharply, 'OK, sir. So you can positively identify that woman as Mrs Rosemary Parsons?'

Stephen looked up, blinking hard. 'Yes, she lived in Springfield Road. Can't remember the number. But I could take you to it. Oh, my God, I was really laying into her this morning, calling her everything under the sun. And she was dead!'

Kate put her arm round his shoulders.

'It's OK, Stephen. You mustn't blame yourself,' Tony said quietly.

'I think we'll take you up on your offer to show us the house now, sir,' Crowther said. He might have been a couple of years older than Kate, but not much more. So he must be very bright, very hard-working. He looked bright, too, with that indefinable gleam around the eyes that said a good brain lurked behind them. '*If* you're ready, sir?'

Kate straightened. Why was the man being so damned officious? As if guidance for such situations had never been given!

And now he was looking obviously, if not ostentatiously, at his watch.

Come to think of it, that neat-featured face under its well cut hair looked, in fact, thoroughly rattled. Perhaps it was the thought of all that TV publicity being in vain. Perhaps he felt he should have been with the team fielding the calls. Now, of course, he'd want to take a look at the house, instead, wouldn't he? And he'd have a hell of a lot of paperwork to round off. But all in all he'd been saved a lot more effort than he'd been caused. Surely he wasn't the sort of person to resent help?

Tony helped Stephen to his feet. 'You OK, now, mate?'

'Sure. Kate – it's such a shock—'

'Of course it is, sir.' Crowther again. 'Now, I think

we should make a move, don't you, sir? Thank you, Sergeant Power.'

Thank you and goodnight. Kate nodded in reply. 'Goodnight, sir.'

She might as well head for home, then. Suddenly she was weary with no adrenalin to drive her. How about supper from that brilliant chippie on the High Street? But before she started out, she had a phone call to make. Yes, she rather thought she'd like to talk to Pat the Path about the autopsy the next day.

So here she was, sitting opposite Patrick Duncan in a Chinese restaurant. It turned out he hadn't eaten either, so they might as well kill two birds with one stone, he said.

Neither of them had ever alluded to an embarrassing incident before Christmas, when Kate had declined to play his sexual games. And now sex was off the menu, they had no difficulty sharing a table and some conversation.

'So have you changed your mind about the p.m.?' Patrick asked, through a mouthful of spare-rib.

She shook her head. 'It's not my case, and there's someone at Kings Heath nick who fancies I've trampled on too many toes already.'

'Nigel Crowther, is it? He's a bright guy – lives with a linguistics teacher at one of the universities. Male,' he added, his voice neutral.

'Do you know him well?'

He shook his head. 'Not socially. I just know he's sharp – quick on the uptake and asks the right questions. Rather like you, really.'

'Thank you kindly, sir. He and I don't seem to see eye to eye about this stiff. He's going for death by natural causes, I – well, I won't tell you it's intuition – we all know how wrong that can be. Even mine!' she said, grinning and toasting him with her saki glass to show she'd got over his being right in another case. 'It's just a funny combination of circumstances. And I'll tell you what, it's an even funnier coincidence that helped us ID her . . .' Her explanation was brief: she didn't want her soup to go cold.

'It's not unknown for apparently healthy people to drop down stone dead,' he reflected.

'You will check every possibility – sorry, I know you will.'

'You know if I find any suggestion of foul play I have to stop and get the Home Office pathologist in?'

'Of course. But you will take every available swab, get the blood checked for absolutely – shit, I'm not being very tactful. You can see why I can't be there tomorrow.'

He dipped his hands in the finger bowl, drying them carefully before he said, 'Just between ourselves, yes. At least now we know who she is we'll be able to check her medical records to see just how fit she was. Not that people axiomatically go to their GP if they suspect something's wrong. I had this guy the other week who'd dropped dead with heart failure in his local Tesco. He was so riddled with cancer he shouldn't have been able to stand, let alone push a trolley. And he'd not been to his GP for months, except to complain about a fungus infection under his thumbnail which he could have cured with a proprietary preparation.'

'Perhaps he'd meant to tell the doctor about all his real symptoms and chickened out at the last moment.'

Patrick nodded soberly. 'Perhaps. None of us likes to think about our last end, as Joyce called it. Now, how's that knee of yours coming on? I can't wait to get you on the squash court ...'

Was it simple kindness that made Kate phone Stephen Abbott before she went to bed? She hoped it was, but she had to admit she might have been sniffing for information.

Stephen seemed genuinely glad to hear her, however. 'I mean, Rosemary was old enough to have been my mother – just – but she was a friend. Well, we were fighting on the same side to start with, but she was so – I mean, she could have bought and sold me and not noticed the small change, but she never shoved her money down my throat. She lives— Oh, God! How many times am I going to say that before I get it into my thick skull she's dead?'

'It's OK, Stephen. It's normal not to be able to take it in. And seeing her ... as you did ... I should think the brain tried to block it out. Have you got something to help you sleep tonight?'

'Apart from a bottle of whisky?'

'That might not be your best friend, you know.' No, she mustn't preach. And there was no need to point out how much harm drink had tried to do to her.

'I know. Alcohol's a stimulant. It might knock me out but it'll probably wake me up. No, I've actually got some homoeopathic stuff. Kate, you will let me know if there's anything—'

She waited a few seconds before prompting. 'Anything?'

'I don't know. There was no reason for Rosemary to die.'

There was something in his voice that worried her. 'If you think of anything – anything at all – you will tell us, won't you?' Every instinct told her there must be something. He'd gone from open to cagey in about three seconds.

'You sound a damned sight more interested than that inspector. He didn't want to know. He just wrote down the number of the house and got the older bloke to take me home. He and I were at the same university. Crowther, I mean. Never met, of course.'

'Which one?'

'Durham. Will he be investigating Rosemary's death?'

'Unless the powers that be decide to send in a special-ist team.'

'You're CID – will you be involved?'

'I'm afraid not.' Yes, she would have liked to be, but at least she could sound positive about her colleagues. 'Look, Stephen, every CID team is full of highly-trained men and women . . .'

On Wednesday morning she'd be late in: that had been agreed. She was going to talk to Simon again. They drifted to a Christian coffee shop a couple of hundred yards up the road. She could make sure that he had a good breakfast, at least. And the bacon sandwich smelt so good she joined him.

'Well,' Simon grinned, after his first slurp of coffee, 'seems I might have something for you. And it didn't cost you much either.' He started to push a tenner across the table to her.

She gestured it away.

He looked at her quizzically, but shrugged. 'Well, if it's who the guy I talked to thinks it is, she was a real old loner. Wouldn't talk to any men at all. Would spit at them if they came near. Not at all keen on women, come to think of it. She came from up Wigan way, originally. She's got – she had – all sorts of pretty horrible nicknames, but this geezer reckons she was really called Sally Bowles.' He caught her eye. 'Hang on, the bastard's been having me on, hasn't he? Isn't she in a film?'

'Mmm. The Liza Minelli character. But the other stuff – do you reckon that could be genuine?'

'Don't see why not. He wasn't quite so pissed then. Trouble is, Kate, he was so happy to be drinking something decent at someone else's expense, he ended up just wanting to please me. I guess when he ran out of hard info he just said stuff he thought I might want to hear. Do you want me to have another crack?'

She pushed another tenner across the table. 'Does the Pope wear a frock?'

Back at the office, Kate pounced on the phone, first ring.

Patrick. 'Heart failure. As far as I can see, it was her first attack. Nothing to show she was anything but an extremely healthy woman. So why the sudden death?'

'The heat of the tennis, the shock of the cold water?' Kate asked. 'When I've showered there the water was extremely cold. Breathtakingly cold. Mind you, it may warm up later in the day.'

'Even if it was still cold, why should it kill her? I know she was in her mid-fifties, but that doesn't mean she was a weak old dear in her dotage. Her doctor's notes make that clear: she went along for a sort of ten-thousand-mile service but there was never anything wrong. BP fine; smear fine; breast scan fine. She seems to have taken her HRT and got on with life. It's just possible, I suppose, that the cold water killed her. Or it may be simple coincidence.'

'Do you think there may be something in all those swabs and blood samples you've taken?' Kate asked.

'I hope so. I sincerely hope so. I hate having to ascribe the cause of death to an act of God.'

'You look very grim, Kate,' Graham Harvey said as she walked slowly along the corridor to the office. 'Fancy a cup of tea and a shoulder to cry on?'

The day she took Graham up on the second half of the offer he'd no doubt drop dead of a heart attack too – brought on in his case by an excess of guilt. Still, the tea sounded good enough. And she was so wound up she might even be better off with one of his herbal brews than with the caffeine-fix she craved.

'Thanks.' She slung her bag on the floor, but was too restless to sit down. Instead she headed for the window. His geranium cuttings would give her something to do – she could prod the soil to see if they were too dry, as usual, and tease round to check the new shoots. Anything to keep her hands occupied.

'There you are: peach and passion-fruit,' he said, putting the mug on the windowsill.

'Thanks.' She jiggled the tea bag until she deemed – as usual too early – that the brew was strong enough. 'I've been talking to Patrick Duncan.'

'You didn't go to the p.m.?'

'Didn't want anyone to think I was muscling in.' Turning so she could rest against the windowsill, she explained what had happened the night before.

'You don't want to put up the backs of the local people,' he said sharply.

So much for the shoulder to cry on.

'Of course I don't. But Crowther's been so slow moving – he—'

'Kate: get it into your head that however good a cop you are, you can't pick up everyone's case-load. OK? You've got enough on your plate with those fires, I'd have thought, on top of all the other stuff in your in-tray. And we're all going to have to pick up more admin with Neville going.'

'You especially,' she observed.

He grinned ruefully. 'But I wasn't talking about me. Any officer can do only so much work. OK, you might not like the pace Crowther's working at, but you can't read inside his head. He might be making an enormous amount of progress, but just doesn't see why he should have to explain himself to a junior officer from another

OCU. I wouldn't, if I were in his shoes. And I can't help noticing there's often something of an edge between you and officers from other squads — you and Lizzie over in Fraud never hit it off, did you? And she's a very good woman. Very good indeed.'

The peach and passion-fruit was a very thin brew indeed. Kate put the mug back on the sill, still half-full. Or half-empty, depending on how you looked at it.

Kate only ate that lunchtime because Colin dropped a sandwich on her lap. Maybe Graham was right. Maybe there was only so much any one officer could do. A quick meeting had established that they still hadn't got a positive ID on the warehouse fire victim despite everyone's leg work. She passed on Simon's suggestion, to some derision.

Closing yet another file, she slapped the side of her head. She'd asked Fatima to chase up something, hadn't she? But Fatima was on some blasted course today. Knowing Fatima, however, she'd have cleared her desk before she went. Which meant there was probably a neat note somewhere in the chaos that had accumulated on Kate's desk since yesterday if only she could burrow through and find it.

Which explained the frantic work and the fact she'd forgotten to eat.

If something was important, Fatima always used an envelope. A sealed envelope. So it might be in the post-pile. No? What about — longest of shots — e-mail?

And there it was. Amidst a stream of other messages. What time was the message sent? And from where? Fatima, bless her, had gone to the trouble of sending it from the course venue.

Kate

Arson attacks

Sorry — forgot to tell you about the art dealer's burns. Seems he was taken into Selly Oak A & E at midnight on Tuesday 30 March. Detained in the Burns Unit. I tried to find out why he'd been starting his garden bonfire at that time of night but wasn't allowed to talk to him — still too ill.

Fatima

Yes, it was indeed a strange time to be starting a fire. Clearly a conversation with the hospital authorities was called for. She e-mailed Fatima back: check where the ambulance collected him from. And, just to make life more interesting, she would phone Kevin Masters, the fire fighter — it would be nice, wouldn't it, to confirm there'd been no outbreaks of warehouse arson since the one she'd been called to last Wednesday morning?

It would have been nice if he hadn't changed shifts and wouldn't be available till seven that evening, by which time she ought to be in the pub saying farewell to Neville. Well, if an e-mail had worked for Fatima, perhaps it would work for her. And fingers crossed that Masters remembered to check all his virtual in-tray when he checked his real one.

Chapter Ten

The noise in the pub wasn't deafening yet. It was still possible to have a conversation without shouting, and without the older officers having to cup hands round their ears and lean intimately forward.

Not that Graham was that old, Kate would have thought. And Rod Neville, who still hadn't arrived, certainly wasn't. But a couple of guys who'd been involved with firearms in the pre-ear-protector days already had strained expressions on their faces, and peered closely at the lips of those they were talking to.

The talk was all of movement, of change. Fine officers retiring, others being transferred. Lizzie Siddal was loudly lamenting that with all the cuts she'd soon reach her original ambition – being Head of the Fraud Squad – without the promotions she'd always expected would go with the job: an ordinary DI, doing detective superintendent work!

No one had noticed that Rod Neville had slipped in. Kate wouldn't ever have associated him with shyness, but he hung back by the door, as if uncertain which group to break into. At last he caught her eye and smiled, starting to push over towards her. Although she tried to make room in the group around Lizzie, he swiftly detached her. In a second, Graham, who'd been on the edge of another group, managed to join the pair of them. Yes, poor Graham liked a bit of status, didn't he?

'How's this tennis court death going, Kate?' Neville asked, with less preamble than if he'd been in his office, where he always observed courtesies, no matter how pressing the business in hand.

'In the hands of the Path. Lab. and Nigel Crowther,' she said.

'I gather you found someone to ID the woman.'

'Kate's buttons man,' Graham put in.

'Buttons?' It was clear the question was directed at Kate.

She explained about her find and about Stephen Abbott's connection with the Lodge and with Rosemary Parsons.

'You've been busy.' Rod nodded his approval.

'She always is: too busy to—'

'And Sarbut says he may have an ID for the guy who died in the warehouse fire,' she put in quickly. 'Not that he is Sarbut, of course.'

As she'd known he would, he ignored the dig. '"Sarbut says". You've got the lingo at least. It's a sort of shibboleth. Rookies tend to say, "My sarbut tells me ..." – quite wrong!' Rod said. He stopped short, staring at his empty hand.

At last Graham took the hint. 'Gaffer?'

'Half of bitter, please.'

'Kate?'

'The same, please.'

They watched Graham push his way to the bar.

Neville leaned closer to her. 'You're really convinced that Rosemary Parsons' death was unnatural, aren't you?'

'I've been wrong before.'

'We've all been wrong at one time or another. And got results at other times. Like you did last December. A couple of fine pieces of work, Kate. You'll make a good cop.'

At least the pub lighting wouldn't show how deeply she blushed, less at the words than at the tone. But she was afraid that as she bobbed her head in a smile, her dimples emerged.

Neville laughed. And then, his face quite serious, added, 'Which is why I want you on this new MIT.'

'What!' She gaped. Would she be pleased or horrified? No, she didn't want to leave her mates, but she'd love to get her teeth into major cases.

'The MIT,' he repeated. 'There's a certain amount of

opposition, of course, but I take it you'd have no objection? Personnel are very keen – after all, they want to build up your CV.'

'I was thinking about pulling out of the fast track scheme, Rod.'

'I know you were. Maybe this assignment will help convince you you shouldn't.'

'What about the warehouse fires?'

Graham, juggling three glasses, reappeared. 'She's making progress with those. Which is why she shouldn't be pulled out tomorrow.'

Neville grabbed a glass hastily – his suit was too expensive for him to welcome a slosh of beer.

'Tomorrow!' Kate repeated. She looked straight at Rod, ignoring the glass in Graham's outstretched hand. 'It's all fixed, then?'

'All bar the shouting, as they say round here. You've been here long enough to understand the natives, Graham? No, you were born here, weren't you?'

'Solihull, actually,' he said, stiff at his sudden exclusion. 'So what's fixed?'

Kate took the glass. He didn't seem to notice.

'That business we were discussing earlier, Graham,' Neville said, so easily Kate suspected their discussions had been rancorous. 'Kate's move to my MIT.'

Graham's mouth was so compressed the skin around it was white. 'My comments are on the Procedure File,' he said, slamming his glass down on a table. With no more than a nod, he turned and was gone.

She turned to follow him. But Neville was shaking his head, and had stretched a lazy arm between her and the door. 'He'll be over it by the morning,' he said. 'Now, come and meet the team—'

'Just a moment, Gaffer. I'm not clear about this. What will the MIT be looking at first?'

'Itself. A day's training. Getting to know one another. And then, back to normal until we have a major incident. Then, just like Superman, we'll don our underpants over our trousers and zip to the rescue.'

'You don't think we've got a bit of a major incident in this fire business? All that property up in smoke, to say nothing of an old woman? To be blunt with you, I think it's more important to sort that out than to sit round bonding. That's probably why Graham—' She jerked her head in the direction of the door.

'Bless you, Kate,' he said, putting a hand on her shoulder, 'you're a woman after my own heart. But I don't think that that's what got up Graham's nose.'

She stared: was the man always so indiscreet?

He was smiling again. 'Maybe the fires will be the MIT's first case? Come on, this is a booze-up, not a policy meeting!' He lifted his glass. 'Here's to our very close association.'

Chapter Eleven

The scale of the MIT organisation amazed her. It wasn't just experienced officers and SOCOs, it was even computer in-putters. And there they were this Thursday morning, in a room usually set aside as an incident room, not just on the diagram projected by Neville's OHP, but in the flesh. And they were all, every one of them, looking at Kate, as she made an excruciatingly late entrance.

'Sorry, Gaffer,' she said. 'But I thought you'd all want to know. We've got another murder on our hands.'

She'd have liked to register accurately all the changes on Neville's face. Certainly they ranged from extreme disapproval, possibly even disappointment, to what now seemed to be comradely amusement.

'Well?' He put down the pointer and nodded to someone to raise the lights.

'This fax from Patrick Duncan.' She held it up. 'Rosemary Parsons – the woman who died at Brayfield Tennis Centre – had in her bloodstream a cocktail of fluconazole and terfenadine, washed down, it seems, with grapefruit juice.'

There was a gratifying silence. The men looked totally blank. But a middle-aged woman – Janet, a computer in-putter according to the name in plastic tiles in front of her – gasped.

The eyes of the room left Kate, swivelling to Janet.

'Is fluconazole the same as Diflucan? The big capsule?'

'Yes. According to Patrick, it is.'

'But you should never take Diflucan with terfenadine—'

'Nor terfenadine with grapefruit juice,' Kate agreed. 'At least according to Patrick. The combination – or in this case combinations – lead to extreme heart arrhythmia. In other words, a heart attack. Particularly if you take twice the recommended dose of each.'

'Someone should bollock her doctor,' said a thin-faced ginger-haired man in his thirties.

'But she didn't get them from her doctor. Not according to her medical records. And the post mortem showed no evidence that she had vaginal thrush, for which, according to Duncan, the Diflucan would have been an appropriate treatment.'

'Pharmacist, then,' said Ginger-hair.

'Terfenadine's prescription only these days,' Janet said.

'I used to have it for my hayfever, only my doctor said it was too much of a risk. I suffer from' – she blushed but continued – 'from thrush. And I sometimes have to use Diflucan to kill that. So I'm on the latest generation of anti-histamine now. And I don't take even that with grapefruit juice.'

'So when did she take it?' Ginger-hair asked. 'Presumably she didn't just pop a couple of pills while she was playing—'

'No, but someone could have popped them to her. In a drink, for instance,' Janet put in. An in-putter!

'But when did she drink it? Wouldn't she notice?'

'Depends what she was doing.'

'Isn't poison a woman's weapon?'

'Quite a sophisticated way of poisoning someone.'

'Not if you're a woman who has hayfever and thrush.'

The whole group was joining in. Rod Neville leaned back against a wall and folded his arms. 'Well, ladies and gentlemen,' he said at last, 'I think we're a team already. Maybe it's time we moved to Kings Heath and put into practice some of the things we've been talking about . . .'

The Victorian house where Rosemary Parsons had lived for the last twenty years was now sealed by the police. There was still no sign of Mr Parsons. *Dr* Parsons, according to an envelope lying on the hall table.

'So maybe we've gone to all this trouble for a simple domestic,' said Ginger-hair sadly, looking round the big square hall. A grandfather clock was clearing its throat to announce that it would soon be three-thirty. Ginger-hair was in fact a detective constable called Mark Wright. What he lacked in colour in his hair and eye-lashes — these were almost white — he made up for in colour in his clothes. He was sporting under his leather jacket a brilliant red shirt, with a highly patterned tie. He also wore several impressive rings, two of which included diamonds amidst all the gold. Whether it was ever wise to draw attention to such an abundance of ginger hair on your hands, Kate wasn't at all sure.

She felt, in her dark suit, like a pea-hen beside a peacock. And then realised she'd made a more precise analogy than she'd liked: Wright proved to have a nasty scream of a laugh, which he emitted from time to inappropriate time. This was not going to be her most pleasant pairing, was it?

She caught up with him in the kitchen.

'Maybe I was wrong,' he said, pointing to a list of numbers pinned by the phone. 'See — dates — first one, yesterday; hotel names. And those are the overseas dialling codes, aren't they?'

'Yes. But why's this list still here? Why didn't Crowther take it with him the other night? Damn it, the poor bastard's probably been trying to phone her, worrying why she doesn't ring back ...'

'If they've got an answerphone, of course. Though I can't imagine an establishment like this not having one.'

'So some poor sap has got to call up Mr — sorry, *Doctor* — Parsons in — where is he today? Berlin? — and tell the poor bastard he's a widower,' she said, feeling horribly that she was leading with her chin. 'And has been since Tuesday,' she added.

'Nice to know it doesn't have to be either of us breaking the news,' he said. 'They'll bring in Family Support or whatever it's called today to do that. What do you make of the place?' He looked round at the kitchen.

'A lot of money here. You could fit two kitchens my size into this.' Hell, she sounded like Stephen Abbott again.

'And five of mine. And it's all good stuff, isn't it? None of your plastic and paper pretending to be wood for these cupboards. The real McCoy.' He tapped a door to prove his point.

The living room came complete with a huge inglenook fireplace, the oak of the overmantel too dark and heavy for Kate's taste, and an intricate plaster-work frieze and ceiling-rose. There was a baby grand in one corner, an elegant hi-fi system in another. Apart from that, there was a wall of floor-to-ceiling bookshelves and a selection of easy chairs, none new. The French doors opened on to what seemed to be an original conservatory. And yes, there was a fountain, and in the furthest corner a tennis court. Some shrubs were already covered with buds or blossom, and there was an army of bulbs ready to break out.

'Loadsa money,' Wright observed. 'But it's not ostentatious, is it?'

'I could live here,' Kate agreed. 'Now, what about the rest of the rooms?'

There were some framed Victorian political cartoons in the downstairs cloakroom, and a pile of reading matter. The dining room was large enough for the table to be kept extended — it would have seated ten with ease, and a quick peer underneath established a couple more leaves could be pulled out to accommodate yet more. Again, a heavy fire surround, heavy velvet curtains, and an impressive ceiling. The pictures on the wall were genuine oils, in big gold frames.

'Not my taste,' Kate said. 'But I bet they'd be worth taking to the *Antiques Road Show*.'

'You bet,' he cackled. 'I wouldn't risk hanging them here in the front room myself — showing Burglar Bill what's on offer.'

'Burglar Bill's more likely to go for the hi-fi, isn't he?'

Wright pulled a face: 'There are specialist antiques thieves, remember. They even knock stuff off to order, don't they? So why didn't they have a burglar alarm, with all this lot lying around?'

Kate shrugged. 'Like those folk who smoke? Never going to happen to you. Now, I like that vase . . .'

Upstairs was more interesting. Two of the five bedrooms had been converted to offices – his and hers, it transpired. His was much the larger, full of books, with a computer with a nineteen-inch monitor on a desk that looked as if it would be happier with quill pens. Beside it lay a couple of quotations from security firms for burglar alarm systems. Mark tapped them, raising an ironic eyebrow.

Kate nodded, before turning her attention to the books.

'Seems as if he's an expert on the Holocaust,' Kate said. 'Shelves and shelves of books about it. Some in German, too.'

'Well, he is in Berlin,' Wright reminded her. 'Hey, you don't suppose there's some anti-Semitic thing here?'

'Why go for his wife, not him?'

'Well, maybe she's an expert, too. Let's check out her room.'

Kate wrinkled her nose as they went in. It was a classic box-room, barely large enough for the filing cabinet and small modern desk it contained. The computer was new, but much smaller than Dr Parsons'. Where he had books, Rosemary Parsons had telephone directories. If his room was a study, hers was an office. Complete, as it happened, with an answerphone.

Kate pressed the play button. Nothing except three messages from a man believing his wife was alive to hear his affectionate greetings.

Pulling a face, she patted the filing cabinet. 'We'd better bag up the files in these. I fancy they should repay a good read.' She opened a drawer at random. It was only half full. 'Now, has someone taken something away, or did she buy the cabinet expecting a long hard campaign?' She checked the other drawers. All of them were practically empty.

'So did Burglar Bill ignore the goodies and take away her files?' Wright asked.

'Come on: there was no sign of a forced entry. And we wouldn't be here if SOCO hadn't OK'd it. Except – hang on – she had no keys in her bag, did she? You wouldn't need to force an entry if you had someone's keys. And, if you do someone in in the evening, knowing she won't be found till the following day, you can spend a happy night working quietly and systematically through a whole house.'

'Wouldn't the neighbours notice?'

'Big detached house, nice thick privet hedge in front, no house within a hundred yards at the back.'

'And, of course, no alarm.'

'Quite. I bet this is the sort of neighbourhood where you get brownie points for keeping yourself to yourself. We'd better get the boffins on to the computer in case someone's wiped that. And the fax, come to think of it.'

'That's it, then. Back to base.'

'Let's just have a shuftie at the bathroom. I know SOCO will have taken away any pills and potions – I'd just like to see it.'

And it was worth seeing. While the rest of the house had been left firmly in period, this had had the full up-dating treatment.

'Wow!' Wright whistled. 'Looks like something in a posh hotel, doesn't it? No nasty pipes visible anywhere, all this nice wood and concealed lighting – my wife'd kill for something like this.'

'So would I. I wonder how much it cost to match the tiles to the carpet? And fancy having a separate shower from that bath—'

'That ain't no bath, lady – that's a Jacuzzi. Or at least one of those massage baths.' Another of those laughs. 'Kate, we're in the wrong line of business. All the overtime in the world wouldn't buy a set-up like this!' His gesture encompassed the whole house.

They looked at the garage before they left. It housed with comfort an M-registered Saab, a collection of tools, a bicycle rack to fasten to the back of the Saab, and a man's mountain bike.

Kate looked around. 'I wonder what she used?'

'Car or bike?'

'Either, I suppose. There was no car left in the car park, remember, and no car keys. That rack would carry two bikes. I wonder if there was a bike lying round anywhere at the Tennis Centre? A woman as fit as her wouldn't balk at bowling down there.'

'A couple of hours on court and she might balk at struggling back up the hill,' Wright said. 'Come on. Time we were heading back. Neville's called that meeting for five, remember.'

Kate nodded. 'Yes, it wouldn't do to be spectacularly late twice in one day, would it?'

Wright looked at her sideways. 'I'd have thought if anyone could get away with it, you could.'

She turned, arms akimbo. 'Oh dear, Rumour's raising its ugly head again, is it? Look, Mark, if we're going to be partners, let's get this straight: I am not fucking my way to the top. I am not fucking Graham Harvey, I am not fucking Rod Neville, I am not fucking Patrick Duncan, I am not fucking Nigel Crowther. I'm not fucking anyone, actually. More's the pity,' she added ruefully.

'Point taken, Kate. Points, in fact. And — because the rumour's bound to reach my wife before you can say partner that I'm at it hammer and tongs with you — I don't fuck my colleagues either. But I tell you what, you want to watch that blonde in-putter — she'd get her hands in anyone's knickers.'

After several false starts — Kings Heath Police Station was a real rabbit warren, despite its imposing modernised exterior – Kate and Wright found the rooms set aside for the MIT's use. One was a splendidly equipped office, with the computers already humming and plenty of phones. The other was a meeting room, with OHP, whiteboard and plenty of display boards. Rod Neville didn't have a separate room, just a glass cubicle off the common space. Poor man, no room for his expensive coffee-making equipment.

He was actually drinking chilled water from a dispenser – now that was a nice idea – when Kate and Mark arrived, both slightly breathless.

'Sorry, Gaffer!'

'OK: you've got three or four minutes, so get yourselves a drink. I take it you've got a lot to report?'

They looked at each other, shrugging. 'Got issues to raise, more like,' Mark said.

'Haven't we all?' Rod smiled.

'Now,' Rod began, 'before we start, just a word about our accommodation. We're here on other people's territory – we must observe the niceties of civilisation, like not purloining other people's parking spaces or hogging the gym.'

'There's a gym? Bloody hell! Where?' This was from a heavily muscled blonde woman.

Mark nudged Kate. Kate was too busy noticing a late

addition to the team to react. What was Nigel Crowther doing here?

'And one word of warning: I know there are hot drinks machines everywhere, but on no account touch the tea. I'm warned it's so vile it could have been the stuff that poisoned Rosemary Parsons. They don't even give it to people in the cells.'

There was the statutory appreciative snigger. But, Kate thought, as she looked at the others, his little jokes were going down well. His speech patterns were often headmasterly, or, at the opposite extreme, lifted straight from a spin-doctor. Perhaps one of the many courses he'd been on recently had been responsible for the change. Or perhaps it hadn't.

'Now, ladies and gentlemen, since our theoretical bonding was so appositely interrupted this morning, we're going to have to work on getting to know each other and our little quirks. I, alas, will be less concerned with work on the ground than with managing the infernal budget situation, but I can assure you it is not my desire to limit your overtime that is at the heart of my next dictum. It's the Service's policy and it's for the good of us all: I want you to work reasonable hours, not excessive ones. We shall meet regularly, not to satisfy an insatiable management desire for meetings, but to brief each other. The officer in charge of day-to-day operations was unable to be present this morning but is now with us – Detective Inspector Crowther.'

Now how had that happened? He was supposed to be running CID on a day-to-day basis here, wasn't he? Hadn't he got enough to do, making Kings Heath a better place to live? Or was someone else doing that now? What was called for was clearly a word with Guljar: he'd know the gossip.

'Now, DI Crowther knows the area like the back of his hand – he was born and bred down the road in Moseley, I gather.'

Pause for a curt nod and not particularly gracious smile from Crowther. Oh, dear. Some men were born to management; others had management thrust upon them. Kate could have wished for Rowley's homely tangle and rather baggy skirts, instead of that uncompromising wing of black hair and the razor-sharp suit.

Neville stepped to one side, sat down, crossing one leg elegantly over the other, and assumed his intelligent listening face.

'Thank you, sir,' Crowther began, picking up a board marker and turning to the pristine white surface behind him. 'Now, I'd like to hear from everyone in the team with something relevant to report.'

Mark Wright fell into step with Kate as they left the room. 'Well?'

'Well what?'

'What d'you think of the new gaffer?'

'I thought he handled the meeting like a pro. Pulled everything together well, shut everyone up at the right time. Very good.'

He looked at her sideways. 'There's a well-substantiated rumour that if it hadn't been for you the scene wouldn't have been preserved and that we wouldn't have ID'd Parsons. Right?'

'I backed up Guljar – he smelt a rat and so did I. And it was only by coincidence I worked out who she must be: the TV appeal must have brought in a flood of responses, so I probably only saved them half an hour.'

'It would have been nice to have been acknowledged for your part so far.'

'Senior SOCO thanked me.'

'And was summarily shut up for his pains. Poor bugger, having to check through all that litter you insisted was preserved. Still, if that's what turns you on. Anyway, what have you done to offend young Nigel?'

'Nothing at all. I'm sure he's just trying to make us into a team. I wouldn't want prima donnas in his situation, would you?'

'No, but in your situation I'd like a bit of what my gran always used to call fairation.'

She nodded doubtfully. 'Mine used to say, "Life's not

what you want, but what you get — so stick a geranium in your hat and get on with it." '

'Only one thing,' Mark said. 'Wrong time of year for geraniums — isn't it?'

And she thought of the exhausted cuttings on Graham's windowsill.

Chapter Twelve

On an evening like this, it would be lovely to have a garden to work in. There was still a stiff breeze, but any rain had cleared and the sun was warm. Kate might almost regret that she'd handed over the coaching of the Boys' Brigade football team – it'd be fun chasing a football around. On impulse, she changed into her running gear. She wasn't going to pound round the streets of Kings Heath. She wasn't pounding anywhere, not if she wanted her knee to stay friendly. She might, however, manage a gentle jog, and where better than the reservoir? OK, she'd have to drive out to Edgbaston, but she'd be able to look at the Lodge.

Parking the car, she looked round. The whole place, although it was close to the city centre, was attractive enough to be enjoyed by whole families out for an evening stroll. She wouldn't be the only jogger out there, but there were far more sailors, hurtling round in small boats, or, quite often, bobbing round waiting to be collected after having been tipped out of small boats.

Yes, there was the Ballroom — dance hall? — that Colin had told her about. And there — that must be the Lodge. Yes, it did look like a toll-house, except most toll-houses she'd ever seen — and she had to admit she didn't exactly have a degree in transport architecture — had been either compact two storied affairs or single-storied with a couple of wings. This was a hybrid, not unattractive, but a bit odd. Someone had tacked on the back what looked like a later extension, which might well reduce its historical value, she supposed. It was in a commanding position, controlling the road to the reservoir and lovely views of a surprisingly rural landscape, dominated by the water. So why had no one got round to knocking it down back in the sixties and seventies, when Birmingham was mad for more concrete? It didn't look to be in bad condition now: so why had Stephen talked about preserving it? Perhaps it wasn't because it was falling down — perhaps someone wanted to help it on its way.

Cursing herself — when would she learn not to make assumptions? — she looked around again. Yes, money, that must be the obvious answer. Big money, to take over either the whole site to turn it into 'leisure facilities' or simply to develop a small and exclusive part of it — a very good hotel, for instance. She'd better talk to Stephen first thing.

She looked more closely – the funny shaped front, the funny chimney matching it. Oh, there'd be technical terms that Stephen would know and use, but she didn't have them. She didn't need words to appreciate the place. And that was what it needed – appreciation and use. Someone to restore it properly, and a job to do. For such an unpretentious place, it generated a lot of protectiveness. In her, for a start, and in Stephen, and in the late Rosemary Parsons. And she had a gut feeling, now she'd seen the site, that it was intimately connected with Rosemary's death. Surely no building was worth killing – or dying – for. And in simple justice no one should profit by both a death and the destruction of something certainly old and possibly precious.

Simple justice. And the Law.

Kate was in sombre mood when she went to see Cassie, and would have liked to join her in a stiff gin. But on an empty stomach it would have been folly. She could always have a beer with her supper. Whatever that turned out to be. Whenever that turned out to be.

'Mrs Nelmes did her best not to be speaking to me today, but she had to come round in the end, didn't she?' Cassie said, gloating. 'She wanted to carry on about young Graham, of course, and who else could she do that to except me? Of course, she still doesn't know he pops in to see me, bless him.'

'Has he been in recently?'

'I was rather hoping he might tonight. What do you think? Does he know you're here?'

Kate said, unblinking, 'I shouldn't think so. I'm not working under him any more. I was transferred temporarily, as from today.'

'Oh, he won't like that, not a scrap. He tells me you shift the work of two. He likes that. And if you ask me, he might have his eye on you — no, not promotion. Not that at all. A different sort of working under him, if you get my meaning.' Cassie cackled and choked, so Kate had to slap her back. The old bones were frighteningly close to the surface.

Eyes watering, Cassie held out her glass. 'Seems I could do with a spot more medicine. That's better. So what's this about a transfer? You been a naughty girl?'

'On the contrary. I spotted something that someone hoped I wouldn't spot, and — well, called the police. And they've pulled together a special squad to investigate what turns out to be a murder.'

'Ooh, does that mean you'll be seeing young whatshis-name? The pathologist?'

'Yes. I told you, we do see each other from time to time. But only as friends.'

'Time you had a proper young man. And some children. That's what a woman needs.'

Kate risked it: 'You never had any.'

'That doesn't mean I wouldn't have liked to. If my Arthur hadn't been married to Elsie Myers, I would have. You see, she had money in her own right. And Arthur was very fond of the old spondulics. Oh, he was generous with me, but only because he could afford to be, see. He had that nice little business, but it was set up with her money, and she never let him forget it. Not that he would have, knowing Arthur. He was an honourable man. In his own way, that is . . .'

'Do you still miss him?'

'Not as much as I miss Edward Read.'

Kate nodded gently. She'd seen photos of a palely handsome young man when she'd been sorting out Cassie's possessions.

'He was the love of my life, you know. And the funny thing is, I've started to dream about him again . . .'

Kate had let Cassie reminisce as long as she could. But she could see the old woman was getting very tired, and she herself was beginning to feel woozy with hunger. So at last she excused herself, stopping on the way out to tell Rosie, Cassie's care assistant, she thought the old lady wouldn't refuse a hand to get into bed. Rosie nodded, absently fingering a bruise on her cheek. Another encounter with a 'door', no doubt – when would the woman do something about her violent partner? But in the past Kate had tried without success to get her to seek help, and now didn't have the right to do any more.

She was turning away to head for the stairs when she saw a familiar figure outlined against the dim corridor lights. Graham. So what would he do? Pretend not to have seen her and go straight into Aunt Cassie's room? Or avail himself of the opportunity to do a little extra-mural bollocking? She certainly didn't expect an apology, even an explanation, for his tantrum yesterday evening.

She gave a neutral, dimple-free smile, and waited.

Graham gave a great show of jumping with surprise, which he probably didn't expect to convince her. It didn't.

'How's the new job?' he asked.

'Fine. Things are coming together. Oh, and we're under Nigel Crowther.'

'Are you indeed? I'd have thought he'd have enough on his plate.'

'What was on his plate is now on someone else's. Don't ask me how. Or you might be able to tell me how,' she added hopefully.

His eyes narrowed. Then his face softened with a smile that started comradely but ended up as tender.

'I'll fill you in if I hear anything. I was just going to see your great aunt. How is she?'

'A bit low. She's been telling me all about the love of her life – he died of TB.'

'Poor bastard. And poor Aunt Cassie. Still, she seems to have found a substitute in that Arthur,' he observed.

The bitterness in his voice told her he was aware that other women found substitutes fast enough too. But it had never been like that between them, not quite, despite all the hole-in-corner measures he'd insisted on to prevent his wife knowing about even the most innocent phone calls, which somehow deprived them of their innocence. And she'd respected his ruling that they could only ever be friends. If anyone had residual problems it was he. Surely.

'But only a substitute,' she heard herself saying. Yes, she was tired, she was hungry. And if she wasn't careful she'd burst into tears.

He looked straight into her eyes. 'Quite.' He flicked a glance at his watch. 'Kate, I . . . Maybe if Cassie's upset I'd better give it a miss tonight. Goodnight, then.' And he was gone, dodging swiftly into a men's lavatory.

No, she mustn't even think about that, about any of it, till she was safely away from the place. The last thing she wanted to do was to have to confront him or his wife, worse still the two of them together, in the car park.

So why was someone phoning her in the middle of the night? She grabbed the handset, Robin's dying eyes still in front of her. She was shaking so much she could hardly speak.

'Kate? Kate? It's Zenia here. Zenia from next door.'

She must have managed some sort of reply.

'Are you all right, girl? Only we heard this screaming – wondered if you needed any help?'

'Oh. Oh, Zenia. I'm so sorry. I must have yelled in my sleep. I was having this dreadful dream ... Did I wake everyone? Oh, I'm so sorry.'

'Well, I'll tell my Joseph he doesn't have to break in and rescue you. You're sure you don't want me to come round, now, love?'

'Sure. Yes, quite sure. I'll go and get some hot milk or something. Then I shall be all right.'

She would. But Robin was gone, dead and gone as poor Edward Read.

Chapter Thirteen

'All these courses they keep sending us on, you'd think at least one would be on rapid reading,' Mark Wright said, pushing away one of Rosemary Parsons' files. He put his fingertips on the back of his neck, and, as if his arms were incipient wings, pushed his elbows back as far as they'd go.

'Not to mention deciphering bad hand-writing. Though to do her justice, Rosemary's wasn't too bad. If a bit – well, sort of childish.' Kate stretched too. 'And no use at all, of course. Just course notes from that local studies course she was on.' Somewhere along the line she'd changed her mind about Mark. They seemed to have become mates. She hadn't even flinched at today's orange shirt and green slacks.

'Go on, that's not a proper stretch: do the job properly.

Stand up – like this, see – and put your arms above your head. That's it. Now turn your hands to the ceiling, link the fingers and push, hard as you can.'

Doing as she was told, Kate was rewarded by a terrifying crunch from her upper chest.

'There! You'd pay an osteopath twenty quid to make them do that to you. My price is half a snifter at lunchtime. And you can show me the joys of Kings Heath. Such as they are,' he added dourly, looking at the rain drumming down on the car park.

'I'd much rather talk to Stephen Abbott – I'm sure—'

'When you two have stopped playing at Darcey Bussell or whoever, you could try getting some work done.' Crowther, his voice so cold with control he might have had advanced lessons from Graham. 'A word, please, Power.'

They snapped to attention.

'Yes, sir,' Mark said. 'Only we were both getting a bit stiff, like. I'll go and get us some water, Kate. Unless you'd prefer tea.'

Since the question was clearly rhetorical, Kate said nothing, simply waiting for Crowther to say whatever he wanted to say. Until it became quite obvious that Kate was expected to make some sort of report.

'The negative stuff first, sir. Mark and I have scanned the files for any sign of pro-Zionist or even Jewish connection which might have attracted the attention of a far right political organisation. As far as we can see, there is none. And though her husband was — *is* — an expert on the Second World War and Hitler's extermination policies, it seems simply to be as an historian. He seems to have no axes to grind.'

'That's the negative. What's the positive?'

'How well do you know Birmingham Reservoir, sir?'

Crowther pulled a face but rallied. 'I thought I was asking you the questions?'

'Sorry, sir. But it is relevant. You see, Rosemary Parsons was on the committee trying to preserve a building out there. What we hope is that these files' — Kate patted a pile of five or six — 'are connected with that. That's our next move, Mark's and mine, that is. To read through them.'

'Maybe you should have started on those first. It's a matter of prioritisation, isn't it, Sergeant? Now, if you're going to meet Doctor Parsons at the airport, you'd better be moving, I'd have thought.'

She stared. 'I thought Brady and Carter were—'

'They're on to something else. There'll be someone from Family Support to back you up, should you need her. I want you to put him under pressure. Yes, Power, a lot of pressure—'

'But the man's just lost—'

'Has just killed?'

Kate buttoned her lip. Putting bereaved partners on the spot had never been her favourite activity. Not that she couldn't, if she thought it necessary. The thing that really worried her was the delay in contacting him. However Crowther had missed that list of phone numbers in the kitchen was beyond her. He'd be very lucky if Parsons didn't whack in a complaint. 'How's the rubbish search coming on, by the way, sir?'

'I'm sure SOCO will let us know when they find anything. *If* they find anything. I still think it's a domestic.'

'A domestic? But he was out of the country?'

'A little naïve, aren't you, Sergeant? I'm sure he'd have ways and means — he's a doctor, after all.'

Patronise her, would he? 'His doctorate is on the Jews of the Warsaw Ghetto, nineteen forty to forty-one.'

A hit. She'd scored a hit.

But he continued without so much as a blink, 'To my mind, his exit from the country the morning before his wife's death is a little too pat to be entirely credible. We shall see. Meanwhile, I'm glad it wasn't I who was responsible for the expenditure of all these resources.'

Now that was impressive — a man who could be grammatically correct even at the moment of bollocking. No doubt he was such an expert he could give Graham lessons. And then the image of Graham's stricken eyes and taut mouth — far clearer than the actuality had been — swept before Kate's eyes, and it was all she could do not to reach for the phone.

Mark was hovering with plastic cups of water. DI

Crowther nodded at him, then at Kate. 'Remember: put him under pressure.' He left.

She dug in her desk. Damn, she'd not personalised it, had she. Back at Steelhouse Lane there'd have been some aspirin in her drawer.

Mark passed her the water and a couple of files before he asked, 'What's he said to upset you?'

She blinked hard. 'Nothing. It's just — well, I seem a bit on edge this morning.'

'I hadn't noticed.'

'I obviously deserve an Oscar, then. You know I lost my partner last summer. I had this dreadful nightmare last night — I'm not quite over it yet.' She took a deep breath. 'Seems he wants us to give Rosemary Parsons' widower the third degree.'

'What's happened to Brady and Carter?'

'He's got them on to something else.'

Mark splayed a hand on the files. 'I'd have thought these had priority. If Rosemary's been busy campaigning to protect something people don't want protected, maybe she's put someone's back up.'

'My reckoning exactly. I had a trip out to the reservoir last night — I'd have thought it a prime site. And where there's a prime site there's developers.'

'And where there's developers . . . It'd make sense. Let's talk about it in the car — we can catch a bite at the airport if we hurry.'

Something clanged in her head as she reached for her bag. 'Best if you drive,' she said.

Michael Parsons might have starred in a movie about World War Two as a brigadier, or perhaps a Royal Naval commander. He had the classic good looks and elegant carriage, even the well-cut clothes and slightly drawling accent, of the upper classes in World War Two movies. So this was where the money came from. Kate told her proletarian hackles to give themselves a rest. All he was at the moment was a man in shock.

'I still can't take it in. I still can't believe it. Will I be able to see her? Did they — make a mess of her?'

To hell with giving him a hard time. Except it was an order. 'You'll be able to see her shortly, Doctor Parsons. After all, we'd like you to identify her formally for us. I take it you haven't any other family who could do it?'

'No. No, we never had children. Too many hostages to fortune, we always said. We always planned a long retirement together.'

'Look, sir, the press'll be waiting,' Mark said gently. 'The authorities here have found an alternative route out for us, but we may have to make a dash for it. OK?'

Parsons managed a shaky laugh. 'I don't think I'm up to much dashing. This sounds so crass. So bathetic. Only I haven't eaten — not since ... I couldn't, last night. The hotel people called a doctor — he gave me something to knock me out. And then I was too ... it was such a dash to the airport. And of course, I'd had no time to tell them about my eggs allergy, so when the in-flight snack was scrambled eggs ...'

'Sit down, Doctor Parsons. We'll find somewhere private and get you tea and a sandwich,' Kate said. 'Anything else you're allergic to?'

'Just eggs. Oh, and nuts. I'm sorry, this isn't a moment to be talking about my health.'

'It's certainly not a moment to be eating the wrong thing and getting ill,' Mark said. 'It may only be an interview room, but we'll sort something out for you to sit on while we find some food.'

'Rosemary used to be a teacher.'

Ah! That explained the handwriting — all those neat sentences on the board, in grubby books.

'She loved teaching. Little children, the sort that run around like little animals and bob up and down with excitement. But then things started to change. She wasn't working in a particularly tough school, but she came home one day with the news that the little boys — five, six, that's all — had a new playground game. Rape. And from there they went downhill. "How can you feed their minds," she used to say, "when they've no one to see they've had a proper breakfast? How can they respect and love books if all they have at home are TVs and videos? How can I teach family values, when ninety-five per cent of them come from broken homes?" So when she reached fifty, I persuaded her to take premature retirement. It was as well I did – they ended the scheme soon after. After all, we didn't need the money. But at least her little pension gave her some independence.' Dr Parsons reached almost blindly for the tea and fumbled it into his hand. 'Not that she needed it. What was mine was hers.'

Kate was ready to pour him another cup: Mark had persuaded someone to produce not airport disposable but china cups and saucers, milk in a jug and hot water to go with the tea. There was a selection of sandwiches spread on a large plate, and a small plate for each of them.

All very civilised. They might have been in a select hotel rather than an interview room courtesy of the Transport Police. But a hotel room wouldn't have held a tape machine recording every breath, every half-suppressed sob.

'She was such an enthusiastic, such a passionate woman.' Parsons spoke almost compulsively. 'She had a career of her own but she was always there supporting mine. God, the long hours I've wasted, when I could have been there with her. What use is all that research, with Rosemary lying dead?'

So Kate was supposed to put pressure on a man with tears running down his face? She passed him a tissue, then, when he'd achieved some semblance of control, more tea. If she could get his blood-sugar level up – persuade him to eat. She passed a sandwich. But his hands were shaking so much he could hardly hold the bread together, let alone deliver it to his mouth. No wonder the German doctor had had to knock out the poor beggar.

She'd better try. 'How long had you been married, Michael?'

'Thirty-one years. Never regretted one moment of it. Not one. Either of us.'

'You never had – disagreements?'

'Rows? Oh, yes, we had rows. Real humdingers of rows,' he added unexpectedly. 'Threw things at each other, especially in the early days. There are some marks on our kitchen wall to prove it. We didn't have them plastered over: we left them there to remind us.'

'Did you have any rows recently?' Mark put in, his voice, his body language as gentle as Kate's.

'Probably – yes, we had a flaming set-to because I'd forgotten to put out the dustbin. Last Friday, that would have been. But it didn't matter – you see, officer, we always enjoyed making up again.'

'You weren't the sort for slow, smouldering disagreements?' Kate put in.

He shook his head decisively. 'That sort of thing breaks up marriages. We're the only pair in our circle with the original marriage partners, would you believe?

"Till death do you part ...".' This time he wept in good earnest.

Kate told the tape recorder they were taking a break.

Back at Kings Heath, she dropped the airport audio tape into the security box and broke open another. Parsons said he was pleased for them to keep a record: all he wanted was a copy afterwards, in case his memory ever needed jogging, he had so much of his wife to remember.

'Crowther'd like him to get a copy via his solicitor – he really wants to nail him,' Mark said, coming back from the MIT office. 'Except I'm sure in his heart he doesn't believe he killed Rosemary – it's almost as if he's repeating things, parrot-fashion.'

'I thought parrots were supposed to be intelligent,' Kate said dourly. She'd forgotten to get any aspirin, hadn't she?

'Miaow,' Mark said.

'Oh, and cats too. Very intelligent. Oh, of course he's good. Has to be to be where he's got as fast as he's got there. If you look at his record, it's exemplary.'

'So why's he off-beam with this one? Because he is, you know. And say what you like, he's taken against you. Is it because your rampant heterosexuality offends his sexual orientation?'

'Jesus – what cornflake packet did you get that off?

You know, until someone told me, I truly didn't realise he was gay. None of my business if he is.'

'And don't look at me in that "none-of-your-business-either" way, either. I may not have been on a rapid reading course, but I've been on my equal opportunities ones. OK?'

Kate nodded and wished she hadn't. The headache was no longer a back-of-the-eyes niggle. It felt as if someone were screwing her eyes out of their sockets. Thank God it was the weekend tomorrow: except somehow, she didn't think that, for all Neville's fine words, it would bring much in the way of free time.

Chapter Fourteen

———◆———

Kate took into the interview room some drinking chocolate and a selection of biscuits, after Parsons had declined the offer of coffee. 'Tell me,' she said, trying not to slop, 'these allergies of yours must be very inconvenient, Michael. What do you do for them?'

'Avoid them, if I can. I'm not one of those people who die if they get so much as a whiff of a peanut — anaphylaxis, isn't it? No, I just get a bit of asthma and some eczema. See.' He produced a spray of some sort. 'And just in here' — he burrowed in an inside jacket pocket for a bubble-strip — 'are my antihistamine tablets.'

'May I?' She held out a hand. 'Doctor Parsons has shown me an asthma spray and a strip of antihistamine tablets,' she told the tape-recorder.

He looked blank, but passed the strip across. 'Telfast,' he said. 'Latest generation. No side effects at all as far as I can see.'

'Did you ever take Terfenadine?'

He looked completely blank.

'They were marketed as Triludan, I believe.'

'My doctor took me off them as soon as these came on the market. I get on with these much better.'

'What did you do with those you had left?'

'I didn't have any left. I finished them and trotted off to the surgery for some more and my GP gave me these. About two years ago, I'd say.'

'You're quite sure you had none left – in some cupboard, somewhere, for a rainy day?' She felt bad, pressing him like this. But she should have done it back at the airport, shouldn't she, as soon as he'd mentioned his allergy. Now she was in danger of making a big deal of it. And taking her eye off other things. What was happening to her brain?

'Quite sure. Rosemary was very systematic. Anything unused for a year and it was out. Clothes and shoes, too. Oxfam did very well out of my old sweaters. And books. Not academic books. But holiday reading, that sort of thing. And if you hadn't read the *Observer* by the end of Monday evening, woe betide you.' He managed a watery grin. 'She did concede that it wasn't possible to read the whole thing on Sunday.'

She tried again. 'Would you describe her health as good?'

'She had just one bad patch, during the menopause. Then she went on HRT and sang her way through life. Almost literally. The energy she put into things — like saving the Reservoir Lodge, for instance.'

'HRT — that doesn't suit everyone, does it?' It was like the Pill, wasn't it? Side effects.

'It certainly suited her.'

'You and she — you sound very happy. Did either of you ever have any — any problems?' If Kate sounded embarrassed it was because she was. But she and Mark had agreed beforehand — medical problems were her questions. Mark would take over later, on more general issues.

Parsons gave a bark of laughter. 'You mean male menopause? Only occasionally, Sergeant. I wasn't knocking on my GP's door for Viagra.'

'I meant things more like your wife's blood-pressure, weight-gain, thrush — that sort of problem sometimes arises with HRT.'

'No. HRT suited her. She never had any of those things.'

'Would she have talked about them with you if she had?'

'For goodness' sake, we're talking about a marriage of thirty years, not a one-night stand.'

'I'm just trying to establish that to the best of your knowledge there were no' – she checked the name – 'Triludan tablets anywhere in your house. Nor any thrush preparations, such as Diflucan tablets.'

'Absolutely not. I don't know what you're getting at. Next you'll be asking me what she kept in the fridge!'

She should be saying something, shouldn't she?

Mark coughed gently. 'Funny you should say that, Doctor Parsons. Because I was wondering, did you or your wife enjoy fruit juice, that sort of thing?'

Parsons pushed away from the table. 'Are we in some sort of mad-house here?'

'Please sit down, Michael,' Kate said. 'There is a method in our apparent madness.'

'OK, yes, she liked fruit juice,' he shouted. Then he took a deep breath. 'We tended to drink orange because I preferred it. There are probably a couple of boxes in the fridge.'

Kate nodded. There had been. Thank goodness Mark had remembered.

'Now – for pity's sake: can you tell me what all this is about?'

'You've been told your wife died of a heart attack, and you must have guessed that we don't think it's as straightforward as that. We think someone introduced various drugs into a drink. Which proved fatal.'

'Poison!'

'If only it were something as traceable as that, Michael. What we think happened is this . . .'

'A tennis partner! Someone she knows well enough to play tennis with wanting to kill my Rosemary.'

'We simply don't know if it was a tennis partner. But we can't rule that out. So if you could let us have a list of the people your wife played tennis with, it would be more than useful.'

Parsons spread his hands. 'It was something she'd taken up since she'd retired. She had lessons — coaching, I suppose I should call it — and then started to play with some arrangement they have for over-fifties — some sort of mix and match arrangement. There's a coach who supervises that. He'd know. And then — especially if she knew I wasn't going to be around — she'd arrange with some of them to play in an evening. A real passion, she'd got. I mean, that was Rosemary. Her tennis and her Lodge-saving. But tell me — who on earth would want to kill a woman like her?' He started to sob, dry, controlled sobs that must have hurt.

Mark, putting his hand on Parsons' shoulder, asked quietly, 'Is there anything we can get you, Michael, anything you want?'

'I want only one thing,' the man cried out, shaking

himself free. 'Can't you understand? Only one thing. The living touch of my wife's hand.'

'But can you believe him?' DI Crowther asked, sitting on a table and crossing his legs slowly, as if he were aping Neville's elegance.

'It would take a lot to make us believe he was lying,' Mark said. They'd agreed that he should take responsibility for presenting their day's results to the late afternoon-evening. Kate's headache was now a full-scale blinder. God, what if Crowther made her angry and she embarrassed everyone by throwing up or keeling over?

'All right. Let's assume for a moment he's a genuine grieving widower. Anyone got anything else?' He'd have made a good teacher, wouldn't he? Or a good committee member – like Rosemary.

Marilyn, a constable in her forties Kate had hardly spoken to, raised a hand. 'So far seven people have come forward to admit that they were at the Brayfield Centre on the evening in question, and they've identified a further five. We start to interview them tomorrow. But no one's managed to sort out the centre's computer—'

'Why hasn't that gone off to the forensic geeks?' Crowther demanded. 'If it's a job for experts, Constable, let an expert do it.'

Marilyn flushed. 'We've also a report of a bicycle seen

chained to the centre's cycle stand at the very end of the evening. Did you check with Parsons whether his wife would have used one, Kate?'

Kate shook her head dumbly. She made a shaky note.

Crowther's face and hands indicated supreme despair.

'I'll go round tonight, sir,' Kate said. 'We had to cut the discussion short because Doctor Parsons clearly couldn't take much more.' No more than she could. 'In any case we had to come up here.' OK, it sounded like an excuse, but it had the virtue of being true.

'Well, Sergeant, when you eventually get round to it' — he paused heavily and an image of Meg Hutchings and her Cornish round tuits flashed before Kate's eyes — 'you might consider asking Doctor Parsons a few other questions that might conceivably be useful — about his past, her past, that sort of thing. Unless you had time to do that?'

'No, sir. Not yet.'

'Dear, dear, and I had it on the best authority that you were a crack detective. Pull your socks up, Sergeant—'

There was a murmur from the others.

Mark was on his feet: 'With due respect, sir, there's only so much we can achieve. We weren't, if you remember, scheduled to do the interview with Parsons, so we didn't have time to bone up on anything beforehand. I mean, like that saying goes, we can do the impossible in five minutes, but miracles take a bit longer.'

'Point taken, Constable.' But it clearly wasn't.

At least they had the support of the others in the team: Crowther was going to blow it if he wasn't careful. But even that knowledge couldn't calm the waves of pain around Kate's eyes.

Carter, a constable who, it was rumoured, played the cello in his spare time, coughed diffidently. 'Since it was originally intended to be our assignment, sir, we did get a bit of background on Parsons. Before you sent us off to check if local pharmacies had sold the drugs in question to Mrs Parsons. A negative report, so far, incidentally.'

Brady nodded. 'We got the bumf from the university. His personnel file. Haven't had time to plough through it yet.' He passed the folder – half an inch thick – across to Kate with a smile. 'All yours.'

'Thanks.' She managed to return the smile. 'By the way, the guy who gave the initial ID – Stephen Abbott: he seemed to know about Rosemary. Has anyone talked to him yet?'

'If you know about something, Sergeant, you're expected to follow it up. Anyone else?'

Tony, who'd been with Crowther when Stephen had identified Rosemary's body, grinned. 'How about a fine set of Kate Power's finger-prints?'

Kate sat up and stared, head clanging.

Tony nodded at her, quite cordially. 'On a plastic drinks bottle. Apparently,' he continued, 'Kate got all the rubbish saved. Right? Just on the off-chance. Well, SOCO found a bottle that smelt of grapefruit juice, they thought, so they had a very careful look at it. Checked it for everything. For a start, they found — and they thought this was very odd — only one set of prints.'

'Sergeant Power's prints? I think it's time we stopped this meeting now. Power — I'd like to talk to you immediately.'

'You're clearly off the case,' Crowther said, sitting behind the desk in his original office, and then getting up again. 'You may be facing a charge of planting evidence. I'll talk to Superintendent Neville about suspending you completely. I don't like bent cops, Power.'

'Neither do I, sir. But if you'd be kind enough to listen to me, I can offer a very simple explanation.' Kate hoped she sounded calmer than she felt. Her head now ached so badly she could hardly see Crowther, let alone focus on him. She gripped the back of a chair — mustn't pass out on him.

'I'm sure you can. A very plausible one, no doubt.'

She made a huge effort. 'Do you seriously think that if I were planting evidence I'd leave my bloody prints on it?'

'Don't take that tone with me, Sergeant. I think it's time you left the building. I'll be in touch with you in due course.'

'With all due respect, sir, we've got a murder on our hands.'

'Which is precisely the reason you will not be in the building. And why you will not be talking to any of your colleagues, either. Get out of my office, Sergeant. And if you're still in the building in ten minutes' time, I'll have you on a charge of insubordination as soon as you can say knife.'

Kate took a deep breath. 'I shall be talking to my Police Federation representative. You'd better be sure, sir, that you're following the approved procedure to the letter—'

'Out! Now!'

The office heaved like an oily sea. She left.

Chapter Fifteen

Painkillers. Now. Something really strong. There was a Lloyd's on the corner opposite Worksop Road. Thank God she'd left the car at home this morning. She wouldn't be safe driving. Not with eyes that hurt too much to open.

Equipped with something – she'd no idea what the pharmacist had given her – she turned for the traffic lights. And leapt back, as a car hooted her out of the way, his passenger yelling at her. Reeling, she staggered into another pedestrian.

'Fucking pissed at this time of day! Should be ashamed of yourself.'

Another voice. 'Hang on, mate. Can't you see she's bad?' And someone took her arm. 'Kate, come on. It's me. Simon. What's up?'

'Simon?'

'Yeah. You know. Down Sainsbury's. Selling the *Big Issue*, right? Come on, chick. Let's get across this lot while we can.'

Someone gripped her arm, quite hard, above the elbow.

'Now, where are you going?' Simon asked.

'Home. Just up here. I'll be fine. Honestly. Thanks, Simon.'

'You got a migraine or something?'

'I don't get migraines.'

'Always a first time. Or even a stress headache. That's what my mum used to get. Now, where you got to go?'

'Just up here. Just up Worksop Road.'

'I'll see you up there. Plenty of time. And if you like, I'll make you a nice cup of tea.'

If she drank tea, if she drank anything, she'd throw up. She knew she would. But he could get her some water for those tablets.

'Which house, Kate? This side of the road or the other?'

'Far side.' For the life of her she couldn't remember the number. Maybe she'd recognise it when she saw it. If she could see it.

'There – soon have you feeling better,' Simon said, taking the empty glass from her. 'God, you got this place looking

nice. I feel – you know – this place is clean. And I'm—'
He picked at his clothes.

'Don't be daft.' And then a bubble of thought surfaced.
'Unless you want to pop your stuff in the washer. And have
a nice bubble bath or something. Only if you want to.'

He flushed scarlet. 'Would that be – I mean—'

'There's a unisex bathrobe. And you can tumble the
stuff dry. So long as you can do it. The detergent's on
that shelf.'

'But—'

'Up to you. A nice private bathroom for you . . .' The
world started to ebb and flow.

'You ought to be having a lie down, not worrying about
baths and washing.'

She managed the tiniest of nods. 'Going to lie down.
See you in a bit.'

Halfway up the stairs, she realised her legs wouldn't take
her any further and she finished on her hands and knees.

It was dark when she woke. It took her a moment to place
herself. Then information arrived quite separately in her
brain, like the names clicking up on a station destination
board. Dark. Bed. Her own bed. The bedroom in the
house she must now call hers.

So why bed? How had she got here?

No. She wasn't dressed. Not dressed?

She didn't remember getting undressed.

The words on the board were clicking more quickly now.

Someone must have undressed her. Simon! Simon must have undressed her.

She was up and out of bed before she remembered her head. Except it wasn't hurting, not apart from a distant dull throb. Yes — she clicked the light — there were her clothes. She picked through the neatly folded pile. All there. All except her bra and pants. Jesus, what sort of pervert was he, to take her bra and pants? It was only as she fished in the drawer for spares that another fact registered. He hadn't taken her bra and pants because she was still wearing them.

Cold. The central heating must have switched itself off. But she'd better go to the bathroom before she could risk the stairs.

It smelt of lavender. Her soap. And was immaculately clean. The only sign that someone had used it was a corner of towel sticking coyly from the linen basket.

The same was true of the kitchen. The washing-machine and tumble-dryer doors were ajar. Someone had used but washed up a mug, a plate and a knife.

There was a note on the kitchen table:

Dear Kate
Sorry, I was really hungry so I had some bread and

cheese. Oh, you need some fresh milk — yours is going off.

Hope you'll soon feel better.

Love

Simon. XXX

What a nice kid. And she'd thought him capable of — no, she hadn't seriously thought it. But why was her handbag open? Well, she couldn't in all honesty blame him if he'd helped himself to a few quid — he'd have lost a lot of sales by bringing her home. Ah! Another note.

Your keys are in your porch-thing. Thought I'd better lock you in.

Chapter Sixteen

⟫◦⟪

The last person Kate expected to see on her doorstep at nine-thirty on Saturday morning was Sue Rowley, clutching a carton of milk.

'It was behind that tub of yours,' she said, stepping inside purposefully. 'Time you turfed out those poor winter pansies and started your early summer flowers. Hm, that coffee smells good.'

Kate bowed to the inevitable. 'Would you like some, ma'am?'

'Sue, at this time of day. Please.' She darted a head into the dining room and moved into the living room. 'Hey, you've got this place looking nice. Is it true what Graham was saying, that you had no water or heating when you arrived?'

'Nor all that many floors, either, actually.' They were

now in the kitchen. 'And this work-surface took for ever to arrive.'

'So no hob, no sink. How on earth did you survive? Well, it's looking lovely now. Oh, I like your table – nice wood.' Stroking it, she sat down. 'I never see ours these days, for homework. A level and GCSE respectively, this summer. Thanks.' Rowley took the mug of coffee Kate was offering and stirred in milk. 'No sugar, thanks. I've put on half a stone since I joined the squad. I've got these sweeteners. Now, sit down and tell me about your fingerprints.'

Kate did as she was told. 'It seems almost a point of honour for players not to use the bins for things like ball-tubes and drinks cans and bottles. I mean, the bins are right by the nets. But come mornings I can pick up five or six things – and that's just off my court. I suppose the bottle with my prints must be one of those I retrieved last Tuesday.'

'"Retrieved?" Where do people put them, then?'

'There are these heavy green curtains at the backs of the courts. They're to deaden the sound and also to absorb the impact of the balls. Some of the balls get under the curtains so when my coach and I are gathering them up, I bin the bottles at the same time.'

'Did you notice anything odd about any of the bottles last Tuesday?'

Kate shook her head.

'But there must have been something odd, surely, for SOCO to notice it?'

'Someone said they were sniffing the contents of each — to see if they'd ever held a grapefruit juice cocktail.'

'With knobs on! So what does that tell us about the bottle?' Rowley had fished a notebook from her pocket and started to scribble.

'That it had been wiped. So inadvertently I retrieved not just any bottle but what turns out to have been a suspicious bottle.'

'Which I now trust is at the lab. And what else does your find tell us, Kate?'

'That Rosemary was probably playing on the court I was on. Or the adjacent one.'

'Only one adjacent one?' Rowley cocked her head.

'The balls tend to stay more or less on your own court — there are heavy nets to stop them going on to the next. And I was playing on the court nearest the door. Jason — that's my coach — and I don't see why we should walk any further than we have to when we're the only ones on court. The important thing is, it should help us work out whom Rosemary was playing with.'

'So why haven't you told Nigel all this?'

'Because he slung me out of the squad — and then out of his office — before I could say anything.'

'I heard words like threatening behaviour and dumb insolence being bandied around.'

The bastard. The absolute bastard. Then it dawned on her: 'But you didn't believe them or you wouldn't be here.'

'Possibly. So now what?'

'What indeed? I know I made a balls-up of interviewing Doctor Parsons yesterday—'

'There were two of you present?' Sue asked.

'Yes, but Mark—'

'Is an experienced constable – despite his taste in loud shirts. OK.'

'There were lots of things someone else said about Rosemary I should have picked up. You see, she was friends with that guy out there at the bottom of the garden.'

'Bottom of the garden?'

'He's the archaeologist who's after my buttons.'

'Not a fairy, then?' Sue rolled her eyes.

'Not as far as I know!'

By this time both women were giggling.

'You'd better ask Colin for an expert opinion,' Sue guffawed. 'Oh dear, thank God I didn't say that at work. Such a nice young man, as my mother would have said. Wasted on another man.'

'Certainly wasted on his present man – poor Colin's going through a really rough patch.'

They were sober again.

'Anyway, this archaeologist who's excavating my site

knew Rosemary. Quite well, I suspect. He's out there now, bristling with potential leads, and I can't even talk to him.'

'No, but I can. Oh, Kate, the sooner we've got this wretched business sorted the better.' Sue pushed herself to her feet.

'How did you hear about it all?' Kate asked, opening the back door for Sue to step into the garden.

'This is between you and me. Rod phoned Graham — asked him what he should do, basically.'

'Eh? A super asking a DCI for advice?'

'Well, I would have in his place. Heavens, Kate, it's a delicate one — an inexperienced DI inveigling himself into the MIT and then cocking up something shocking.'

'"Inveigling"?'

'Forget you heard that. Oh, all right. But I haven't said this either, mind. The word is that someone high up phoned Personnel, who then put pressure on Rod. Who seems to think I'm some sort of Mother Confessor, for all I'm only a couple of years older than him. Hey, what's that?' She patted a mini-wheelie bin by the back door.

'My wormery.'

'Worms? God bless us all!'

'I had these problems with maggots, you see. And had to have therapy. I mean, someone in my job not coping with maggots! So — just to prove I could — I bought this.

You put worms in the bottom and rubbish on top. The result is high quality organic compost.'

Eyes dancing, Sue started to giggle again. 'Jesus, that sounds like a parable of our times. Oh, dear. Oh, dear!'

'The difference is that my compost is good, healthy stuff. Or will be. Oh, Sue!' Kate wailed, doubling in laughter.

The older woman made a visible effort. 'The trouble is, should we protect Crowther's ego or yours? What I shall recommend to Graham and Rod is that it's put about that you're on sick leave — Mark said you'd got a migraine or something.'

'The jungle drums haven't half been beating,' Kate observed.

'Mark was on the phone to Graham before Rod was, as it happens. So with a bit of luck you can go back in after a discreet break—'

'Break!'

'Oh, say, tomorrow, if I can fix it with Rod. Monday, anyway. And no one'll say anything more about it. What do you think?'

Kate pulled a face. 'Are you sure I wouldn't be better off back with you and Fatima sorting out those warehouse fires?'

'Well, Fatima's on sick leave. She tried to interrupt some bar brawl and got two lovely black eyes for her pains. So, God help us, we've got a MIT on the fires.

Bloody crazy – you know all about them and you get plucked off the case and shoved in another MIT. Bloody administrators. Now, lead me to this fairy.'

The garden path being as short as it was, there was very little leading. In fact, Kate was afraid that Stephen, despite the radio beside him playing classical music, might have heard Sue's suggestion. If he had, he gave no sign of it, and he jumped authentically when Kate spoke.

'Let me get this straight, Stephen,' Sue said, in a tone suggesting that she was exercising the greatest self-control. 'Correct me if I've misheard you or got anything wrong. OK?'

Small boy in a corner, Stephen nodded.

Sue counted on her fingers. 'One. Rosemary was afraid that she was being followed. Two. She was sufficiently convinced to go to a police station and ask for advice.'

The air was buzzing with suppressed exclamation marks. Not for one minute would Sue spell out that she thought he'd been criminally irresponsible not to tell someone all this. But he was getting the message, no doubt about that.

'And was sent off with a proverbial flea,' Stephen confirmed, lifting his chin.

'Any idea which police station?' Kate asked, forgetting she shouldn't.

'No. But Kings Heath would be the logical one, given where she lived. Wouldn't someone have kept some sort of record?'

Sue made a non-committal noise.

'Well, they should have done!' he said, on the offensive at last. 'She was making a serious allegation!'

'An allegation like that has to be against someone before we can act. You've no idea, Stephen, the number of nutters who're convinced that MI5 are tailing them. So have you any idea whom she alleged was stalking her?'

He shook his head.

'You're quite sure? Even the longest of shots?' Sue prompted him.

He shrugged angrily: 'The sort of enemies she'd made wouldn't tail anyone themselves.'

'Enemies? That's a very strong word. Come on, Stephen. What enemies?'

'How do I know? You're the police!'

'What enemies?' Sue pursued.

'Look, I said all this to that bloke the other night, when I was showing him Rosemary's house. Tried to. I should have told him something else, if he'd listened.'

Kate asked, 'What's that?'

'Oh, I said — it was a joke, really — I said if she was worried she should write everything down and send it in a letter to her bank. Look, I would have told that guy the other night.' He turned to Kate, hostile. Probably with guilt. 'You said the bloke in charge was the best. Some best, not to take any notice of what I was saying.'

'DI Crowther wasn't involved in the investigation at that point—' Sue began.

And in any case Kate had meant Rod. So why had Sue mentioned Crowther?

'Which must mean he is now. So why doesn't he get his sodding finger out?' Stephen turned his back on them, and fiddled ostentatiously with a peg and a measuring tape.

'Which organisations had Rosemary annoyed?'

Stephen straightened and turned. 'Well, I offered that guy a sight of all the Lodge Preservation Committee records, but he didn't seem interested.'

'I am. Very interested,' Sue said. 'In fact, I'll take you home now, to pick them up.'

He dug in the pocket of a donkey jacket hung on one of the few remaining fence posts. 'I don't want to leave this site. I'm working in my own time, as Kate knows. And Kate also knows she wants her garden! So why don't *you* go and pick them up? You and Kate. You're policewomen, after all. This is the front door key – right? And this little chap's my filing cabinet key – the one on the right of my office. Don't bother about the other one – just rubbish. Oh, and the burglar alarm code's the date of the Battle of Waterloo.'

Kate raised her hands in despair. He knew this was

urgent and yet he was still prepared to fart around.

'Ah. 1815,' Sue said crisply.

'I suppose it could have been a more obvious date,' Sue said, unfastening her seat-belt. She peered upwards. 'Are you sure this is the place? It's huge!'

'Obvious?'

'It's obvious if you have kids doing that particular era of history, anyway.'

'I didn't think schools bothered with such trivia as dates,' Kate said. And she'd been too ignorant to be able to talk sensibly to Graham about the Victorian Army and its buttons.

'I do. So my kids learn them, syllabuses or not.' Sue set her jaw.

Kate had no difficulty believing her. 'Maybe Stephen lives up there.' She pointed to a coach house, cheek by jowl with an enormous Victorian pile, still a family house by the look of it. 'He said he'd hate my house because it was overlooked. He wouldn't be overlooked there. And probably he'd get a corner of what is no doubt a huge garden for his own use.'

'Let's try, anyway. Oh, isn't that obliging of him.' Sue pointed to a neatly printed name above his doorbell. And then at some jemmy marks. 'And isn't obliging of someone else, to spare us having to use these keys?'

Chapter Seventeen

'Burgled! Why should anyone want to burgle my flat? Well, you've seen! There's nothing worth nicking!' Stephen sat down heavily at Kate's kitchen table.

'There isn't now, certainly,' Kate said. 'Especially not in your filing cabinets. Either of them.' She heaped sugar into a mug of tea, and passed it to him.

Stephen drowned in a long slow flush. As the colour receded, he was left so pale she was afraid he might faint.

'Head down. Right down. Long deep breaths,' Sue Rowley said. 'Better? Right, now, Stephen, we'll get on to this straight away. But it'd be a big help if you could tell us precisely what's missing. So I suggest you come back to the flat and have a quick look round and tell us. You know, just routine.'

'It isn't just routine, is it? You don't get a detective inspector and a detective sergeant every time a yob nicks your telly. You're tying this up with Rosemary, aren't you? And with what happened to Rosemary?'

'They could be connected,' Sue said mildly. 'It'd help my colleagues if you could remember the names of the other Lodge Protection Committee members—'

'My God, yes! We need to warn them!'

Kate passed him paper and a pencil; he started to scribble.

'One thing, Stephen — whom do we need to warn them against? Come on, stop playing games with me!' Sue leaned forward so the tip of her finger was almost touching his nose. 'You're on the committee. You're the big cheese. You know whom you've annoyed.'

He licked his lips. 'I don't know any names. Honestly.'

'I don't believe you,' Kate said flatly. 'You know you should have given us this information as soon as you'd identified Rosemary.'

Sue pulled back an inch or two. 'I'd very much like to know why you didn't.'

'I didn't because I wasn't asked. That's why. I mean, you don't tell policemen like Crowther how to do his job, do you? And at the time everyone assumed it was "natural causes"!' He mimicked an official-sounding voice. He assumed a bit of self-righteous anger. 'What I'd like to know is why I wasn't questioned earlier. Kate—'

186

'Was ill yesterday. I'll check out the rest of what you said later. Meanwhile, Stephen, the names, please. Come on, if you don't want to protect your own skin, you might think about others'. What about committee members with kids? Don't they need a bit of consideration?' she added, her voice rough, not with anger, Kate thought, but with anguish. Having kids changed things, didn't it?

'The obvious conclusion,' Kate put in, 'is that it's the people who own the land round the reservoir. Who's that?'

He laughed mirthlessly. 'That? Oh, that's you and me. The city council. Apart from the bit the house stands on. That belongs to some big girls' school.'

No guesses for which. She'd bet her pension it was the Seward Foundation. But she wouldn't interrupt.

'So why should anyone be trying to knock down the Lodge?' Sue demanded. 'They should be trying to preserve it! And surely the council would want to preserve it.'

Stephen shrugged. 'Don't be so bloody naïve! The city council can't preserve everything old. Not while there are kids who need schools.'

'OK. So how would it benefit the council to pull it down?'

'Not at all. The benefit lies in what goes up in its place. The poor old Lodge brings in nothing, because it's derelict. A spanking new development would bring in loads of jobs. Need I go on?'

'You've made your point, Stephen. So who wants to

develop the site — and what do they want to put on it, just as a matter of interest?'

'There are two main contenders. Behn Developments, and something called Hodge Associates.'

Sue wrote them down. Kate sat on her hands: which MIT needed this information more? Rod's or the one investigating the arson? If she was right and the Lodge was indeed on Seward Foundation land, they'd need it equally. And ought to be working together.

'That was what I call an interesting morning's work,' Sue said, as they watched Stephen out of sight. Abandoning his work on the button workshop, he'd gone back to his flat, which he'd find watched over by a uniformed officer. On Sue's firm instructions he was to come up with a list of what was missing. 'What was he hiding, do you think?' she continued.

'God knows. My instinct would be to say porn, maybe paedophile porn, but people don't keep that sort of thing in ordinary filing cabinets, do they?'

'Not if they've got any sense,' Sue said, popping her notepad into her bag and standing up. 'Right, time I wasn't here.'

'Gaffer' — Kate could hear the pleading in her voice — 'how long do you reckon it'll be before I can get back into harness?'

'Look, Kate, you're still looking peaky. Eat well and sleep well today: that's my advice.'

'But—'

'Meanwhile, I shall toddle up to Kings Heath nick and talk to Rod Neville. Come to think of it, I might as well leave my car here and walk.'

'That's what everyone says,' Kate said darkly. She pointed at the road. 'And, as you can see, that's what everyone does.'

'Thanks for the milk, Simon. And thanks for everything else, too.'

There were too many lunchtime shoppers pouring into and out of Sainsbury's for a long conversation, but Kate thought that was best. She was embarrassed, and there was no doubt that Simon was, his blush lasting even longer than Stephen's, half an hour ago.

'I wondered—' He stopped to let a family push past, mother, father, three kids under five, all grossly overweight – not, she thought, with overeating, but with the bad diet of poverty. He grimaced, and continued, 'I wondered whether to ring your bell. Then I thought you'd be better having your sleep out. So I tucked it behind that flowerpot and hoped you'd spot it before anyone else did.'

Another family, three kids, not babies, their faces stuffed with dummies . . .

'It was very kind—'

'No more than you've done for me. I mean – you know, the washing and that. By the way, are you still interested in that bag-lady? Only my bloke was positive it was Sally something.'

'Not Sally Army?'

He grinned. 'After that Sally Bowles business, I was on to that, wasn't I? Got a clip round my ears for my pains. Thanks, love.' He pocketed a pound coin, but the woman gestured away the *Big Issue*. 'How about Blake? Only he was wittering away about "Pity, like a new-born babe" after his second snifter, and I just wondered ... May be a red herring.' His grin lit up his face. 'Or a Tiger, more like!'

'Are you sure we haven't had enough of things "burning bright"? Now, what would you fancy for lunch – are you still trying to be a veggie?'

'After that bacon the other day? But there's no need, Kate, honest. I'm making a bit—'

'The sooner you can get a deposit for a bed-sit, the happier we'll all be. OK? What would Sir like for a sandwich filling? Cheese or tuna or—?'

A quiet look round the High Street shops might be one way of passing the time. But she turned down the idea. Firstly, she certainly didn't want to run into any of her colleagues, not if the pretence were to be maintained.

Secondly, despite the proud Victorian architecture, it was all too depressing: slow moving families straggling over the ill-maintained pavements. If the kids weren't sucking on bottles full of garish liquid doing vile things to their teeth, they were stuffing crisps and dropping the packets. She looked at the graffiti, the broken pavement, the beggars. Not that it was different anywhere else in a big city. It was just that she didn't want to be part of it this afternoon. No garden to retreat to? There was only one place to go.

Aunt Cassie was in the television room, watching an old film. She acknowledged Kate with a flap of the hand, and a terse instruction to sit down and be quiet for five minutes. Kate responded with a gesture of her own – she was going to walk round the garden and would be back soon. Anything rather than sit with the other old people, most of whom were, she suspected, less alert, less well, than Cassie. And today – should she obey Cassie's perennial instructions to tell her? – there was a distinct smell of urine in the air. Urine and old bodies.

The garden was idyllic. Despite the sensibly placed chairs and gentle slopes, it was also unoccupied. Perhaps the old might think the wind chilly, but the sun was warm on her face. If she sat, she might go to sleep, so she walked gently round, recording the names of things in flower — all clearly labelled for the ignorant like her.

Her five minutes up, she turned back. Coming out of the door she had to go in was a trio of figures, two familiar. Graham Harvey, his wife, and — she presumed — Mrs Nelmes. She would try a vague and general smile and see where that got her, as she moved aside to let pass the old lady and her Zimmer.

Mrs Harvey — Flavia — stopped short. There was more grey in her hair than last time they'd met, but it was still beautifully — if severely — cut. 'What are *you* doing here?'

'Visiting my great-aunt.'

'I don't see her.' Mrs Harvey's fine eyes scanned the garden ostentatiously.

Graham looked acutely uncomfortable. Mrs Nelmes might have rubbed her hands in glee had she not needed them to hold the Zimmer.

So why was Mrs Harvey going to the trouble of being so rude? She and Kate had only met once, when Kate had taken to the Harveys' house a get-well message from the squad for Graham. Ever since then Graham had gone to humiliating lengths to prevent her knowing if Kate had phoned, always, as it happened, on the most innocent of business.

And how rude would Kate be in return? She was on the point of letting rip when she remembered that whatever she said would no doubt rebound in some way on Graham.

'You will when I bring her out here,' she said. She nodded to Graham and his mother-in-law and headed inside.

Threatening Mrs Harvey with Aunt Cassie was one thing, cajoling the old lady into the garden would be entirely another. But the film was over, and Cassie was prepared to be entertained.

But wanted a wheelchair.

'Cassie – you don't need one! You're more spry than Mrs Nelmes!'

Cassie regarded her slowly. 'Never heard of the sympathy vote?'

In the event, the clash of the Titans was averted. Aunt Cassie needed the loo, and an outdoor coat and a hat, and by the time the whole process was underway, the sun – and the Harvey-Nelmes party – had gone in. Kate took her for a brisk tool round, barking her own shins on the wheelchair, which had all the steering charm of a badly maintained supermarket trolley. Cassie seemed to enjoy the displays of bulbs and polyanthus, but Kate was all too aware that she considered them pale entertainment. Cassie versus Mrs Harvey – now that would have made the old woman's weekend memorable.

But, as Kate knew, it would have made completely impossible the chance of Graham slipping out to phone her about the current crisis. Except it was impossible anyway. Wasn't it?

There were several phone messages waiting for her when she got back home. The first was from Mark: 'There's all sorts of shit going on here, but we don't know quite what it is. Any road, the rumour is you'll be in tomorrow, so I'll see you then. Oh, and don't forget to bring some Anadin or something with you. For me.'

From Sue Rowley: 'How would you be fixed for a meeting at Kings Heath nick at eight-thirty tomorrow morning? I want to fit it in before Graham goes to church.'

So what did that mean? It certainly meant that things weren't as straightforward as she'd hoped.

Colin: 'I was going to come round and take you out on the beer, but – well, things aren't too good here, so we'll have to take a rain-check. Lots of love, though, Kate. Take care of yourself, now.'

A night on the beer. Now that would have been good. Even if, with that eight-thirty meeting, half of the beer would have had to be water.

So what would a sensible young woman do on a Saturday night in? Her washing and her housework, that was it.

Chapter Eighteen

Kate had just loaded the machine and was hunting for the plastic bubble for the detergent when the door bell rang.

Rod Neville.

'Sir!'

'Is there a chance of a quick word, Kate? I'm not interrupting anything?'

Gesturing him in, she grinned. 'Only the washing, sir.' Under the hall light he looked weary. No doubt he'd only just come off duty. He dropped a briefcase and a Safeway carrier by the coat-hooks. 'Would you like a coffee with the quick word? Or a beer? This way.'

He stepped inside her living room: she had a sense that he was appraising it. 'Beer sounds wonderful,' he said at last. His smile suggested he hadn't found her decor completely wanting.

'Would you care to sit down, Gaffer?'

'I'd rather be Rod and I'd rather not stand on ceremony.'

'In that case, come into the kitchen and get the beer out of the fridge while I set off my machine.' It all seemed suddenly so easy. 'Or there's the tail end of a nice Chilean Sauvignon Blanc. Whatever sort of glass you want, this cupboard.'

'I thought you were owed an explanation,' he said, leaning comfortably back on her new sofa as if he were there for the duration, 'of some of the recent events. I'm not, of course, at liberty to tell you everything.' He sipped at his white wine, smiling his appreciation.

'The most important thing, Rod, is whether I'm back on the squad. Or which squad, more to the point.'

'Which? Which should it be?'

'I gather there's a meeting first thing tomorrow with Graham Harvey and Sue Rowley.'

He smiled and shrugged. 'That will be purely to up-date them on your original case-load. There's no question of your coming off the MIT. Absolutely none. Not until we've sorted out the tennis centre business, when we all return to our respective units.'

'That's great! Er – how – what—?'

'How has the little local difficulty been resolved? If you

are prepared to accept a verbal, informal apology from DI Crowther, and you're prepared to go along with the notion that today was sick leave, I'd like you back first thing tomorrow.'

'I'd like to be back.'

He raised his glass. 'To our continued association, then, Kate.' He smiled, as if he meant it.

She raised hers, but confined herself to a guarded smile.

'Now, have you eaten? I'd say,' he said, 'from the pristine state of your kitchen that you haven't. Or at least that you're not in the middle of preparing a meal.'

She shook her head. Now what?

'Perhaps we should eat together and I'll brief you on today's developments.'

'That would be great. The only trouble, Gaffer, is that I'm not the sort of woman to knock up an interesting meal for two while talking about crime.'

'That's fine. Because I've taken the liberty of booking a table at that restaurant in York Street. Kings Balti. I trust you like baltis, Kate?'

Liking baltis was one thing, enjoying one in the company of a detective superintendent who happened to be your boss's boss's boss was quite another. Not that he was at all in boss-mode. He was charming, God he was charming.

All that eye-contact. All that deference about her choice of food. All those witty – and slightly risqué – remarks about the tropical fish that darted in a tank next to their table. She'd always assumed that someone like him would always try to maintain what he'd probably call a professional distance. Unless – unless … Surely this was a man who wanted sex with a woman. And – oh, yes – she was a woman who wanted sex with a man. But sex with him? His occasional pomposity still irritated her, though not as much as on their first encounters. He was a good cop. And he was good-looking, in a slightly studied way. Nice body, too, as if he used weights. Very nice body.

Their meal chosen – he produced lager from the carrier-bag since the place was unlicensed – he leaned forward. 'It didn't take Sue Rowley to alert me to what was going on,' he began. His voice was low, intimate, quite wrong for the words he was saying. 'When Crowther told me he'd had to suspend you for insolence, alarm bells started to ring. Tell me, though – had you noticed any untoward hostility between the two of you?'

She shook her head firmly.

'Mark – you understand, I spoke to him entirely off the record – asserts that DI Crowther has had a down on your from the start.'

'Perhaps he didn't give praise where praise might have been due, but I thought he wanted to make us into a team with no prima donnas. I don't need ticks and pats on the head.'

'You're in the wrong job if you do.' He produced that charming smile. Held it.

'But I don't want to be publicly bollocked for doing a job badly when I haven't had a chance to do it properly.'

'I gather he switched people's assignments at the last moment.'

'That's right.' She paused. A kind-faced waiter was bringing poppadoms, an assortment of dips and a bottle opener. 'But I think you should be talking to him about his management style, not me. After all, he's quite young for such a big assignment, quite inexperienced. He's got a lot to prove – perhaps he's over-anxious.'

'I've already spoken to him . . .' He looked her straight in the eye. 'You sound very understanding – not the sort of person I'd associate with homophobia.'

She gaped. 'My—' She stopped abruptly. She wasn't about to reveal Colin's sexual orientation to his superior. 'One of my best friends is gay. I know that doesn't mean everything, but it does mean something, surely.'

'You mean on the lines of some of my best friends are Jews? No, of course it doesn't. But I know Colin's absolutely happy with the way you treat him. He *does* admit that his best friend's heterosexual. In fact, there's only one person who seems to have less than an entirely happy relationship with you, and that's Graham Harvey.'

'Sir!'

His smile was both weary and apologetic. 'Rod. And I'd say that's more to do with him than with anything you have or haven't done. You know he keeps a pair of your gloves in his desk?' And the thought excited him, didn't it?

She raised her hands, palms towards him. 'No more.' So that was where they'd gone. Oh, poor, poor Graham. 'This is not something we should be talking about.' If he persisted, boss or not, sex or not, she'd be out of there. She owed Graham far more than she owed him.

'I'm sorry. I was completely out of order there. Please – forgive me.' He waited.

She nodded, infinitesimally. But she kept her mouth tight, her eyes cold.

'May I pour you some lager?' He sounded as ashamed as he looked.

'Thanks.' If she sounded off-hand it was because she felt it.

'I really am sorry. I didn't mean to upset you.'

Oh, God, he was getting it more and more wrong! 'It isn't a question of upsetting me. It's breaking a confidence – someone who can't defend himself . . .' She lifted her chin defiantly. 'He's a friend, Rod. A good friend.'

'I'm sorry. It's none of my business. Hell, this is what happens when you mix business with pleasure.'

'Maybe we should get back to business. Or was that business?' she asked.

'Certainly not pleasure.'

They ate in silence for a few moments, till the poppadom she was trying to break into manageable sized pieces exploded all over the table.

She had to laugh.

He laughed too. A delighted, unbuttoned chuckle. 'Thank God for poppadoms – no one can maintain a dignified silence with one. Any more than you can with spare-ribs.' He mimed nibbling one. And the absence of a finger bowl.

Soon they were laughing like old friends. Old friends with lust in their eyes.

The atmosphere in the restaurant had become far too loud and jolly for them to exchange any more confidential information without yelling it in an entirely unconfidential manner.

She made him laugh over her house disasters; he reciprocated with lost luggage at international airports. The hands that had feigned battles with spare-ribs became animated, slowed, hesitated as they approached hers. Her dimples refused to stay concealed. Their eyes locked. She wanted that mouth on hers.

Would there be any condoms in the men's loo? There weren't in the ladies'.

As if reading her mind, he excused himself. He

returned with a slightly abstracted expression, asking almost abruptly for the bill.

They'd be passing a pharmacy on the way back to her place – where he'd conveniently left his case. It didn't close till ten. Now which of them would pretend to need tissues or aspirin?

It would be less embarrassing to go in than to hover outside while he did. And she could come out carrying tissues – no pressure on either of them. She could still say no if she wanted to. Assuming he asked.

As soon as they got back, he fielded his briefcase, looking as fresh and alert as the Chief Constable could have wished.

'The kitchen will be warmest, and the light's good in there,' she said, equally business-like. But not, to be truthful, feeling it.

He was already unpacking notes by the time she'd taken off her jacket. Her answerphone was flashing. On the whole she thought it better to leave it unanswered. She dropped her shopping on the stairs.

'There,' he said, 'is our list of contacts at the Tennis Centre – you can see your colleagues have been busy. And I understand from Sue that you were playing on this court.' He unrolled a plan, and pointed. 'Right?'

'I rather think it was this one … yes, the one with the Bluebeard's doors: *Plant*, from which, incidentally, the cleaner's trolley was emerging that morning, *Cleaners*,

Coaches — I always want to snatch one open and see what falls out!'

Turning to her, he laughed. 'At least Bluebeard didn't keep his dead women in the shower . . .'

And — which of them moved first? — it was quite clear that no more work was going to be done that night. And he no more wanted to go home than she wanted him to.

At some point he said, 'Do you have an alarm clock? Working day tomorrow.'

'And I've got that meeting with Sue and Graham. Eight-thirty. I suspect it would look better if we didn't arrive anything like together.' Well, one of them had to say it. And then she laughed. 'Especially as I made it quite plain to Mark that I wasn't sleeping with anyone in the service.'

'Mark!'

'He was making it plain he only slept with his wife.'

'Did you want to sleep with him?'

'Certainly not. The man's got white eyelashes!'

'And — and did you want to sleep with me?'

'How can a woman possibly answer while you're doing that? However much I might have wanted Rod the person, I certainly didn't want Detective Superintendent Neville. Not while he had my future in his hands.'

'I'd rather have in my hands what I've got now . . .

Shit! My car's still at the station and I've still got to brief you.'

'Do you know enough about cars to prevent them starting? Well, maybe when I arrive tomorrow all I should see of you is your legs and bum as you try to repair the car – such a nuisance, and I'm sure the damned thing's under guarantee. And as for filling me in on all I need to know ...' She meant to tell him that breakfast briefings were what all bright young managers had these days, but who cared when he was doing that?

Chapter Nineteen

So how did Kate feel about Rod using Robin's razor? She might tell herself that it was simply a matter of practicality, but she still felt uneasy. Robin had been her partner in every sense, would have been with her for life but for that accident. Rod — well, he was a charming and exciting sexual partner, but she couldn't imagine their relationship being more than that. Or either of them wanting more. Could she?

She moved Rod's neat piles of notes from the kitchen to the dining room and laid them on the newly French-polished table, one of the few pieces of Cassie's furniture she'd wanted to keep. No, if either of them jotted anything down, the pressure would damage the table. Better use that heat-proof sheet to protect it. What was this, a new housewifely Kate? She pushed the thought to join Robin's razor at the back of her mind.

Breakfast was a perfunctory affair of toast and coffee. Seven on a Sunday was scarcely a romantic hour, and they both had work on their minds. Possibly. Kate told herself she needed Rod's information, and that Rod needed to get away. Going back to bed was not an option.

Meanwhile they both had to come up with some sort of goodbye and thank you line.

'Now,' Rod said, leaning over the dining table and checking his notes, 'the bottle was found somewhere in this area. Right?' He pointed to the sketch-map.

'That's right. The nearest court to the doors. The walkway goes across here. And at the far side of the walkway is another set of doors leading to the further four courts.'

'As I recall, they have no cubby-holes, however interestingly named, but are attached to a new fitness suite.'

'That's right. So I'd have found the bottle behind the curtains at one end or other of that court – or just conceivably on the adjacent court, if one of the balls we'd been using had slipped past the netting between courts. What's happened to the bottle, by the way? DNA testing?'

'On what grounds?' He was in cold, alert mode.

'Well, sometimes people share a bottle. And I can't see Rosemary as the sort of woman who'd ignore a litter bin.

Perhaps her partner – I don't know, I'm grasping at really thin straws here—'

'Carry on.'

'I'd think the person she was playing with had a small swig, then pressed it on Rosemary. Oh, God, this is such guess-work! Perhaps Rosemary's own bottle had – I don't know – perhaps been "accidentally" knocked over. Or X had drunk from it "by mistake".'

'I'll go for the former. According to SOCO there was a damp patch on one of the courts – yes, Court One – which couldn't be attributed to the leaking roof. So you think there might be two lots of DNA to be found?'

'Rosemary's and X's. I know it's a long shot—'

He nodded. 'The acid from the juice would considerably reduce the chances of DNA surviving. But it's worth a try. Yes, I'll authorise a test for that. I'll get it prioritised and hang the expense! All we've got to find is someone with whom to match up any DNA we find.' He smiled encouragingly.

'We can assume that – unless whoever disposed of the bottle – both bottles? – wiped them and ran on to another court to sling them away – Rosemary was playing Court One. How would that tie up with the witness statements?'

'You know the answer already, don't you, Kate? No one we've spoken to appears to have been on Courts One or Two. Everyone we've spoken to so far was playing on one of the other six.'

She pushed back her hair, still, like his, damp from the shower. 'Are we talking about a conspiracy here? You'd expect one person to remain steadfastly quiet. The one who laced the drink. But there might have been two more, if they were playing doubles, or even another four if doubles were in progress on the adjoining court.'

'Exactly.'

'I suppose the people on Court Three wouldn't recollect how many there were next to them?'

'They seemed singularly vague. Said they were so absorbed in their own game that they can't remember. Though it might have been two women, they think. Certainly a woman had to retrieve a ball from their court. Very well-spoken, they said.'

'It might be worth talking to them again, see if their memory improves.'

'Two of the team will be doing that this morning, I would assume. But not you. I've advised DI Crowther that he should consider asking you to continue your conversation with the bereaved husband. Mark said he – Doctor Parsons – was quite anxious about you yesterday. And you know as well as I do a sympathetic approach can often produce excellent results.'

'With respect, I don't think he'd got anything to do with it. Whatever DI Crowther's theory. The Parsons might have had rows, but I'm inclined to believe him when he says they were quick to flare, quick to subside.'

'A decent man, stunned by his terrible bereavement?'

She looked at him sideways. 'You've got something up your sleeve.'

'Only the information that when he was younger he was a star of the OUDS.'

'That's not a police acronym,' she observed.

'Oxford University Dramatic Society,' he said.

'You're Oxford?'

'Wadham. Which means,' he said, with a smile that would have had the clothes off her back in ten seconds, had they had the time, 'you got your Master's the hard way, while I only had to pay for mine. But at least Doctor Parsons' doctorate is the result of scholarship. We've not been able to find anything untoward in that. Not any political enemies, of whatever persuasion. So apart from his thespian abilities, I'm inclined to back you in your judgement.'

'In that case, I think we should put pressure on my buttons man. Sue Rowley will have told you about his burglar.'

He nodded. 'A very unsubtle burglar compared with whoever stole all Rosemary's files.'

'So they were stolen!'

'According to Doctor Parsons, there are unlikely empty spaces in her filing cabinets.' He glanced at his watch. 'So, there's the list of tennis players. The list of what Stephen admits to having had stolen—'

'"Admits"?' Her eyes scanned the list: papers concerning the Lodge, headed paper, personal writing. Personal writing?

'You and Sue thought he was hedging, didn't you? So do the people talking to him. Crowther and Tony Mills, as it happens. It might be ... awkward ... to change that arrangement. Particularly since you know him socially.'

'More professionally than socially. Which reminds me. Sarbut. Not-Sarbut.' She grimaced.

He produced a dry smile.

'— may have something worth following up. Just for the sake of the Coroner.'

'It's something to take up with Harvey and Rowley this morning. Before you report back to Crowther.'

Kate bit her lip. 'This apology business ... Can't it just be taken as read? If we're going to have to work together, the fewer grounds for mutual hostility the better.' Damn, she was sounding like him again.

'I was hoping you'd say that.' He smiled. But then for the first time seemed much less assured. 'Kate — last night. If it's to happen again — and I hope it will' — he reached to touch her cheek — 'we have to be either terribly discreet or absolutely open. The problem with discretion is we could still be found out. The problem with openness is you may be taken out of the MIT. Which on strictly professional grounds I should dislike intensely.'

'It's put you in a very awkward position.'

'It's put us both in an awkward position. You more than me, I'd say. And for that, I'm sorry. But I don't regret a minute of what passed between us. And I'd very much like to repeat it.' He kissed her. She responded with more ardour than was sensible. 'But everything has to be your decision,' he added.

'A mutual decision,' she corrected him.

'So long as you understand you have the casting vote.' He looked down, grinning ruefully. 'As you can see, I'd rather be heading back upstairs, but it had better be out through your front door. We'll talk later?'

'Later,' she nodded.

'Kate spent a lot of time at the hospital when Simon was recovering from a serious assault,' Graham explained. 'And she found him a place at this hostel. Dreadful place.'

'Poor kid,' Sue said.

'Every time I look at my spare bedroom I get these guilt pangs,' Kate said. 'You know, just me rattling round my house. And all these people homeless.'

'I can't see that offering Sarbut a roof over his head would do much for your social life,' Sue observed.

Despite herself, Kate shot her a glance.

'It's not as though it could be a house-share on equal terms, is it? Ask yourself if you'd want him to lodge with you if he wasn't homeless. If it's just the guilt of privilege talking – no, keep out of it, Kate.'

'After all,' Graham added, to her astonishment, 'you never know when Colin will need it. He and his partner were having a hell of a row over the phone the other day. He told me you'd once offered him a bolt-hole.'

'Poor bugger,' Sue said, shaking her head. 'Oh, God. Oh, sorry. Sorry.'

None of them laughed. There was a silence that threatened to grow. At last, Graham seemed to realise that it was his meeting and he ought to move it along. 'Sarbut problems apart, I really could do with you back in our squad. And moving you back immediately would paper over any awkwardness with Crowther.'

It would solve a lot of problems, wouldn't it, not least the Rod Neville situation. If they weren't working together, they could bonk each other brainless and no one would have any grounds for concern. By the time he returned to the squad, they'd have had time to sort out the way their relationship was going.

'It's not as if we haven't enough work,' he added. 'You've probably heard that Fatima was assaulted. She's likely to be off all this week.'

'She's so conscientious she'll be in the moment she can,' Kate said. 'You know, when she was on that course of hers she even took the trouble to e-mail about information she'd picked up. Hell!' She smacked the side of her head. 'I asked her to check on something – I bet she never had time!'

'What was that?' Sue asked.

'Someone was admitted to Selly Oak Burns Unit late one night, remember?'

Sue nodded. 'Fatima was going to find out—'

'Who it was and why. It turned out to be an art-dealer – I'm sorry, I don't think I ever heard the name – a middle-aged man. Who seemed to be having a bonfire in the small hours. I asked her to find where the ambulance had collected him from.'

'OK, I'll get on to her. And if she didn't manage to – fancy a kid that size wading into a pub brawl!' Graham broke off, shaking his head.

Sue and Kate exchanged ironic glances. Would a male officer have evoked such sympathy?

'If she didn't manage to, then the MIT can sort that today.'

'And there's another thing too.' Kate had e-mailed Masters about the fires and had never checked for a reply. OK, another MIT was busy on that case. But that one fragment— 'You don't suppose DI Crowther would mind if I used his computer, do you?'

Graham looked alarmed. 'What on earth for? Surely – the situation between you ... He wouldn't want you sifting through his files.'

'I just want to get at my e-mail,' she said. 'In fact, I'm happy for either of you to do it.'

He overrode something Sue was about to say. 'If it's that important, just get on with it.'

She sat down and switched on.

'You cunt — what the fuck d'you think you're doing?'

Three heads whipped round as if caught conspiring.

Kate had only ever seen Graham do it once before. He didn't even bother to pull himself to his full height: simply asked, very quietly, 'Do you have a problem with DS Power accessing her e-mail under my supervision, Inspector?'

The man had presence of mind, she had to admit it. 'Not at all, sir.' He produced a natural-looking smile. 'It was just rather a surprise to see her at my desk, that was all. Can I help, Kate? Oh, are you feeling better?'

If he could play a part, so could she. 'I'm fine, thanks, sir. And here's my e-mail coming up now. Do you mind if I just print it all off?'

'Go ahead. Do I take it you'll be going back to DCI Harvey's squad, then?'

Graham spoke across her. 'I'm afraid a decision hasn't been made yet, Crowther. And I'm aware Superintendent Neville would prefer her to stay here. Perhaps you could give us another couple of minutes?'

It was tantamount to an order. Crowther, however,

seemed too interested in what his printer was producing to respond.

Graham repeated, very quietly, 'Just another couple of minutes on our own, if you don't mind.'

In case Crowther hadn't understood, Sue opened the door.

She shut it firmly behind him.

'Well?' Graham asked.

'Nothing much. Just confirmation that the outbreak of warehouse fires seems to be over. Which I'm sure the appropriate MIT will know anyway. The funny thing is – which again I'm sure they'll know – is that the arson seemed to stop the night that highly respectable art dealer ended up in Selly Oak Hospital Burns Unit.' She passed Graham the print-out.

'Just to make sure, I'll put it in their Super's hands myself,' he said. 'And Kate, don't take this the wrong way, but I think you should stay on this team as long as Neville wants you. Don't you?'

Chapter Twenty

'Bent! Crowther bent!' Rod Neville sat heavily in the chair Kate had vacated behind Crowther's desk. 'No. No, surely not. Inexperienced. Rattled. Making bad moves. But not bent – no!'

Graham leaned forward, enumerating on his fingers. 'He doesn't want to believe there's a case. He asks no questions at all of the man who identifies Rosemary – shuts him up, rather. And when Sue repeated Stephen Abbott's allegations yesterday, he tried to shut her up too.'

'Oh, yes. Despite the burglary at Abbott's flat. Well,' Sue said, spreading her hands, 'you saw. Didn't you?'

Graham waited, as if for Rod's response. There was none. He continued: 'He gets himself on to the MIT. He changes people's assignments at a moment's notice so they can't work at their most efficient. He tries to get DS

Power off the team. And this morning he explodes like a young volcano when he sees her at his computer.'

Sue Rowley nodded home each of his points. 'You should have seen his face, sir.'

'He wouldn't be such a fool as to leave anything incriminating on his computer,' Neville said. 'Even if he were bent.'

Kate said quietly. 'If you don't want to make an issue of it, sir, would you like me to make his computer impossible to use so it has to be sent to the geeks? Who could take the opportunity to check it over thoroughly.'

Neville frowned. 'Could you?'

'Someone once showed me how to change the password. That should be irritating enough for him to ask for it to be repaired.'

'But not immediately. He's not officially using his room. He's one of the team, mucking in with the rest of you. Us.'

'It'd be even more interesting if he did notice it straight away, wouldn't it?' Sue observed.

Neville looked at each one in turn. 'You're convinced that something is – shall we say, at this juncture, amiss?'

Graham and Sue nodded.

'Kate?'

'I don't want this to seem like – like some sort of revenge on my part.'

Neville nodded. 'Easily prevented. Would you be kind

enough to work on the computer? And then leave us to finish the discussion without you. I think we would have had to do so anyway. Otherwise working with him would become untenable for you.'

Mark, resplendent this morning in a gold shirt and clashing khaki jeans, greeted her with a huge grin and an affable hug. 'Welcome back. Migraine better?' he asked, very clearly. So he didn't quite buy the sick-leave business, and there might be others who didn't, either.

'Much better, thank you. Until I saw your outfit, at least. You know, I was out cold for about twelve hours. Never had anything like that before. Now, what's on the agenda?'

'The DI and Tony are talking to that archaeologist chap.'

'Stephen Abbott? Right.'

'Now, I suggested that all the tennis players we've got so far should be invited on court tomorrow evening for a reconstruction. We could get a Rosemary lookalike to play with a tennis machine – don't want to put any ideas of age or gender into people's heads. They get to play for an hour for free, then we'd give them tea and biscuits and the third degree.'

'Sounds the obvious thing. But do I sense a "but" hanging in the air?'

'You do,' he said grimly. 'A "but" from on high.'

'How high?'

'DI Crowther high.'

'Well I'm blowed. What a surprise.'

'Quite. Meanwhile today we're back on Parsons, again. Though I for one am convinced it's a complete waste of time.'

'In what way?' She slung her bag on to the desk and helped herself to water from the chiller.

'If he did it, I'm a Dutchman.'

She passed him a cup too. 'Is that the line that you've been pursuing? That he did it?'

'That's the one I was told to take. Orders is orders.'

'Direct from Crowther's mouth, I dare say. I had the same ones.'

'So, much as I'd have liked to talk more extensively about her friends—' Mark shrugged.

'How's he coping with it all? After all, he's been bereft of what seemed to me like a dearly loved wife, and now we're trying to pin her death on him.'

'No one's ever actually suggested it—'

'The man's no fool. He must know what you're after.'

'He's – I know it sounds weird – it's as if he's treating all this as therapy. He keeps saying how good it is, to remember things.' Mark shook his head sadly.

'Therapy! Some therapy if he gets sent down for life!

Not that it'll come to that. We'll get the bugger that did it first.'

'You hope.'

Like Graham before her, she counted off items on her fingers. 'So far there's not a shred of evidence against Parsons. All the stuff at the tennis centre – the Blu-tack in the changing room, the duff computer, the sudden changes of personnel – we're talking conspiracy here, Mark. I think Neville's buying the theory. And – having seen him in action – I can assure you he usually gets his way.' Oh, and in more senses than one.

Mark shook his head. 'In yesterday's briefing meetings he was a hundred per cent behind Crowther.'

That brought her up short. 'I suppose he feels he's got to support him – new manager, that sort of thing,' she said doubtfully. He'd been quick to defend him this morning, too, hadn't he? Oh, to be a fly on the wall, listening to the arguments, and to the ultimate decision.

Perhaps she'd made a terrible mistake last night. No. Whatever the situation, she'd have been excluded as too lowly anyway. Wouldn't she?

'I'm afraid I'm what P. G. Wodehouse would have called a non-doing pig,' Dr Parsons was saying. 'I'm not interested in sport of any sort, Sergeant.'

'But your wife was?'

'Became, would be a better term, I think. When she reached fifty, she started to put on weight. A combination of retirement and HRT, she said. Oh, it was nothing gross, but enough to make her want to lose it. She loved her food, you see. And she was such a good cook. Dinner parties for twelve were nothing.'

'What sort of people did you invite?'

'Academics. Lawyers. Health and media professionals – doctors, social workers, the odd writer. They're known in some quarters as the Moseley Mafia. And Rosemary's teaching colleagues.'

Kate registered the distinction. 'No tennis players amongst them?'

He shook his head. 'I'm afraid none of our friends joined her, despite her efforts to cajole them. She started almost from scratch, you see. Had regular coaching, and then got involved with what she called community tennis. For the over-fifties.'

'"Community tennis"?' Mark intervened for the first time.

'The idea is that a coach gathers together groups of players of similar ability and gets them to play mixed doubles,' Kate explained. 'Certain times and days of the week. I'm surprised she didn't play at a proper tennis club, Doctor Parsons.' She could certainly have afforded it.

'She said she didn't need the social life. More to the point, she didn't think she was good enough. And the Brayfield Centre's very convenient. She made friends amongst that over-fifties group – used to play occasional games in the evening, especially when I was away. Kept her out of mischief, she used to say.'

'What sort of mischief?' Mark asked.

'It was a figure of speech, Constable,' Parsons said wearily, looking with distaste at Mark's rings.

'But not necessarily only a figure of speech,' Kate said. 'Some people might have regarded her efforts on behalf of the Lodge as mischief ... Did she ever speak about – did she ever suggest she might have made enemies?' It would be nice to have Stephen's allegations corroborated.

'You can't be a thorn in the flesh of big development companies without irritating people. But surely – we live in a civilised society—'

'Someone killed your wife, Doctor Parsons: I wouldn't call that civilised, would you?' Mark asked, his rings flashing.

Kate raised a warning hand. 'Did your wife ever voice any fears about her activities? Or mention which development companies?'

For the first time that morning Parsons looked harried. Guilty? 'She did. But I pooh-poohed it. So did she, in daylight. Said it was her age. But one day – oh, my God

— she swore someone was following her on her cycle. She threatened to get a car. You don't think—? If I'd done something?' There was a long pause while he pulled himself together.

Kate said quietly, 'Other people knew that she was afraid. You don't have to feel guilty.'

Another long pause. Then, almost as if he were merely an interested bystander, he asked, 'Did you ever find her cycle?'

Mark shook his head.

'She must have used it to get down there. Someone must have noticed it.'

'Someone did. But someone else did more than notice, I'm afraid, sir,' Mark added. 'Someone removed it from where it was chained. It hasn't been recovered, to the best of my knowledge.'

'Did she ever feel tempted to report her fears to the police?' Kate asked.

'She did mention it. But they didn't take it any more seriously than I did.'

Kate nodded. Sounded familiar, didn't it? 'I suppose you've no idea which station she might have gone to?'

Parsons sat forward. 'It would have to be this one, wouldn't it? Dear God, you people knew about it all along, and did nothing.'

Mark was about to say something, but Kate silenced

him with a glance. Meanwhile, Parsons was gripping the table, repeating with increasing horror, 'Nothing!'

'It would be remarkably interesting,' Rod Neville said slowly, 'to find out to whom she spoke. Such an allegation wouldn't have gone unrecorded, would it, now? Even if the officer she spoke to found it spurious.'

'It confirms everything Stephen Abbott said, Gaffer,' Kate said.

Mark nodded.

'It's interesting that you should have thought it necess-ary to bring it directly to me,' Neville continued.

Kate said nothing.

'My idea, sir,' Mark said. 'It's seemed to me in the past that if DS Power suggested anything, some of our senior officers saw fit to deride it.'

Neville's speech patterns must be universally infectious. Kate stared at her shoes.

'Point taken, Mark. And not an easy one to make. In fact, when Abbott made his allegations on Saturday, we took them extremely seriously. Investigations are already in train.' He let rip the sort of blazing smile that had guaranteed his popularity despite his quirks. 'Thank you for bringing this to me.'

Kate wondered if he would call her back. He did not.

❋　❋　❋

Kate and Mark were just returning to the Incident Room when they ran into Guljar Singh Grewal.

'How are you doing, Kate? Heard you were bad,' he said.

'I'm OK now. Tell me, Guljar, you must know all the gossip round here.'

'Just off for a slash,' Mark announced, as if she'd somehow pressed an invisible button.

Guljar looked apprehensive. 'Gossip?'

'I'd bet you know who's bedding who, who's shedding who.'

'Might do.'

'Bet you know who's getting what job.'

'Might do.'

'Who's got friends at court, who's in, who's out.'

'Might do.'

'Might know whom Nigel Crowther got to pull strings to get him on to this MIT.'

'Can't you ask Rod Neville? He ought to know.'

'It'd make it a bit heavy, going straight to the Big Boss, wouldn't it? It's just something that interests me.'

Guljar looked around him. The corridors were empty, all the doors shut. 'The word is it's his mother.'

'Mother!'

'Big on the Police Committee. And maybe close, like, to a Big Gun. Oh, much bigger than Neville. Wants her little lad to shoot up the tree faster than any of the other monkeys.'

Kate nodded. 'Maybe someone should talk to dear Mrs Crowther.'

'About pillow-talk promotions? Anyway, her name's not Crowther. She remarried a year or so ago. I remember him going to the wedding.'

'Thanks. That's very interesting.'

He looked at her shrewdly. 'This isn't the Power revenge for being suspended, is it?'

'Me? Suspended? I was off sick with a migraine.'

'That too. OK, so some deal's been done behind the scenes. But I'd hate to think of you trying to score off him.'

'Why?'

'Because you're a decent woman. You shouldn't stoop to cheap revenge.'

Cheap revenge? No, with a bit of luck this would be very expensive revenge. But not for herself. For poor Rosemary Parsons and her grieving husband.

And maybe for Stephen Abbott, who phoned her as she was eating chicken tikka in a naan. If she'd hoped it was Rod Neville, she hoped equally that her voice betrayed nothing but an overfull mouth.

'I can't hack it at work tomorrow,' he said. 'Not

after the grilling they gave me. So I thought I'd come and work on your site, if I may. A bit of peace and quiet.'

'Was it so very bad today?'

'It's like they want to pin something on me, Kate! I liked her, remember. We were friends. And they keep on going over and over the stuff I've had stolen. They don't seem to realise it's nothing to do with the case.'

'In a case like this it's terribly hard for us to tell what's relevant and what isn't, Stephen. That's why we go all round the houses when we question people.'

'I don't see why they should want to know what was in my filing cabinet. My private one. It's as if they think it's — I don't know, hard porn.'

'You can see why they should be interested if it were. Is it?' she asked, as lightly as she could.

'No. But I wouldn't want other people — look, will you be there to let me in tomorrow? You or Alf?'

'If you want to catch me, it'll have to be horribly early. Before eight.'

'Before eight it is. Provided you give me a cup of tea. With sugar, not sweeteners, remember.'

Poor Stephen, thinking he could get away with working on those buttons without Kate asking another set of inconvenient questions. Yes, they had to find out what was in those drawers, and if the hard men couldn't manage it, she'd see what the soft touch would do.

The naan had gone cold and leathery. She picked at it with distaste, until she was saved by the doorbell.

Rod with his briefcase and a couple of carrier bags. One chinked on the hall tiles. The other emitted good and familiar smells.

'I thought you'd be too knackered to cook,' he said, picking up the carriers and taking them through to the kitchen. 'So I brought you some of our regional speciality.'

'You're a King Kebab fan too!' She meant it as a sociable observation. It sounded more like the eager sharing of a lover.

'Of course.' His smile suggested he took it as it sounded. And the smile intensified as he produced a bottle. 'And something to wash it down with afterwards – they wouldn't go together. Only first I want you to promise me something. Not a single word about work.'

'One single word only,' she said, reaching plates for new portions of chicken tikka in naan, and shoving the champagne in the fridge, 'before we deal with any of this. And that's it. Promise.'

'And what's that word?' he asked, sinking to a chair and rubbing his neck.

'Sweeteners,' she said. 'Oh, and perhaps one more. Backhanders.'

Chapter Twenty-one

'The hardest part of this relationship is trying not to talk shop with you,' Rod said, tracing a trickle of sweat between her breasts.

'You're sure it isn't the second hardest part?' Kate asked, with a sexy giggle. 'Going by the evidence, that is.' And then she stopped giggling. Although she knew it was inevitable, the last thing she wanted at that moment was a sober discussion.

He produced that devastating smile. Just for her. 'And the third hardest is trying not to let my feelings for you affect my judgement about some of our colleagues. And what to do about them. And not to break confidentiality when I'm with you.'

She tensed. 'You're saying that the relationship is a mistake?'

'A tiny, tiny part of my head's trying to tell me that. But the rest of me just isn't listening.'

But it might, one day, mightn't it? And how would she feel then?

He brushed her cheek with a finger that smelt of her. 'I've broken my promise, haven't I? And talking like this in bed is in the worst possible taste. Oh, please lie down again.'

She shook her head. They'd done things in quite the wrong order, hadn't they? They should have talked before they fucked. She and Robin had worked things out, not clinically, but clear-sightedly. That's why they'd been so good together. In every respect.

'Oh, Kate, Kate. Don't you see, I want it to work, you and me? But there are issues.'

She scrubbed her face and turned to him. 'Not the least of which is my late partner. You must have read my file.'

He nodded. 'Is this – am I – the first since – since you lost him?'

Her turn to nod.

'In that case we have all the more to work through. Together: I want us to deal with all this together.' He pulled her gently down, cradling her head on his shoulder. 'Let it all go, Kate – I'm here.'

*   *   *

She woke to find the bed empty. The bastard! Not even saying goodbye. But then she could see his clothes still on the chair where he'd flung them. Part of his brain had clearly wanted to fold everything meticulously. The other part had simply wanted to leave things where they'd fallen. A compromise: his trousers should be OK, but she didn't hold out much hope for his shirt.

And there he was, wearing the unisex bathrobe last worn by Simon.

'Tea in bed! What a luxury!'

'But it presages my early departure. There are things I must collect from home. And I can't fake the car again.' Putting the mugs on the bedside cabinet, he perched on the side of the bed. 'Cold shower time, Kate. Enjoy your tea. Only before you do, tell me when I can come and meet Aunt Cassie.'

'Whenever you want,' she said. 'She's always happy to entertain attractive young men. Trouble is,' she added more soberly, 'there's always a chance you'll meet Graham Harvey there.'

'Graham Harvey! Visiting your aunt!' His smile faded.

'More particularly his mother-in-law. He consulted Cassie before he booked Mrs Nelmes in, and he still pops in from time to time.'

'Whether you're there or not?'

'More often when I'm not there, I'd say. He's fond of the old bat.'

'Is she like you?'

'Heavens, isn't that stretching the laws of heredity a bit far? I'll say this, she's a tough old bird, my great aunt. With a heart of gold.'

He looked at her sideways. 'You may think you're tough, Kate, but I'd say you're more vulnerable than you care to admit. God!' He kissed her, gently then very hard. 'Kate — you have this weird effect on me. I want to protect you from the harsh winds that blow.'

She reeled. No one had ever said anything like that to her. She looked away. And managed a cracked laugh. 'So long as you protect all the other Lodge Committee members too.'

Biting his lip, he looked her straight in the eye. Whatever he meant to say he cancelled. This time his smile was his professional one, and it became grimmer. 'It was a job I delegated to — to someone. Perhaps it would be advisable to check that measures have in fact been put in train.'

She cobbled together some breakfast while he was showering. A trip to Sainsbury's was called for if he proposed to stay more often. Milk; eggs; bread. Even loo rolls.

'I thought,' she said, scraping the very last from the Marmite jar, 'that I'd stay and talk to Stephen Abbott for a few minutes. See if softly-softly will extract from him what was nicked from his filing cabinet.'

'Good idea. Of course. I'll let Mark and Nigel know.' He started to make a note.

'No, you won't. Not unless you and I have started to practise telepathy.'

Kate didn't broach the subject while she and Stephen were drinking tea in the warmth of the kitchen. She thought she'd wait till he was off his guard, hunkered over the bricks at the bottom of her garden. Alf hadn't arrived yet. There was no point, as he said, in busting a gut if he couldn't get on with the path. And he'd got other jobs he could get on with.

'I'm just off,' she said. She might well have been, with her jacket buttoned firmly over her working clothes. Bright though the sun was, it was still pretty feeble — only seven-thirty, in its own terms, which were nothing to do, after all, with British Summer Time. 'You'll help yourself to tea and everything, won't you?'

'And I'll remember to take my boots off when I go in.'

'Thanks. You're still feeling ... bad?'

'This,' he said, waving a tiny trowel, 'is very therapeutic. Better than writing reports, any day. I've been wondering if any of your neighbours have similar sites. Where you have one workshop, you tend to get a cluster.'

'Enough to make quite a landmark? Did you ever

find out about Worksop Road? If it is a corruption of Workshop Road?'

He stood. 'It's on my list.'

'If this road is worth investigating, think how much the neighbouring one would – Goldsmith Road.'

'If you know how many precautions jewellers take not to lose one iota of gold dust, you wouldn't expect much,' he said.

'I don't know about losing gold. I do know I found a packet of diamonds under my study floor,' she said. 'Oh, my Aunt Cassie had put them there for a rainy day—'

'Downpour, more like!'

'Quite. Anyway, they'll pay for another year in that home of hers. You live in an old place. Anything interesting under your floor boards?'

'I wish.' His sigh gave her the opening she'd been edging towards.

'What they took – was it insured?'

'Not intrinsic value, really. Photos, mainly. And some letters.'

'Anyone special?'

'A woman.'

Well, that was one theory blown out of the water. Possibly. He squatted again: had she lost him?

'Must have been someone pretty special – you were very upset about it.'

'A woman. Just a woman. Oh, the sister of a friend of mine. I — got too fond of her.'

She waited.

'You know how intense things get when you're young. You lose a sense of proportion. I thought she cared for me as much as I cared for her.' He broke off to ease up a dandelion root. 'Turned out she didn't. But I couldn't quite — well, maybe the burglar did me a good turn, getting rid of that stuff.'

'What was she like?'

He put the root on what would become the path — then thought better of it and slung it over the fence into the entry. 'Beautiful. No, I mean it. Beautiful. She was. Extraordinary. Why I should ever have expected her to want to stay with me—' He shrugged. 'And very clever. Intelligent. Whatever. Got a double first a month after she'd dumped me.'

'You were both at Durham?'

'No. I suppose that was one problem. I was a year older than she was, so I went off to Durham a year before she went to Cambridge. And I remained absolutely faithful to her, all the time. We wrote — just a note, sometimes — every day. And when I'd got my degree, and started work on a project in Lincoln, we still wrote. Until the Easter of her last year. And then that was it. Full-stop.'

'Just like that?'

'Just like that.'

'What happened to her?'

'She's already a senior civil servant. Going to fly very high. Home Office, I think. Your boss,' he said, managing a grin at last.

She nodded. 'So all Burglar Bill got was her love letters and some snapshots.'

'Oh, no. Snapshots they weren't. Studio portraits. I'm a very good photographer – though I says it as shouldn't,' he added, dropping into a Birmingham accent. 'I use photography a lot in my work,' he said, in his normal voice.

'Studio portraits? We're not talking what amateur photographers will call "glamour", are we?'

'Silly tarts wearing nothing but a basque and a pout? Do me a favour! Oh, there was some nude stuff. But, as the amateur photographers would say, "all very tasteful".'

'But she might not have wanted them lying around.'

'They were in a locked drawer,' he snapped.

Get his trust back. 'Where did you meet her?' she asked.

'The county youth orchestra. We were both viola players. Now, I know there are pages and pages of viola player jokes on the Internet, but we're not all sad old gits. At least, she isn't!'

'So you'd be very young – still at school?'

'That's right. Both swots, of course, but with lust and loyalty. We'd study together, until I went up north. And half of her letters are about work she'd be doing – ideas for essays and so on. But she was good fun, Kate. We laughed a lot. Of course, her parents were loaded compared with mine, but they quite liked me. Didn't discourage me, at any rate.'

'Were you at the same school?'

'No, I was at the local comp. She – I told you she was a high-flyer – she was at a girls' public school.'

'Oh – now, what are they called here in Brum? One of the King Edwards' schools?'

'No. Neither of us is a Brummie – can't you tell? The accent? We were both from Lichfield.'

Lichfield! 'The Swan of Lichfield'! And the Seward Foundation and all its land!

Not letting her voice change, keeping the tightest control over her face, Kate asked, 'Now, would that be an Anna Seward Academy, out there?'

'That's right. Know someone there, do you?'

'Someone was telling me about the foundation, just the other day. They were saying it was surprising there weren't Seward Academies in Brum.'

'Suppose it is, really. Still, like you said, there are other good girls' schools. Now,' he said, pointing swiftly, 'how about that for a bright little button?'

It seemed Stephen, slender though he was, was a man for

second breakfasts. If all his work was done in weather like this she could hardly blame him, even if making him toast did finish off the bread.

'My colleagues need to know all about the problems with protecting the Lodge,' she said, passing him the butter. 'All.'

'They didn't seem very interested. Or in the fact that the committee papers had been nicked. In fact, that sleek bastard Crowther thought that part of the burglary was just a bit of vandalism, that all they really wanted were sellable things: the video and TV, and the computer.'

She looked at him steadily. 'Are you sure?'

He shifted. 'OK. Probably he didn't. What he really wanted to find out was what I've just told you. And I suppose you'll have to go and tell him, won't you? He is your boss, after all,' he added wearily.

'What I'm more interested in now,' she said, 'is the Lodge. The Lodge documents that were stolen.'

'No need to worry about them. There'll be copies of everything in Rosemary's files,' he said. Her silence must have told him what he didn't want to know. 'Oh, God, don't say they've taken all her stuff?'

'Enough,' she said mildly.

'When? No, don't tell me. The night she was lying dead in the shower. Fucking hell, how callous can you be! They kill her, they nick her keys, they break into her house and take her stuff. Jesus Christ. God save me from big business.'

'From what?'

'Stands to reason. We were trying to protect the Lodge from being "redeveloped"—'

'Not simply protect it from general dilapidation?'

He shook his head. 'So it doesn't take much detective work, does it? It's got to be one of the firms that wanted to develop it.'

She nodded. At least someone was now taking it seriously.

'Then there was the Tax Office—'

'Tax!'

'Yes. She'd been on PAYE all her life, of course. But she reckoned someone at the Tax Office kept on querying her returns. And she'd have been punctilious about something like that. I suppose I should have told that woman on Saturday, shouldn't I?'

She didn't deny it. Why hadn't he?

'Someone else you should talk to,' he continued, as if relieved to have everything out in the open, 'is whoever it was in the Planning Department that messed up our application to have it listed.'

She pounced. 'Any idea who?'

'Rosemary went to see her. Yes, some woman. She wrote a report – and that was in my files, see?'

'Any guess at a name?'

He shook his head. 'I've got this blind spot about names. Hereditary according to this article I read in *New Scientist*. So everything's written down in there. If that's gone—' He flapped his hands in resignation.

'Ever talked to a hypnotist?' she asked.

Chapter Twenty-two

The five-minute walk up the High Street gave Kate enough time to worry about reporting her next move. She wanted to go to the Planning Department. Stephen might have difficulty with names, but he'd had no problems describing the woman who'd delayed their attempts to list the Lodge.

So she ought to tell someone what she was up to. Nigel – to whom she was officially reporting? Or Rod? With whom she was unofficially sleeping? Both? Both would be best. Separately? So in which order? Nigel first, as was usual? But what if he vetoed it? She could scarcely go over his head to Rod without it becoming an issue.

And what about Rod and herself? A cleanish break now? A couple of nights of fun, no hard feelings? That would be best. He seemed to want a relationship, but certainly saw problems. She — well, she hadn't realised how much she enjoyed having a warm body in the bed beside her. Or how much she'd missed sex.

Jesus, she wanted him now. Now.

Or did she want Robin?

No. Mustn't even think about Robin.

Think some sense. It would be better to put the whole thing on hold for a bit. Wouldn't it? Until this case was over, at least. And don't admit that that would be an excellent incentive to solve it as quickly as possible.

Ahead of her, an old woman stumbled in the road. No wonder: there was a pot-hole some four or five inches deep. No need for her to do anything, by the looks of it. A couple of other people were steadying her, and Kate could hear words like 'reporting' and 'council' being bandied about. She hoped the roads were better wherever the Sargents were now living. She couldn't, come to think of it, imagine them being less than perfect if that barrister daughter and her round tuits had any influence. So what would be happening to their claim? And had Guljar managed to pin anything on the driver or his employers? She'd have a word with him the moment she could make a chance.

Why not make that moment now? It would put off making a decision on the other stuff. She headed not for the Incident Room and the MIT's quarters but for

Guljar's office. Which was occupied by him seated at his desk and Rod, standing, clutching a file.

'God, you CID people work tough hours,' Guljar said, looking ostentatiously at his watch. 'Fancy having to get here for ten. Such a strain.'

'I know. And I shall be leaving in half an hour, absolutely exhausted. That's if it's OK with you and DI Crowther, Gaffer? Something cropped up with Stephen Abbott. Did Mark tell you I was talking to Stephen this morning?'

'He mentioned something.' Full marks for his acting. 'Anything interesting?'

'Only the contents of his drawer – the one he was keeping schtum over. And a possible lead.'

'Well – what are you waiting for? Tell—' Rod shoved a chair at her, but then seemed to think better of it. 'Ah, hang on. I've got a meeting with Crowther in a few minutes – my room. Room! Gold-fish bowl, more like. You can brief us both at the same time. OK? See you in five minutes, Kate.' He nodded and was off.

Nice and brisk and impersonal. Good. But what was he doing closeted with Guljar? An unlikely combination. And why in Guljar's room, not his own? Because Guljar's had solid walls and a wooden door?

She grinned at Guljar, and took the seat Rod had pushed forward. 'No need to look so apprehensive. I'm not after any more gossip. Just wanted to know what was happening to the lorry driver that flattened the cottage down the back of Moseley.'

Guljar stared. 'Ah, the budgie people! Well, we're doing him for careless driving.'

'Not dangerous?'

'No injuries resulting.'

'Oh, come off it – they could have been killed. And he went into that place like – what was it you called it? An aries?'

He nodded in acknowledgement. 'We're doing his boss for overloading, as well. The thing is, the forensic people in Traffic went over it with the proverbial fine-toothed comb and couldn't find much wrong with the vehicle itself.'

'So they'll get off lightly?'

Another nod. 'I must admit that that barrister-woman – you know, the daughter – she's not happy. And she's now alleging that someone was harassing the old dears. Nothing serious. Just enough to have made them think about moving down south. Tim Brown in our CID's on to it, if you're interested.'

'I rather think I might be,' Kate said. 'Thanks.'

Tim Brown was a comfortably padded man in his mid forties, with fading blond hair, a snub nose and big, baby-blue eyes. Big shoulders and short legs – once a rugby prop, perhaps.

'Someone wanted the Sargents out of that place,' he said flatly. 'The person who watered their front garden with weed-killer, who put dog-shit through the front door, and who – *allegedly*' – he stressed the adverb ironically – 'allegedly rammed the front of the cottage with a bloody great lorry. Well, the lorry and the cottage certainly came into intimate contact. And the latter is no more.'

'Who are you after?'

'You tell me.'

DI's could play that game, couldn't they? All of them.

'The people who own the site next to their cottage,' she said briskly. 'Who probably own the site being developed at the top of the hill – from whence cometh our lorry,' she added, a fragment of Sunday School surprising her.

'Hole in one. And I'm sure you could come up with some names?'

'Behn for one. And possibly Hodge for another?'

He looked totally blank. 'Why them?'

'Because they want to develop a prime site out at the reservoir.'

'Do they, by Christ?' He jotted.

'But it isn't them?'

'Not unless there's been a recent change and the Land Registry hasn't caught up with it.'

'So would the Land Registry have on record the Anna Seward Foundation?' she asked.

The baby-blue eyes opened wide. 'I think we need to talk,' he said.

'Not just us, but the MIT on the warehouse arson cases. And maybe, just maybe, the MIT I'm in.'

'Quite a lot of conversation, one way and another,' Tim observed, smiling broadly, and rubbing fat paws.

Rod Neville was still deep in conversation with Nigel Crowther when she arrived outside his office. She caught his eye, nodding as he held up a splayed hand – five more minutes.

Enough time for her to make a phone call then. One she'd rather not make in the office. Or even in the building. She ran downstairs; only to find, out in the street, that her mobile was being temperamental. Thank goodness for the payphone by the library.

Graham picked up his phone first ring.

'Gaffer: do you have any hard news about why Nigel Crowther got moved into the MIT?'

'Morning, Kate. Yes, it's a nice day, isn't it?'

'And I haven't all that much change,' she retorted. Trust this to be one of Graham's affable days.

'Phone box call?' His voice was suddenly serious. 'OK, fire away.'

'The rumour this end is that his mother pulled rank. She's on the Police Committee and married to someone with even more clout.'

'Name?'

'Remarried last year. Guljar remembers that Crowther went to the wedding. Don't know what her new name is. Gaffer – this could be important.' Why did she add that? Didn't she trust him to take it seriously.

'I know. I'll deal with this myself, Kate. You – you just keep out of this.' He said this as a plea, not an order. Then, more briskly, 'Anything I should be looking out for?'

'Whether she's associated with developers called Behn or Hodge. Oh, and Gaffer, much more important – see where she went to school.'

Her money ran out.

If Rod Neville noticed the rain splashes on her jacket, her damp and ruffled hair, he gave no sign of it. He nodded her to a chair next to the one occupied by Crowther, who, as far as she could tell, didn't look at her at all.

'First of all, Power, I have to ask you if you in any way interfered with DI Crowther's computer when you used it yesterday,' Rod said, grim, intimidating.

'Sir?' She sat up straight.

'You heard. When you were getting your e-mail or whatever.'

She spread her hands in disbelief. 'All I did was get my e-mail, sir. You'll find it in the computer's trash bin. And I printed it off. As DI Crowther saw.'

'You didn't infect it with a virus, anything like that?'

She allowed herself a short laugh. 'I'd have thought we'd got the best anti-virus system going, sir. Of course, PC's are notoriously unstable. I can never open my e-mail until I've had a moment tapping away in Word. Don't ask me why.'

'I have your word on that, Sergeant?'

She nodded. No problem: she did always have to go into Word first.

'OK, Crowther, it seems the best thing we can do is get a technician to have a look at it for you. And — well, until we can get you a replacement, there are all those in the incident room for you to choose from.' He spoke with an air of finality — this wasn't a suggestion that he expected Crowther to argue with. 'Right, now that's out of the way, to MIT business. How are your interviews with Doctor Parsons progressing, Power?'

Kate shook her head. 'It depends how you look at it, sir. Neither Mark nor I can see anything in his demeanour to suggest he's anything but a bereaved husband. We see neither motive nor opportunity. The way we see it — with due respect, Inspector Crowther — is that person or persons unknown prepared a lethal brew, left Rosemary to die while they searched the house, and then made a follow-up visit to Stephen Abbott's place.'

'The modi operandi are completely different,' Crowther said.

Now that was something Rod could adopt: a full-length Latin term with, presumably, the correct ending for the plural.

'Nothing was taken from the Parsons home except files,' Crowther was saying. 'And we've no idea how many files or what they may contain. Abbott's was a straightforward breaking and entering, according to SOCO. TV, video, hi-fi: a whole tranche of objects taken. Oh, and his computer, of course. All highly saleable.'

'And the contents of his filing cabinet. Cabinets, I should say.'

'A few porno magazines!' Crowther scoffed.

'Is that what he says?' Neville asked.

'He wouldn't answer. Consistently. I'd say he was scared shitless the scandal would lose him his job.'

'He confided to me what had gone, sir,' Kate said, direct to Rod.

'Well?'

'Portraits of his former fiancée. Letters to and from her. That's the one cabinet. The other contained his files for the Lodge Preservation Society. I thought they were just trying to stop it falling down. It seems I was wrong. There's someone trying to knock it down. And though it should have got listed at the last council Planning Committee meeting, somehow it got missed off the agenda. So it's terribly vulnerable.'

'I wonder how that happened?' Rod mused.

Kate waited. Would Crowther take the bait?

'Everyone knows how inefficient local government is,' he said. 'Remember what Tony Blair was saying. Still got the marks on his back from when he tried to institute change.'

Yes! Yes, and yes, and yes! She looked to Rod for a gleam to answer her own, but his eyes were totally expressionless.

'I think it would be helpful, Power, if you and Mark were to go and find out why, in this particular instance, the council staff were inefficient.'

'Sir.' She got to her feet.

'There is just one other thing, Crowther. The other Lodge Protection Committee members — you have taken appropriate measures to protect them?'

'Sir.'

'Perhaps — thanks, Power, you'll need to be on your way to the planning office, won't you? — perhaps you'd be kind enough to tell me what you've done so far.'

Dismissed. Fine. Well, if that was the way he was going to deal with it, that was up to him. Wasn't it?

But she rather thought, as she closed the door, that he was asking about Crowther's computer needs.

* * *

She hadn't mentioned Stephen's allegations that Rosemary was being harassed by the Inland Revenue, had
she? Presumably they'd be in the letters she'd sent to
her bank or her solicitor. She checked — no, no one
had collected them yet, goodness knows why, though
Parsons had obviously told someone which bank, which
solicitor.

'Penny for them, Gaffer,' Mark said, coming in and
dropping a pile of papers on to an already toppling in-tray.
Today he was resplendent in turquoise and grey. The man
must spend a fortune on his gear.

'Don't know which order to put jobs in,' she said.

'Give me one, do one yourself. We'll haggle over the
third. Come on, don't want you going sick again.'

She managed a smile. 'True. Now, can you get on
to Rosemary's bank and see if she sent them any
papers? If she did, we collect them. You and me.
No one else. I'll do the same for the solicitor. First
one to finish can phone the Inland Revenue and find
which officer handled Rosemary's tax returns. Then
— it's a nice sunny morning — we'll go into the city.
Right?'

As she finished her first call, Crowther left the gold-fish
bowl. His face gave nothing away. Neither did Neville's
as he closed the door from the inside, and returned to the
far side of his desk.

'One thing,' she said, as Mark put down his handset,

'that we ought to do, is let DI Crowther know exactly where we're going this morning.'

He looked her straight in the eye. 'Shall I do that while you deal with the Revenue, ma'am?'

Chapter Twenty-three

'Rosemary's bank's the Midland, in Moseley,' Kate said, grabbing her bag.

'HBSC, rather. I liked the name Midland,' Mark said. 'I don't like initials and anonymity. I like names.'

Moseley was on their way into the city, for their talk to the anonymous planning officer.

'We'll stop off en route, then,' Kate said. 'And deal with the Inland Revenue after the Planning Department.'

'What about the solicitor?'

'Let's assume he's got the same letter. No. We'll deal with him on the way back. Leave nothing to chance.'

They headed for the car park.

'Do you mind using your car?' she continued. 'I left mine at home. To be honest, it stayed at home. People had parked so tightly it would have taken me all morning to wriggle it out.'

'No problems. God, look at the traffic. I'll tell you what, there are days I feel like getting my bike out again ...'

'And then you imagine what it would be like to be a cyclist in all that mayhem?'

'I've got a helmet.'

'Helmet? You'd need a suit of armour!'

'Newsagent's! What the hell for?' Mark demanded, standing by his car outside the bank. He held his car key ostentatiously.

Kate kept her gaze steady. 'Because I'm suffering from paranoia. Because—'

'Oh, I think paranoia's enough. OK, let me work out why we need a newsagent's. Because we've only got one copy of Rosemary's papers. Because we could be in a fatal RTA and we'd get blood all over them and—'

'Something like that, Mark. You're right. We're going to photocopy them. You'll have one set, I'll have the other.'

'Sure this isn't overkill?'

'Just paranoia,' she grinned.

'Why not make it three sets? Leave one in the car as bait?' he asked.

'Are you serious?'

He looked straight at her: 'On the basis of what's in this letter of Rosemary's, never more serious in my life.'

They watched four single-spaced pages of accusation go through the copier. Rosemary had recorded the numbers of cars and a motorcycle she'd seen parked near her house. Plus descriptions of drivers. She had listed near misses on her bike. She'd had phone calls on the hour, every hour, on days when her husband had been away. Letters with nothing inside but blank sheets of paper. Harassment – no, that probably wasn't too strong a word – from someone at the tax office: someone who had omitted to type in a name after an illegible signature. Someone had kindly sent her photocopies of newspaper descriptions of car bomb incidents. She'd knelt by the car to check it every time it had been parked outside her house.

It would have been easy to dismiss some of her allegations as neurosis: cars could park anywhere, for goodness' sake – look at Kate's problems in Worksop Road! But it seemed hard to disbelieve some of the others. If only the evidence to substantiate them had been left in her filing cabinet.

'Poor cow,' Mark said at last. 'Come on, let's get the bastards that were doing that to her.'

Kate nodded. She'd while away the journey getting those registration numbers tracked down.

Finding a space without too much difficulty in a car park near Baskerville House, home of the Planning Department, Mark cut the engine and turned to her. 'You've been very quiet. Do you want a full-length lecture on Baskerville and typefaces to cheer you up?'

'You could tell me about that little bronze guy sitting near the fountain in Chamberlain Square. First time I came across him was late at night and I tell you, I nearly tucked my hand under his arm to help him up.'

'Thomas Attwood — he wanted full adult suffrage, full-employment, prosperity for all, didn't he? Ah, we've got some interesting ancestors, us Brummies.' He turned to her, his face quite serious. 'It wouldn't do you any harm to go to night class to learn about your adoptive city. Local history. You know, the sort of course Rosemary was on. Brum University — extra-mural classes, they used to call them. Continuing studies, or something, these days.'

'On top of the promotion exams?' she retorted. 'Thanks, but I'd rather practise my tennis. Which reminds me, I'd better cancel the lesson tomorrow — I can't see anyone in the MIT being overjoyed if I turn up ten minutes late.'

Again, he surprised her. 'I wouldn't cancel. Absolutely not. But I'd bloody watch my back.'

'You mean, OK it at the highest level?'

'I mean, watch your back. I might even come and pick you up from the Tennis Centre. Just to make sure, like.'

She stared at him, eyes narrowed. 'You really are serious, aren't you?'

He blushed slightly. 'Look, you make a good partner, and I don't like the way Crowther's doing things. Hell, he only got the job because his mother was fucking someone at the time.'

'Married to someone, was what I heard.'

'Well, the two aren't mutually exclusive, as Neville would no doubt say. If I pick you up from Brayfield at – say – five to eight? I know it means missing a bit of coaching but we'd be at work almost on time, specially if I got the old siren going. You know it makes sense. Go on, laugh – that was my Margaret Thatcher impersonation!'

She laughed, obediently, then demanded, 'Have you any idea what time I shall have to get up if I'm going to walk down there? OK, Mark – you're quite right. Thanks, mate. And now,' she said, unfastening the seat-belt, 'we'd better go and check all the planning officers and see if any of them match young Stephen's description. Could be fun if we've got protective bosses and a strong union.'

'Bugger fun. My kid wants me to get something from the museum shop — if we can wangle the time for that I'd be grateful.'

'No problems. OK. *Avanti!*'

The Personnel Officer to whom they presented themselves was a sari-clad Asian woman in her forties, who sat them down and listened intelligently but was clearly not going to give an inch unless she had to.

'All we want to do at this stage,' Kate said, still calm, 'is talk to someone. No accusations, just questions.'

'In my experience, questions all too frequently lead to accusations, Sergeant.'

'And if they did, Mrs Gupta, would that be a problem? After all, none of us wants to see the law broken and law breakers get away with it. But I assure you, at present, all we want to do is find out who this woman might be. And talk to her.'

'If I say no, you can't look at my files, you'll have to go off and get a warrant.'

'You've no idea how much paperwork that generates,' Kate sighed. 'And how much time and energy.'

Mrs Gupta came to a decision. 'I can't show you my files. Data protection, and all that. But I can invite you to walk through the offices with me, and to check out those officers who have dealings with the public. See if one matches the description … Is it a very clear description?'

'Even to the length of her finger nails, Mrs Gupta.'

They set off together down the corridors of local power. Before they had to look at anyone's manicure, however, Mrs Gupta froze. 'That man there – the short one, with red hair. That's the Chair of the Planning Committee. Mr Benson.'

Benson turned, apparently hearing his name. He smiled, pleasantly but with reserve. Presumably a man with that much power would learn to smile like that very early in his career.

Mrs Gupta's answering smile was embarrassed to the point of shifty. Kate and Mark produced courteous, efficient ones. After a tiny hiatus, Kate stepped forward, showing her ID. She offered a brief explanation.

Benson frowned. 'Could you find us a private room somewhere, please, Mrs Gupta?'

'Let us be quite clear about this,' Benson said sternly, sitting sideways to a heavy table, and hitching immaculate trousers. He was as slight as he was short, but not lacking in dignity. 'Just because an application for listed building status misses a particular meeting, that does not necessarily mean that anything sinister is afoot.'

Mark mouthed, 'Rod Neville lives!'

'Most planning applications,' Benson continued, 'are quite properly dealt with by a planning officer – some eighty per cent, in fact. Only the controversial or borderline ones go to Committee.'

'We're not talking planning applications – we're talking about listing a building,' Kate said. She didn't have time for prepared speeches. 'Would it be possible to – persuade – an officer not to submit an application? Assuming you wanted – say – to knock down a building without fear of retribution?'

Benson shrugged. 'We're all human. However incorruptible we like to think we are, we're all susceptible to something.' He looked hard at Kate and Mark in turn.

'Even the police.'

Might Benson – and this was the merest possibility – be hinting that he knew something she didn't, about Crowther, for instance? No. Nonsense. He was simply throwing the usual stuff about the long since disbanded Serious Crime Squad in her face.

'Of course,' she agreed briefly.

'It might help me to help you,' Benson continued, 'if you could be more specific about the case in question. I can assure you that I will treat all this in absolute confidence, provided I have your word that you'll do the same — to anything not directly involved in your investigations.'

Kate nodded, waiting for Mark to follow suit. 'Who wants to develop the Lodge site?'

'Out at the reservoir? No one, as far as I know. I mean, it's an historic building.'

'But not for long. Not if it can legally be knocked down because someone didn't get it listed.'

Benson frowned. 'Give me two minutes.' He was on his feet and out of the room.

Mark raised an eyebrow. 'Brisk and efficient or scared?'

Kate wrinkled her nose. 'I'd go for the former.'

'God!' Mark raised his eyes heavenward. 'Are you another graduate of the Neville School of English?'

Not to mention of the Neville School of Sex. Or was she really half-way through the course? Making an effort, she pulled a face. 'It must be the building. It has that effect on Benson, anyway. He seems quite young to have all that power — forty? Forty-five?'

'The latter, I'd say.' He stuck out his tongue. 'The skin under his chin's a bit saggy, isn't it?'

A tap at the door silenced them. A young woman had brought tea and coffee in silver pots. The cups and saucers were china. She put the tray on the table and smiled her way out.

Mark was about to pour when Benson returned. 'Tea or coffee, sir?'

'Tea, please. Lemon, no milk.'

Kate hadn't registered the lemon slices. She had the same. Mark settled for coffee and both looked at Benson.

'Things are never as straightforward as they look, in the world of planning applications,' he began, crushing the lemon against the side of his cup, and replacing the spoon in the saucer with meticulous care. 'Oh, if you want to extend your property, that's no problem. There is a very clear set of guidelines about what you can and cannot do. The same applies to most small traders. They want to do something to their shop, we can tell them what they can, what they can't. If they want to change the use of their premises, however, things get more interesting.'

'"Change the use"?' Mark repeated.

'Say it sold ladies' clothes in a nice quiet side road. But it changed hands and the new owner wanted to operate a take-away pizza service.'

'The neighbours might object!' Kate said.

'Quite. So the new owner has to get permission. Now, all this is common knowledge, more or less. But of course the players aren't always small guys. Sometimes it's very big guys.' He allowed his pause to swell. 'Now, sometimes very big guys play games with each other. X owns a piece of land that Y wants, so they'll negotiate. Now, somewhere in the city – don't ask me where, because it's absolutely not relevant to the case — is a lovely old building on a corner of a highly desirable site. We grant planning permission on the grounds that the building is rebuilt brick by brick and someone can live in it. Fine. So then the developers sell on the piece of land — and house — with planning permission to another consortium, who argue that they are by no means bound to rebuild this house.'

'But that's dreadful!'

Benson smiled. 'But legit. Now, what I did probably isn't legit. I took out the MD of the first consortium and reminded him how much he depended on planning permission. So, hey presto, his company buys back the whole shebang and are currently doing up the house. No names, remember, and absolutely no pack drill.'

Nice story, spot how it helped the present situation. Kate smiled politely.

'Now,' Benson continued, 'it seems to me as if the same sort of thing might be happening at the Lodge site. Yes, we do have an application from the owners to develop that parcel of land. And an application has been made for an hotel complex.'

'Jesus — what a wonderful site!'

'Exactly. But I'm very surprised that the people putting in the offer should be interested in hotels. I can only assume that there's a bit of this bartering going on. Land for land. Site for site. Why else should a charity be trying to build hotels?'

Kate smiled grimly. 'Because the charity that owns the land is the Anna Seward Foundation?'

Chapter Twenty-four

Kate and Mark stepped out of Baskerville House and stared over Centenary Square, blinking in the midday sunlight. She seethed with anger. She was sure Mark did too. So the planning officer that fitted Stephen's description was on leave, was she? Back-packing through Greece? Well, it was all too bloody convenient. And it would take time to get at her file through official channels. Time and effort, that was. And then the long wait for the woman herself.

As she opened her mouth to swear, Mark pointed at the Hall of Memory.

'My grandfather's in there,' he said. 'In the Book of Remembrance.'

Kate waited. It wasn't at all the remark she'd expected.

'Monte Cassino,' Mark added. 'He fought all through

Egypt, all the way up Italy – and then a sniper got him. I always think about him, days like this.'

'Days like this?' It didn't sound as if he meant bright spring days.

'Days like this.' No, his voice was very grim.

She tried a different tack. 'But you could never have known him.'

'No. Nor did my dad. His mother talked about him a lot. Must have been a nice guy. Just ordinary, mind, nothing special. Had an allotment, played soccer in the winter, cricket in the summer. Worked five days every week and Saturday mornings. And then he went and joined up, because he'd heard stuff he didn't like and he got very angry and wanted to do something about it. Now, I've heard stuff I didn't like.' Mark paused. She thought he might be rubbing his eyes. 'What next, Gaffer?' he asked at last, his voice hard, brisk.

For now, she would take his tone. Had to. There was work to be done. But later she would buy him a drink, encourage him to talk. 'We go off towards the museum, like we agreed. But instead of going with you to the shop, I stop off in Paradise Forum and buy one of those cheap-o cameras – the disposable sort. And I walk back to the car, and drop the third set of papers into the car and wander off, tutting and looking at my watch as if wondering where the hell you were.

In fact, you're hurtling back, clutching a dinosaur or whatever.'

'So you lurk in the shadows of the car park, ready to take a photo of anyone showing an unnatural interest in my car.'

'Spot on.'

Mark shook his head. 'Don't like that. We work as a pair.'

'Two can't lurk as well as one. And I tell you, Mark, once we've had our nice gentle amble to the Forum, you go off like greased lightning to do your shopping, and come back like the bloody clappers. OK?'

'We couldn't do it the other way round?'

'Whatever happened to your equal opps. training? Come on, you don't have to protect me.'

'Not because you're a woman, I don't. I do because you're my mate.'

She touched his arm lightly. 'Thanks. Now, give me your keys and go.'

Kate strode back to the car, throwing an A4 brown envelope on to the driving seat and relocking it. At the last minute she'd had a rush of sense. If she messed up, someone would have a lot of information she didn't want anyone to have. So the envelope now contained several sheets of the day's *Birmingham Post* photocopied specially for the occasion. The original photocopies were crammed into her bag, now safely slung round her neck, lest she had to give chase.

Tapping her watch, she peered round, sucking her teeth in irritation. Everything about her, she hoped, wondered where the hell Mark was. And said she was going to look for him.

It didn't take long to slip round to the car park from the other direction. No, she didn't want to look furtive, more like a snap-happy tourist. Pity there was very little touristy stuff to look at just here. Just act casual. Uninterested.

Yes, there was someone near her car. Probably innocent. But worth a look.

Feigning interest in the commercial skyline over Broad Street, maybe panning in to Symphony Hall, she edged closer. A crow-bar! Jesus! Hardly your streetwise break-in gear! Well, Mark wasn't going to like having his driver's door jemmied, but it all tied up with what Graham had said about the fires — that the whole thing smelt amateur.

The poor camera was amateur too — not really up to the job. The shutter was audible, there was no motor-drive. But she had him, there, on record. And now she was going to get a nice snap of him grabbing the decoy papers.

There was someone behind her. She waited as long as she dared, then feinted to the right. Then to the left. The knee screamed. So did the man following her who fell flat on his face. She bounced off a bonnet, pushed

herself upright. Somehow the camera stayed in her hand.
She closed the other one round it, to make sure.

Crowbar man ran towards her. Hell, where would an
amateur strike with a crowbar? Not to maim, that was
for sure. To kill. She took off to her right, bouncing
off a Volvo wing, and hurtling down the exit lane. Not
tarmac here. Cinders. Not good. The footsteps behind
were getting closer. Mustn't look back. Think feet. Dodge
reversing cars, leap pot-holes.

And a voice to the right. 'Kate! Kate! To me!'

Swerving took a second off her speed. Another second
to register Mark, running parallel to her. And then she
was brought down. As she fell, she slung the camera, still
clutched in both hands, sideways. Thank God – yes, roll
to protect the head and face – thank God for all that
training.

Nothing would protect the knees, though, even her
trousers.

Several people were hauling her to her feet. She must
fling them off, chase the bugger who'd tackled her. Only
someone else was doing that, hotly pursued by Mark. He'd
better have that camera safe!

Safe enough. Chummie jumped into a car that emerged
from nowhere and accelerated fast enough to shake off
Mark and the other man, who walked back together,
apparently too deep in conversation to think about radio-
ing for back-up. Better do it herself, then, and hope Mark

would remember he'd need to tell her the car make and number. Amateurs might not have nicked one specially for the job.

'You really should go to casualty, with those poor hands,' a woman with a kind Brummie voice was telling her.

'Casualty? She should be going to Twickenham,' Mark's new chum said, all Welsh charm, turning her gravel-rashed hand and kissing the back with aplomb. 'I haven't seen a dive-pass like that since Gareth Edwards retired. Mind you,' he added, more seriously, 'he didn't practise on a surface like this. Anything broken?'

She shook her head. She found herself returning a twinkling smile. He must be nearly old enough to be her father, and here she was, flushing like a teenager under the gaze of those blue eyes . . .

'I've got a first-aid kit in my car,' he continued. 'You should swab that gravel rash. Come on. It's just over there. You did very well, you know. I was afraid your face would be hurt.' His tone told her that that would have been a shame.

She followed. She had, after all, to take his details as a witness.

The bruised and exposed flesh quivered as she dabbed with the wipes he offered her. Both hands. Then he found Melolin dressing pads. All the time they were talking the sound of mobile back-up was coming closer. She didn't expect it to come in the form of Rod Neville, or to come while the Welshman — Martin, his name was, disappointingly English — was applying adhesive to the dressing-strip.

'Kate!' If he'd stamped his foot, Rod couldn't have made his displeasure more obvious.

Martin smiled easily. He produced a card from a slender wallet. 'I should imagine you may want me as a witness. Yes, I'll be happy to make a statement. And believe me, Sergeant Power, even happier to come to the trial as a witness. Provided you'll be there.'

Rod glared.

Martin melted obligingly towards a uniformed constable. Pity: she'd have enjoyed — but Rod was already asking her something.

'Sorry?' she prompted him.

'Graham Harvey wants us to meet him in Steelhouse Lane nick,' Rod said at last, as the last response vehicle drove away. No, there's been no sign of what he clearly found difficult to call the scrotes. His mouth curled fastidiously as he used the term.

'Not until I've bought some new trousers,' Kate said emphatically.

He stared.

'I'm going to have to soak these off, and even I don't go

into meetings wearing a towel as a kilt,' she said, pointing to the bloodstains on her knees.

His voice dropped. 'Oh, Kate – I didn't realise. Let's get you to casualty.'

'Casualty wouldn't solve the trousers problem. Come off it, Gaffer, there are enough people back at the nick with first aid training to sort out playground knees.'

The word 'Gaffer' brought him up short. 'OK. How long will it take?'

'Ten minutes to walk into the town centre. Ten minutes to shoot into Rackhams and out. Ten minutes to shower these off and dress whatever's underneath.'

He checked his watch. 'Two, then. My room.'

She pressed her luck. 'Since it's a lunchtime meeting, will there be sarnies, Gaffer? 'Cause Mark and I haven't got round to having any lunch.'

He leaned slightly towards her, as if to bollock her. 'Look here, Sergeant—' he said loudly. Then he dropped his voice: 'When you talk like that, what I want to do is take you home and fuck the arse off you.'

Rod's eyes gave her much the same message when she turned up in his Steelhouse Lane office wearing not the usual neat trouser-suit, but a dress. The thought of spending the rest of the day with tight fabric chaffing her sore knees had been too much, and the sun was now warm enough to tempt her into buying something less severe, more feminine, indeed, than her usual line. The bonus was that it was long enough to wear with knee-highs, so she didn't need tights.

There was a welcome smell of coffee in the room – it hadn't taken Rod long to start up his favourite machine – and a pile of sandwiches. Kate grinned, but said nothing, taking her place beside Mark and Graham. There were a couple of spare chairs, one for Sue Rowley, no doubt. But the other?

'Has someone seen to your injuries, Kate?' Rod asked, almost absent-mindedly, as he opened a file and picked up a ball-point.

'Injuries?' Graham repeated sharply.

'Someone tried a flying tackle on her in the car park at the back of Baskerville Place,' Mark said. 'Lovely pass she threw me, though. And here are the photos, Gaffer, that the scrotes wanted.' He laid a wallet on his leg. He laughed. Funny, she couldn't recall being irritated by his laugh, not for a couple of days now. 'Mind you, I should think it'll be a bit hard for you to hold a racquet tomorrow, won't it, Kate?'

'Racquet?' Rod asked.

'My tennis lesson,' she said. 'And however stiff I am, I think I should go. Don't you?' She looked round at the three men.

'Dead right she should.' Sue Rowley, making an impressive entrance. 'So long as the place is stiff with the rest of us. Discreetly concealed about the place, of course.'

'Why?' Graham asked.

'Because,' Sue said, sitting down and helping herself to egg and cress on brown, 'we should have most of our friends tied up then, and those we haven't may want a last despairing go at Kate.'

'Or a spot of revenge,' Mark amended grimly.

Rod nodded. 'I'd like to postpone any discussion on this till we've heard everything else. Henceforward, none of our decisions can be taken in isolation. In fact, after the work Graham has been doing this morning, I've taken the liberty of inviting my opposite number in the MIT investigating the warehouse fires to join us. I think you know why, don't you, Kate?'

Chapter Twenty-five

A sharp tap, and the door opened to admit Rod's opposite number in the MIT dealing with the warehouse fires. Detective Superintendent Dick Ford was a man near to retiring age, with a face with as many vertical lines as the outside of Birmingham Town Hall. He scanned each person in the room, giving the distinct impression that he found most of them wanting, especially Kate, in her light dress, and Mark in his peacock plumage.

When Neville, presenting them in order of seniority, introduced Kate as the lynch-pin of the investigations, she could have cursed him for his tactlessness. Ford was clearly the sort of man who preferred to make up his own mind. Which in turn preferred white sandwiches to wholemeal, and stewed tea to coffee. A room which had been full of colleagues at ease with each other was suddenly on edge.

To her surprise, Graham took the lead. Not, she thought, because he wanted to puff his own status, but because he too seemed to sense the older superintendent's disdain for the younger and his trendy assertions of power.

'I originally asked Sergeant Power here to represent us at that outbreak of warehouse fires, Superintendent Ford, because I wanted to widen her experience and because I knew she was a damned good cop. It was her investigations that enabled us to discover that all the premises concerned were on land owned by the Anna Seward Foundation. And it's she who – as you know – has just slotted into the jigsaw the fact that we have an adult male currently hospitalised who was picked up not from his home' – he paused to smile at Kate – 'but from a phone box near Spaghetti Junction.'

'Ah. The poor bugger tried to get home but collapsed in pain,' Ford said. He grunted. 'Pity you didn't think of it earlier, Power. Still, better late than never, I suppose.'

She wouldn't bite. 'What's the latest on him, sir?'

'Still touch and go whether he pulls through. A Mr Blakemore, by the way. Jeremy Blakemore. Has a fine art shop out Lichfield way. You know the sort of place – one picture on an easel, tastefully lit and no price, so you know it'll cost.'

Not for anything would Kate allow her eyes to drift to the Feininger print on Rod's wall. But she couldn't resist shooting Rod himself a glance when she was sure the others' attention was on Ford. She was rewarded by the merest flick of a wink from an eye suddenly gleaming with affection.

'So what's a man like that doing starting fires in less than lovely parts of Brum?' Sue Rowley asked.

Ford's shrug wasn't the elegant shoulder twitch that Rod had mastered: Ford's gave the impression that someone had hitched a coat-hanger upwards and then let go. 'Still not talking. Well, not able to talk, according to the quacks. But at least we've got his clothes off to the Forensic Science people. Poor bugger,' he added reflectively.

'What's known of him, sir? Apart from his taste in art?' Mark asked.

Ford shook his head. 'A highly respectable man. Always the Tory agent, never the candidate. A Mason. Governor of some boys' public school. And a trustee of a high-profile charity.'

'Don't tell me,' Kate said, before she could stop herself. 'The Anna Seward Foundation.'

Ford looked at her coldly: she should have known better than to steal his line. 'Which owns the land on which all those premises were built,' he concluded for her. 'So we now know there's something up. Precisely what we're working our arses off trying to find.'

'Which is why we agreed on this meeting,' Neville

added smoothly. 'You see, my MIT has found other Anna Seward activities. We've got the death of a woman opposing the development of a site owned by — guess what — the Anna Seward Foundation.'

Kate slapped the side of her head. 'I think another officer should be here too, sir.'

'Who's that, K—?'

Silly man. Why hadn't he used her first name? Suppressing it was far more noticeable than using it.

'Tim Brown, sir, back in Kings Heath. He's been making investigations concerning the old people whose cottage was knocked down.'

'The budgie people? Go on.'

'You'll never guess who owns the land next to their home, sir.'

'Spit it out, Power: OK?'

Ford grunted. 'Obvious I'd have thought. The Anna Seward Foundation.'

Graham leaned forward. 'I'd like to contribute my mite here, if I may. At — at Kate's behest' — bless him for giving credit where it was due. Even if the effort had been palpable — 'I've checked the identities of several women on the Police Committee. One of them, a Mrs Coutts, is quite interesting. Apart from being the mother of one of our officers, she is married to a very senior local politician. A very powerful man.'

Ford shifted in his seat. 'Well?'

'She's a very bright woman. Very bright indeed.'

'No doubt a product,' Kate said, 'of the Anna Seward Foundation.'

Graham's eyes opened wide. 'Why on earth should you think that, Kate? No, she went to Cheltenham Ladies' College. Then to' – he checked his notes – 'Girton. Where she got a First.' He said it so flatly no one would have guessed that he himself had once been a high-flyer too. With a Starred First. If not from Cambridge. 'She did her doctorate at the Sorbonne, some aspect of education, as it happens, and then became, of all things, a teacher.'

Sue frowned. 'An ordinary school teacher?'

'If you call teaching at a succession of girls' public schools ordinary, yes. And ending up as Chief Mistress of—' He waited, as if to gather them into a chorus.

'An Anna Seward Academy,' all but Ford chanted obediently.

'But only one academy,' Kate put in.

'That was then. Now she's' – Graham gestured quotation marks – '"retired", and has taken on another role. She's—'

'Don't tell us: she's big cheese of the whole fucking lot,' Mark said.

His face straight, Rod said, 'Which is precisely why, Ford, we needed to get together. The only question in my mind is who goes to talk to Mrs Coutts. More precisely, who goes with Kate to talk to Mrs Coutts.'

Ford stared. And then a slow smile spread across his face and he rose to his feet, proffering a stately arm. 'May I have the pleasure, Miss Power?'

Chapter Twenty-six

'The wife and I do a lot of ballroom dancing,' Ford volunteered, as he unlocked the door of his Rover. 'Exhibition standard, actually.'

Kate got in, fastening her seat-belt. While they were heading for Lichfield, and the headquarters of the Anna Seward Foundation, the unlikely combination of Mark and Rod were setting off for the Tax Office. What Graham and Sue were doing, she'd no idea: but she'd been glad of their presence at that meeting. And of their support over the weekend. Two good, kind friends. Not a lot of bosses would have come round as Sue had done to sort things out. Not a lot of bosses would have leapt into action after a hasty phone call.

And not a lot of bosses would have wanted to fuck the arse off her.

'Sequins and everything?' she asked.

'My wife sews them all on herself,' he said. 'It's tricky, fitting the competitions in with work. When there's a panic on, of course, I have to let her down. But it's a nice thing, to work in partnership with someone.'

'Have you been married long?' she asked idly.

'Eighteen months come next Wednesday,' he said. 'My first – she died a while back. And I thought the world would end. Wanted it to, to be honest. Then I met Irene—' He gave it all three syllables. And stopped.

He might as well have said, *And my heart stood still.* The grim contours softened. Could she ever say the same about her and Rod? The best she could say was, *My vagina salivated.* And she'd no idea whether he'd be round tonight. He better hadn't be, come to think of it, till she'd laid in supplies. Or would they steer a romantic trolley round Sainsbury's, as Robin and she had once done?

Her mobile cheeped.

'Kate? It's Stephen. Kate. Get round here. Quick.'

'I'm working, Stephen. I'll—'

'Get round here quick. I've called the fire brigade but it may be too late.'

Ford looked at her. 'We'll use a rapid response vehicle. Out of the car.' Seat-belt free, he opened the door.

Closing the phone, she shook her head.

'Come on, woman!'

She took a deep breath. 'What can I do if I go? I

don't want to watch my house burn.' She swallowed back tears. 'I want to go and get the bugger that's responsible for all this.'

He turned full towards her. 'You mean it, don't you?' Eyes narrowing, he appraised her. At last he nodded. 'Jesus, but you'd better not have had that phone call. Officially. I never heard it, of course. I certainly didn't hear that remark about getting the bugger responsible. Or you'd be off the case. Let's just assume, young lady, that you've got a chip fire or something. We're pursuing our enquiries into two deaths. Not your house fire.'

She nodded. 'No, Gaffer.'

'You understand?'

'Yes, Gaffer.' Like a schoolgirl to the head.

'OK.' He smiled. 'So let's go get her.'

It was early enough for the traffic through Spaghetti Junction to be light. Ford obeyed the Highway Code in every detail, but still conveyed urgency.

'Tyburn Road already,' Ford said briefly. 'That name – still strikes a chill, doesn't it? I wish I knew about capital punishment,' he added. 'Some scrotes don't deserve to live, do they? And then you get the people who want them locked up and the key thrown away. That might be worse. I've seen "natural lifers": nothing to live for.

And while you can say . . .' He continued the debate until well down the A38.

Talking to keep the victim's mind off things. That was what he was doing. She'd done it herself often enough.

'How do you want to play this interview, Gaffer?' she asked, in a gap in his monologue.

'Soft cop, hard cop? I used to be the tough one, Kate. A natural, you might say. But I'm out of practice, remember. Spend too much time chasing budgets. I should have got one of my lads to come with you, shouldn't I?'

She couldn't deny it. Questioning suspects was so much a matter of practice. That's why it worked well, doing a two-hander with a good colleague.

'Mark's very good,' she said briefly.

'With that shirt?'

'You should see the other shirts. He dazzles the info. out of the suspects,' she said, trying to laugh. 'Hey, it's nice out here, isn't it? Real countryside.'

'And a real villain at the heart of it.'

The trustees of the Anna Seward Foundation certainly didn't stint themselves. The general office, in a lovely building bent asymmetrical by age, hummed with mod.cons. Ford looked sternly out of place in a reception area replete with palms, discreet lighting and up-market magazines. Kate felt equally inappropriate, in what she now felt a totally regrettable dress. She shifted in the low chair: to sit elegantly in anything like that, you had to cross your legs. Now the bruises were coming out, crossing was the last thing her legs wanted. She picked at the edge of a dressing on her left hand.

Dick Ford caught her eye. She stopped.

'Mrs Coutts will see you now, Superintendent,' the receptionist cooed. But not especially warmly.

The office said simple power. The lines of the desk, the angles of the chairs said power. The empty grate, now filled with an arrangement of silk flowers, echoed it. No fuss. No ostentation. The sort of desks and chairs Kate had seen in country houses, five quid a head for the tour. Regency or Georgian, weren't they? Maybe Mark would have known. As for Mrs Coutts, she was standing beside her desk, extending a courteous hand to Ford.

If asked, Kate might have predicted a grey-haired woman, stout to matronly, in a dress cleverly cut to conceal a spread waist. What she saw was a woman almost as compactly built as herself. Her hair – like Rosemary's, Kate reminded herself – had been coloured, but Mrs Coutts' showed far less grey. Her complexion must have been admirable without make-up: it was flawless with. A fuchsia-pink plain top was covered by the sort of suit Kate wore to court: simple and elegant. But better cut than anything Kate could afford. Like the shoes. She'd seen shoes like that in Selfridges, and rejected them, even in the sale, as too expensive.

'I must say, Superintendent,' she was saying, 'we seem to have been seeing rather a lot of your colleagues recently. These outbreaks of arson – terrible, aren't they? All those jobs gone overnight. And, I understand, a death.'

'Indeed. A very sad business. I hope my team haven't hindered you in your work.'

Hard cop indeed! That man was eating out of her well-manicured hand!

'Such a lot of responsibility, educating the young. And of course,' he added, 'we have this life-long learning business, now. I was saying to my sergeant here, I've taken up ballroom dancing myself.'

Kate nodded on cue, realising slowly which role she'd been cast in. The silent, anonymous one, so far. How long did Ford want her to sustain it? Certainly his – the charming, slightly bumbling middle-aged gent – wasn't entirely convincing Mrs Coutts. How long should Kate wait before jumping in as nasty cop? He'd give her the opening, sure, but it would have been better to rehearse the moves first. Except he'd been too busy chuntering away to keep her mind off her house – and her fire. Oh, yes. She could do nasty cop. But she must take extra care over what she said. That neat, friendly woman was bright enough to be taping everything, wasn't she? And she could certainly employ lawyers ready to pounce on every weak word.

'Ballroom dancing,' Mrs Coutts repeated, as if to prompt him.

'Indeed. Excellent exercise, of course, as well as being very pleasurable.' He paused.

The pause grew into a tense silence. Kate's eyes never left Mrs Coutts' face. Yes, however bland her smile, Coutts must know which way the questioning was going. And she was planning to outwit them, wasn't she? By simply remaining silent.

Whose nerve would snap first? Ford – he'd be unflappable, surely. And Kate herself had only to think of two dead women to be able to button her lip.

Coutts. Yes, she was going to break. She looked at her watch as if to hint at more urgent things on her schedule than standing in silent conflict with two police officers. And then – yes, they'd got her – she said, with a silly giggle she'd regret till the end of her life, 'Surely you're not here to discuss exercise, Superintendent.'

Kate's turn. 'I assure you we are, Mrs Coutts. Precisely that.'

Chapter Twenty-seven

'But,' Kate continued, 'before we do that, Mrs Coutts, I'd like to talk about your health. You look a very fit woman. All that exercise we're going to talk about, no doubt. But I sense you don't always feel as well as you look. Now,' she paused to look around, 'I can't help noticing that there are no fresh flowers in this room. I simply cannot believe that your secretary couldn't produce some as easily as she types your mail. And that fireplace simply cries out for live gladioli, not silk ones. I'd say you suffer from hay-fever, Mrs Coutts. But I'm sure you keep it well under control. What do you use, Mrs Coutts?'

'It's none of your business, but I use a nasal spray.'

'And? If your allergies are so bad you can't even keep cut flowers in a room, I'd bet in the summer you need more than a nasal spray. You'd need antihistamines. What sort do you use, Mrs Coutts?'

'This is a gross impertinence.'

'You do use antihistamine tablets? Yes or no, Mrs Coutts?' Ford shot in.

She glanced at him. 'I wouldn't know the name.'

Kate continued: 'I'm sure your pharmacist will be happy to tell us, to spare you the trouble. Are there any other ailments you might suffer from, from time to time, shall we say? After all, we women have all sorts of problems, don't we? PMS; cystitis; thrush: that sort of thing. If it weren't for the presence of Superintendent Ford, I'm sure we could have a nice womanly chat. Your homely remedies. My homely remedies. That sort of thing. But since we wouldn't want to talk about them in front of Superintendent Ford, maybe we should return to the subject of exercise.'

Ford said politely, 'I'm so impressed with the way these young women keep fit, aren't you, Mrs Coutts? Now, Sergeant Power here—'

Yes! A tiny gasp, a slight dilation of the eyes: Kate shouldn't be here, she should be back in Kings Heath watching her home in flames, that was what those minute signs said.

'– she's got, I'm told, an injured knee. And the police physio takes it so seriously he's got her exercising regularly. So I'm told. But it has to be light exercise, none of your jogging on mean streets. No, she exercises on a proper surface. A tennis surface.'

'Of course,' Kate observed, 'exercise makes you very thirsty, doesn't it? I wonder what you drink when you're thirsty, Mrs Coutts? Water? Or do you prefer fruit juice?'

'This whole conversation is quite bizarre, quite surreal,' Coutts said. 'You'll be aware—' She stopped short. Yes, she was rattled, wasn't she?

'Aware of what, Mrs Coutts? I didn't quite catch that,' Ford said politely.

Coutts shifted her weight to the other foot. All three were still standing. Kate forced herself to unbrace her bruised knees. The more relaxed she was, the better she could react.

Coutts was reacting, too. Trying to retrieve what must have been a gaffe, she smiled, dropped the pitch of her voice. 'You'll be aware that I have other appointments—'

'At five o'clock? Most people are packing up to go home,' Ford said. 'In any case, I'd like to talk a little more. Why don't we all sit down? Maybe your secretary could organise a pot of tea. I'll just ask her, shall I?' As he turned, he flickered a minute wink to Kate. Hard cops, it said, were not asked to organise tea.

Neither did hard cops normally wear light summer dresses which fell in soft folds as she sat on one of those elegant chairs. She might just manage a feminine cross at the ankles.

What would the house be like? What would she find when she got home?

Ford was back. He sat heavily in the other chair. Mrs Coutts withdrew to hers, the far side of the desk.

Mistake. They'd made a big mistake. OK, she wouldn't be the sort of woman to keep a firearm in a desk drawer, but there might be other things—

Kate was on her feet. She headed for the window behind Coutts, as if to throw it open and let in spring air. But stopped, turning swiftly. Ford's eyebrows moved up and down. She nodded curtly. If only they were a team, not two colleagues thrust together by chance.

Kate's new position seemed to throw Coutts even more than it threw Ford, however. The only way she could see both was to push back from the desk, and turn her chair through ninety degrees. Good. She couldn't reach the desk drawers even if she wanted to, not quickly and easily.

A knock at the door. The secretary with a tea tray: teapot, water jug, fine china. Ford, facial lines more austere than ever, stirred the tea and poured three cups. 'Milk and sugar, Mrs Coutts?'

'Neither, thank you.' She produced a bleak, self-derisory smile. 'A milk allergy, Superintendent.'

Was this the start of a confession? If so, the tension between them was broken by the bathos of a mobile phone chirrup. Ford's. Whatever the message from the other end, he kept his face completely impassive. The monosyllables he grunted revealed as little.

'Very well,' he said at last, ending the call. He looked first at Kate, then at Coutts. 'I think it would be better,' he said, 'to continue this conversation back at Steelhouse Lane. Mrs Coutts, if you want your solicitor present, I think you should phone him.'

Wherever Mrs Coutts was languishing, Kate was damned sure it wouldn't be a standard cell – not a member of the Police Committee and the mother of a detective inspector. But languish she must, until what Rod Neville – why wasn't he back in Kings Heath with the MIT? – referred to as a little local difficulty was sorted out.

Face unreadable, he ushered Kate into his room. There his poise deserted him. He faced her, apparently wanting to kiss her but unable to. At last, he reached a tentative hand to her face, pushing her hair behind her ear. 'Oh, Kate ...'

'What is it, Rod?'

'God, I don't know what. I think you're the bravest, gutsiest woman I know. You hear your house is on fire and you carry on doing the job. But you shouldn't have, Kate, you shouldn't have. What if the other side find out you were personally involved?'

His fingers still in her hair, she considered. 'Rod: that call never reached me. Dick Ford and I never had a call. I kept my mobile switched off, didn't I?'

'Have you thought of the consequences of lying under oath?'

'You sound like Graham Harvey,' she said flatly. 'Of course I have. But no one will ever know about the call, so I won't have to perjure myself. But,' she added ruefully, 'clearly I know now, so I won't be questioning her, at least.'

He shook his head. 'No.'

She looked him straight in the eye. 'What's the damage, Rod? What did they do to my house?'

His other hand gripped her shoulder. 'Enough. Could be a lot worse. That tiled floor in your vestibule saved you. But there's smoke and water damage to the front of the house. The back's relatively untouched. Habitable, the fire people say. And Guljar – he phoned in ten minutes ago. Habitable.'

'It wasn't our art-dealer friend who did that.'

'No.'

'Any idea who did?'

He shook his head. Not because he didn't know, she thought. More because he didn't want to say. Her insistence on going to Lichfield had shocked him more than she'd expected.

'Rod?'

'It's out of my hands, Kate. Bent policemen don't get investigated by their day-to-day colleagues, do they?'

'So what now?'

'You go back to your house. Sort out insurance and security and whatever. Take a few days off if needs be. Compassionate leave, whatever. Why not?'

She was shaking her head violently.

'I'll do what I have to do to the house. But there must be something I can do, behind the scenes, to help tie up this lot.'

'You'll have to let me think about that. I'll have to take advice.' He pulled away his hands, shoving them deep in his pockets like a guilty schoolboy.

'Think about something else, then, Rod. Tomorrow is Tuesday. Tennis coaching day. I still want to play tomorrow. I want it known I'm playing tomorrow. To everyone.'

'You want to be a *decoy*?' His eyes widened.

'A bit more active than your normal tethered goat, but yes, a decoy.'

'What sort of predator are you expecting to attract?'

'I've no idea. What interests me more is who will be there to catch the predator. Without him knowing they'll be there.'

'Leave that to me.'

So how was he speaking? Superintendent to sergeant? Or man to woman? She doubted if he knew any more than she did.

'Of course. The plan was I should walk down to the centre, and Mark would collect me. You'll let me know if you want changes?'

'Jesus. You'd be so bloody vulnerable . . .'

'Quite. Which is where the team comes in, as Sue suggested. I take it someone will brief me? Or is it more convincing if I don't know the details?' Despite herself, she had to stop. Biting her lip, she turned away. Her house. The house she'd worked so hard to make her home. She wailed with the pain of it.

Knowing in another single agonising second that the man she'd slept with wasn't going to comfort her, she opened the door and fled from his room.

Chapter Twenty-eight

———❦———

Sue one side of her, Colin the other, Kate stared at her house from the road. Habitable, was it? Well, she supposed it was.

What she didn't expect was to see Alf emerging from her entry. 'Soon sort that out.' He jerked his thumb at the tarpaulin where the front door had once been. The inner door, which she'd been to such pains to have re-glazed with stained glass, was a shell of burnt wood dumped on her front garden. 'I'll get a door for you now – no time to hang it properly tonight but I'll fix it, inside and out. You'll have to use the back door for a bit. Kettle's on, as a matter of fact.'

She didn't expect to see Stephen ready with a teapot, either.

His smile was embarrassed. 'I think I may have made

it out to be worse than it was,' he said. 'There's actually not all that much damage. Considering.'

Apart from muddy footprints and something chuntering away in her washing-machine, the kitchen was just as she'd left it. So, as she pushed her way gingerly through, was the living room. Apart from the smell of smoke and burnt paint. But beyond the living room were the tiny hall and the vestibule. Both stinking messes. God knew what the dining room would be like. Not to mention the front bedroom.

'The FIT have been in, have they?' she asked Colin, who had his hands on her shoulders.

'Yes. Complete with dog,' he said.

'Did they say anything?'

He shook his head.

'Did the dog get excited?'

'It wagged its tail a lot.'

Did that mean it had found petrol? Well, that was the usual m.o. for domestic arson. Nothing to get excited about. Excited! This was her own house. But better be interested than appalled.

'I gather your front bedroom's not very well. But Stephen's been trying to sort out the damage,' Sue, who'd not followed them, announced. 'Ready to see?'

He'd propped up the carpets to dry and set a fan heater going. He'd actually saved the curtains, Sue said, and set them to wash.

'If I know you, you'll insist on staying,' Sue added. 'But you know there's a bed for you at my place.'

'Thanks, Sue. But you're right. I do want to stay here.'

'I'll go get my sleeping bag,' Colin said.

And with that she couldn't argue.

No Rod in her bed tonight. A good job he'd chickened out, really, considering that Colin was occupying the living room. Perhaps Sue had told him. Not warning him off – no, she couldn't have guessed – merely passing on news about two of his squad. But Kate would have liked a phone call. Some reassurance that – well, she didn't know what she wanted. Clearly things had gone pear-shaped when she'd carried on to Lichfield and Mrs Coutts; but Ford had at very least connived with her. If he'd insisted on turning back, she'd have had to go. But Ford had not only continued to drive her, he'd worked with her.

No. She mustn't try to blame anyone except herself. She deserved a flea in the ear from her boss. But not silence from her lover.

Whisky; a warm bath, complete with aromatherapy oils Colin had conjured from somewhere; homoeopathic sleeping pills courtesy of Stephen, who'd joined her and Colin in a balti – she ought to sleep, oughtn't she? Just as she was resigning herself to a night of insomnia, however, the phone rang. Rod.

'I'm sorry. I'd no idea it was so late. I've been busy setting things up for tomorrow. I promise you, you'll be quite safe, whatever happens. And we've no reason to believe they'll do anything. But you — Kate, you must promise me you'll pull out if anything worries you. Anything at all.' His voice gave little away until that last sentence.

She might as well be honest. 'I'm scared, Rod. And what really scares me is I don't know what I'm scared of. It's one thing looking down a barrel of a gun and working out a strategy. It's quite another—' She took a deep breath. 'I'm sure I shall have a perfectly normal lesson.' No, that didn't sound right. 'Rod — what about Jason, my coach? He's a nice kid—'

'I'm coming round—'

Oh, yes! 'You can't.'

'Don't you want me to?'

'Of course I do. But you'll fall over Colin if you do. Maybe literally.'

She was surprised when he laughed. 'Only Colin? Well, maybe I can go to bed a slightly happier man. But if you can't sleep. If you want me — to hell with everything. Just phone and I'll come. Promise?'

She promised.

*   *   *

Some of those vans would be concealing her colleagues. Some might be concealing other people. But she must do as she'd done before. Simply trust the organisation. Trust Rod. Who would have come round if she'd asked.

The lesson went surprisingly well. OK, her knees were sore, and the palms of her hands quite painful. But she could ignore that. So her forehands were good, the backhands – oh, yes, there must be other backhands to investigate – pretty efficient. Her serve had improved beyond measure. But as the end of the lesson approached, everything went to bits.

'Kate – are you OK?' Jason came to the net and peered at her.

'Fine. No. Not fine. I'm scared. And I tell you, I don't know what I'm scared of.' She looked at her watch. 'Let me pay you now. Then just scarper. Don't wait for me. Don't try to leave the building with me. Understand?'

'No – I—'

'Just do it anyway. Just look as if you're in a hurry, pack your things, wave me goodbye. And go.'

'Are you sure? – there's a good five minutes—'

'Same time next week? OK? Now, go!'

Shaking his head, he gathered his gear – mobile phone, drinks bottles, huge bag – more slowly than she thought she could endure without screaming at him. At last. Now to her own kit. Just the tracksuit to pull on. Racquet and water into the bag. And walk towards whatever it was that was waiting. In the foyer? In the car park? Or just in her mind?

One familiar face: the woman on Reception was the one who'd been helpful — was it only a week ago?

She smiled at Kate. 'Same time, same court next week?' she asked, activating the computer. She was a pretty kid. Fine blonde hair, in a straggly bun. Good skin. Good features. A book on child psychology to read when things were slack.

'Please. A coaching session with Jason. Shall I pay now?' Kate heaved her bag on to the counter. Fumbled for her purse.

Slowly, slowly fumbled for her purse. Because there was someone behind her. A man in a tracksuit — she could see his reflection in the office door behind the computer. A man in a tracksuit with a drinks bottle. Which he was casually opening as he waited.

This bottle wouldn't have juice.

The bag! 'Get down,' Kate yelled. She threw the bag hard at the girl who screamed. And whirled back herself to elbow him hard in the guts as the liquid flew in a silent and sinister parabola.

Chapter Twenty-nine

'Amateurish from start to finish,' Rod was saying coolly.

No one else in the tennis centre was cool. There was a mass of frantic activity from police and paramedics. Even the Fire Service was involved, mopping up the acid. The receptionist was having hysterics. Good old-fashioned hysterics. Kate herself had never indulged in them. But she would have liked to now. Jason, the man whom she'd trusted enough to want to protect, had tried to throw acid in her face. Indisputable. OK, he'd missed. And by some miracle had missed the receptionist — what was the girl called? Sylvie? — had missed Sylvie too. But he'd tried. Tried to burn her face, her eyes, with acid. He was in tears now. He wasn't confessing, so much as blabbing. He was pouring everything out. Non-stop. To a ring of interested listeners. Blackmail, coercion — the words flew from him.

Did she want to howl like Sylvie because Rod had let her down? Not just as a man but as a colleague, whose terrible error of judgement had let Jason approach Kate again. Except, for God's sake, he'd seen Jason teaching her kindly and patiently for nearly an hour. No. She couldn't blame Rod for that. Nor, come to think of it, for putting professionalism before concern for her as a woman. No, as a policeman he had to detain the accused, supervise the whole operation, in fact.

But he hadn't spared her a single word.

The word he threw her back at Kings Heath nick was, 'No.'

'He's mine, Gaffer. I've earned him. And he knows it.'

'You should be having medical attention,' Rod said. 'Shock. Bruises.'

'Mark and I have earned him. We deserve him. We wasted all that time talking to that poor bastard Parsons. It's only right we get a chance at a real scrote.' Except it wasn't a scrote, it was Jason.

'But you know Jason White. You're involved.'

'I shall know him even better when I've had a nice long talk to him. Me and Mark.'

He dropped his voice. 'Even if I give you a direct order, in this mood you're quite capable of disobeying, aren't you?'

'It's not a mood, Gaffer. It's a simple case of me and Mark being the best ones to do it.'

'I don't need to remind you about procedures.'

'No. You don't. Nor to remind me that he's only the very bottom of Coutts' heap.'

Kate had given Jason a cup of drinking chocolate. She knew it was much less good than the cup he'd organised for her back at the tennis centre the morning she'd found Rosemary's body. She was still in her tracksuit, but acid had splashed back and burnt his: he was in a paper overall. Jason's solicitor – a mousy young woman whose severe black suit and even more severe bun made her look about thirteen – looked askance at Mark, a perambulating carrot in bright tan trousers and green shirt. Mark inserted the tape and did the introductory spiel.

'Jason,' Kate said quite kindly, when he'd finished and sat down, 'what on earth has happened? I thought we were well on the way to being friends. I like you. You're a brilliant coach. What's gone wrong?'

The solicitor shot out a warning hand.

Jason ignored it. He was under control now, but very near to tears.

As Kate suddenly found she was. She swallowed and sat on her bruised hands.

'I'll tell you everything. Everything I know,' Jason said, pushing his hands through his hair.

'That's a very good idea,' Kate said, settling into the grey anonymity of the room and trying to be as neutral as the furniture.

'Mrs Coutts and my mum are old friends. Go back forever. Though they don't get on so well these days. Mum doesn't make the fuss of herself that Mrs Coutts does – face lifts and implants and what not.'

Whoever had done them had done a good job, hadn't they?

'Mrs Coutts says Mum's let herself go . . . I know Nigel. Not all that well. We went to the same school, but he was way above me. Five or six years. And he was clever. I just scraped along. I was good at tennis, that was all.' He paused to sip the chocolate, more, Kate thought, to have something to hold in his hand than because he wanted to drink it. 'The trouble is, when you're a kid, you think you know it all. And I – well, to be honest I had a dabble with some of these performance enhancing drugs. Only they weren't.'

'I'm sorry?'

'I bought a – a substance – from a friend. It was supposed to build muscle and endurance. In fact, it gave me a bad trip. A dreadful trip.' He shuddered. 'Anyway, whatever I'd taken wasn't the sort of thing the Lawn Tennis Association would have approved of.

And I've always sort of had it hanging over me. Know what I mean?'

'Like the Sword of Damocles?' Mark suggested.

Jason shook his head. 'If you say so. Anyway, somehow Nigel found out. And so did his mother. Oh, about two years ago. It was ancient history then. But not to her. Or to me when she'd finished.'

'Two years ago? Has all this been brewing that long?' Kate asked.

'Not exactly. She rang me just before a big tournament and told me to lose it. And threatened to go to the LTA if I didn't agree.'

'Losing a tournament? Are you saying Mrs Coutts was into match-fixing?' Mark put in.

'I don't see her as part of a gambling syndicate,' Kate said.

'No. No, I don't think it was like that. I think – she just likes bossing people around. Manipulating them. Just because – because that's what she likes doing.'

'And did you lose this match?'

'I told her I didn't have a prayer anyway. In the first round I was up against a guy with a huge serve. OK, she said. So I could save the favour for another day.'

'Favour?' Mark asked.

'Her word for blackmail,' Kate suggested.

Jason nodded. She told the tape-recorder he'd nodded.

'How did you get on in the tournament, as a matter of interest?' she asked.

'Went out in the first round. That big serve. But she said she'd tell everyone I'd blown it deliberately if I didn't agree to help her again. I told her to get lost. Said I'd go to the police.'

'And?'

'And she laughed. She phoned me last week to tell me what she wanted me to do ... to do to you. I said I wouldn't. Honestly, Kate. I tried and tried. I even said I'd go to the police. And then she said nasty things happened to people who went to the police with silly stories.'

Kate flicked a look at Mark, who nodded. The nod said, 'Rosemary Parsons.'

'Did she give you any idea of what might happen?'

'Not until after Rosemary died. And then I knew all right. Kate, there was no one on duty that night who should have been there. She must have tipped them all off to do things. Like me playing in Handsworth. You've got to talk to everyone else. She's got so much power that woman. Sorry.' He managed a feeble grin.

'Be my guest,' she said, grinning back.

'Any idea how she got it?' Mark asked.

'She's – just ... When Nigel was at school, he was never – you know, into rebellion. Mum used to tell me what a good boy he was, how obedient. Not like me. I reckon he was afraid of her. And maybe other people are too.'

'So when Rosemary died you got a fair idea of what happens to people who get in her way?'

'Not just a fair idea. Chapter and verse. How this woman was being a right pain and how she'd been making allegations to the police and look what had happened.'

'Was she specific in what she said?'

He shook his head. 'She just said, look what had happened. That's how she does it, see. She tells people what to do, and they do it.'

'The entire Tennis Centre staff?'

'No. Just the one drawing up staffing schedules. One or two others. That's all she'd need. She'll have found out their weak spots. Organised her friends or – or other people – to play that night, so you wouldn't get witnesses.'

Kate straightened. 'I'd like to take a minute's break here,' she said. She signed off the tape-recorder and smiled at Jason. 'Thanks. You're doing very well.' Outside the interview-room door, she turned to Mark. 'Whoever's talking to Crowther needs this. Can you tell Rod? Get him to pass it on?'

'Me tell Rod?'

'That's what I said, Constable,' she said. And then shook her head. 'Sorry, mate. Shouldn't have snapped. But I'd still prefer you to tell him.' And she retired to a lavatory to think.

*　　*　　*

'So you were scared by Mrs Coutts' threats?' Kate prompted Jason, as they resumed their interview.

'Yes. Funny,' he said, picking at a spot near his ear, 'how you get to call all your mates' mums and dads by their first name. Nice and casual. Like it is with my coaching these days. I mean, you're Kate. And Rosemary was always Rosemary, never "Mrs Parsons". But Mrs Coutts was always Mrs Coutts. Always Mrs Crowther, rather.'

'Not a motherly sort of woman?' Mark suggested.

'Cruella de Vile, more like. And if she finds out I mucked up this morning—'

'"Mucked up"?'

He squirmed. 'I was supposed to make sure you got it full in the face. Go round and stand behind the desk and let you have it. In the face. But I couldn't. Not after yesterday.'

There was no need for the recorder to tape all his sobs. Kate paused it. The solicitor looked anguished, but didn't seem able to do the obvious thing: put her arms round Jason and hug him. Kate would have. Would have even now. If ever anyone needed forgiveness, Jason did.

When he'd collected himself, she restarted the tape. 'After yesterday?'

He looked up, tear-stained, anguished. 'Your fire,' he whispered. 'Your fire.'

She could feel the colour draining from her face. 'My fire?'

'I had to, Kate. I had to. But – to be honest, I was wetting myself. Like I was this morning. And I couldn't do it. Not properly. God, what a waste of space! Can't play tournament tennis, can't say no to burning someone's house, can't say no to burning someone's face. And Kate – I really like you, you know.' He produced an angry, watery smile.

She tried to smile back. How convincing her effort was, she didn't know. What she did know was that Rod would go into orbit if she continued with the interview now. And, more to the point, she didn't know if she could stay in the room with Jason and pretend what he'd said didn't matter to her.

She told the tape-recorder she was taking a break.

If she wanted a bolt-hole, she couldn't find one. The best she could manage was the canteen, empty but for a huge TV screen purveying some sporting fixture the far side of the world. Mark looked for a way of switching it off, even turning it down, but shrugged and settled for getting her coffee.

'Well?' he said, unwrapping a Kitkat and giving her half.

'Well, what a God Almighty mess,' she said. 'Poor kid.'

'Poor kid my arse. Your house and your face might never have been the same again.'

'Not to mention that pretty kid Sylvie's face,' she added. 'But how do you resist a monster? That Blakemore guy – assuming he did start those warehouse fires – couldn't resist her, and he was a grown man. I wonder what she had over him?'

'Jason's not a baby. He's a grown man too.'

Twenty-four? Twenty-six? That's all. I wonder who did over Stephen Abbott's flat? I think you should stick with Jason, and I'll get Rod to allocate someone else to partner you.

'You reckon Jason's not above a bit of breaking or entering?'

She shook her head. 'I'd guess someone else did that: Jason would be coaching on a Saturday morning. Nothing to say he couldn't cancel a session, of course. If forced. God,' she slammed her hands hard on the table, hurting them and slopping the coffee. 'To take over a decent man's life like that. Not to mention her own son's.'

'And I'll bet she can afford the trickiest lawyers in town,' Mark agreed. 'OK, Kate, are you going to talk to Rod Neville or am I?'

She grimaced. 'Better be both of us,' she said.

*　　*　　*

Rod was on his own in his gold-fish bowl. He didn't seem to be in smiling mode, so Kate nodded briefly back and outlined their progress.

'But I don't think I should continue now, sir. I'm beginning to lose my grip. Mark now – if you could find someone else to partner him—'

He looked at his watch.

'A break won't come amiss now anyway. Don't want to be seen to bully White, do we? And I was minded to call the team together. There are other developments we should be sharing.'

Mark flushed: 'I think Kate should be taking a sickie, sir.'

'What you and I think, and what Kate thinks are entirely different matters.' He produced a sudden smile. 'But I don't think I could force her to miss this meeting.'

The rest of her colleagues seemed more subdued than she'd have expected on a successful day like this. More apprehensive. And there was a distinct avoidance of eye contact. Not just between them and her, but amongst all of them.

There was no sign of Nigel Crowther.

At long last, the door was flung open and their senior colleagues strode in, for all the world like schoolteachers out to impress dilatory kids. Rod headed straight for the far end of the room and the table kept by common consent for him and Ford. Ford, on the other hand stopped in his tracks, scanning the room.

He headed straight for her. 'You're all right, my wench?'

Before she knew it, he had her on her feet and into a grand, kind, hug. Which brought tears to her eyes faster than she'd feared possible. There was a general stamping of feet, thumping on tables. She didn't look at Rod.

'We could have called this Operation Queen Bee,' he was soon saying, sleek and elegant by the whiteboard. 'Because as you'll have gathered at the heart of this web of intrigue was a woman. My apologies, ladies and gentlemen, for the mixed metaphor. I think her position is best expressed diagrammatically.' He printed Beryl Coutts' name in the middle of the board. Then he drew a series of lines radiating from it. 'Let us start – inevitably, I fear – with her son. DI Crowther is currently helping the anti-corruption team with their enquiries. He no longer has any part of ours.'

That was what had caused the unease, then. No one would have known, not for certain. But the rumours would have been rampant.

'It appears that Mrs Coutts, who enjoyed considerable influence in areas other than the Anna Seward Foundation, was moved by two motives when she – arranged – to have DI Crowther moved to this MIT. The first was to have another very swift promotion to decorate his

CV – though that might have been counteracted by the other thing she wanted, which was for the investigation to falter.'

'Hang on, Gaffer,' Mark said. 'Murders don't just go away.'

'They might do if a verdict of accidental death goes through,' Rod said. 'Which was no doubt the original intention. Thanks to Sergeants Grewal and Power, however, that was foiled: and imagine how difficult the whole enquiry would have been had not the scene been preserved.'

'He was really pissed off when I got Stephen Abbott to identify her so quickly,' Kate said.

'One of his instructions, no doubt, was to protract everything. So one deduces that the next move was to try to pin the blame for Rosemary's death on Doctor Parsons. By the time the trial came round, and, one hopes, a not guilty verdict, one imagines that DI Crowther would have acquitted himself so well in other cases that a slight glitch in this could be overlooked. I once read,' he continued, 'a study of the playwright Christopher Marlowe called *The Overreacher*. That's how I see Mrs Coutts. She was running an extremely successful organisation, investing money wisely, planning ahead well, and then somehow forgot that the trust was simply a charity. Now, the duty of every trustee of every charity is to make money for that charity. That is a duty in law. But she became obsessed with it. Warehouses paying inadequate ground rents are in the way. Get rid of them.'

'Except she didn't do the dirty work herself,' Ford put in. He took the board marker and inserted another line. At the end of this he wrote, 'Blakemore'. 'It seems that Mr Blakemore wasn't always careful enough to check the whatd'youcallit – the provenance – of some of the pictures he sold. Put it another way, he lied through his teeth. The Fraud people and the Art and Antiques Squad are having a picnic up in Staffordshire. Somehow or other,' he said ironically, 'Mrs Coutts persuaded him to run a couple of errands for her.'

'But where would she find out about his fraud?' Mark asked.

'Probably bought a wrong 'un from him,' Kate said. 'And had a little revenge.'

Rod nodded and resumed his narrative. 'He'd no idea how to go about them, of course. Which is why he's still in the Burns Unit, with – well, very little hope, to be honest. And since he'd in all probability do a great deal of time for the murder of one Sally Blake – thanks, Kate! – perhaps one can't hope he will recover.'

'Come off it, sir,' Mark said. 'A bit of justice – that'd be nice.'

'Perhaps he's had a bit of natural justice,' Kate said quietly.

For the first time, Rod looked at her. But he slid his eyes back to Ford, who gestured him to continue.

'Thanks,' he said. 'Now, Mrs Coutts wanted to develop the prime site out by the reservoir. If she could get outline planning permission, then the land was worth much more to developers. But someone was already ahead of her. The Preservation Committee. Who'd applied to have the building listed. It's a curious little building that deserves a better fate than ending as rubble under the foundations of an hotel. But Mrs Coutts didn't see it that way. She suborned one the Planning Officers.' He drew another line, this one ending in the words, 'Planning Department'. 'An ex-Seward Academy girl as it happens. Who had a lesbian relationship in her past and doesn't want it to become general knowledge.'

'Oh, come off it,' Kate said. 'What century are we in?'

Rod shrugged. 'Might not be a problem to you or me, but it seems some people still find it so. To continue.' He consulted his notes. 'How did Mrs Coutts find out? I should imagine she had reasonably free access to confidential school records.'

'How come a school wants to build a bleeding hotel?' Mark demanded.

'I don't think it did. Investigations into planning applications suggest that what the Seward Foundation did want was to expand one of their other city sites, currently owned by Behn Associates. So they would have done a bit of wheeler-dealing with them. Mutual back-scratching. And possibly it was considered a little more "respectable" if a charity was making the application.'

'So why harass Rosemary? She was just one of the committee?' Kate asked.

'Because she was certainly one of the most vociferous. A lot of committee members had problems, not least Stephen Abbott, the archaeologist whose flat was burgled the other day. Naturally all the committee members have been interviewed. Most admit to nuisance phone calls, that sort of low-level harassment. But Rosemary's was certainly more extensive, if half the allegations she made in her letter to the bank have any foundation. Inland Revenue are currently checking which of their staff was dealing with her tax returns.'

'Someone educated at a Seward Academy?' Kate suggested wearily.

'That's the line we'll be pursuing. Meanwhile, there have been some recent developments. Sergeant Power – I believe you have something?'

The team was euphoric, ready to head for the pub, but Rod held them back. 'And there's yet one more success to celebrate. We've heard from the forensic lab. There's enough DNA on a certain plastic bottle to match against other samples. One from Rosemary Parson's body is already on the way. So is one, ladies and gentlemen, from Mrs Coutts. So then we'll have good scientific evidence to match good solid police work. Well done, everyone.' He might have added, 'Especially Kate,' under his breath, but if he did, she didn't hear him.

Chapter Thirty

However much Kate had fought against sick leave, she'd
ended up taking a few days. It was the paperwork that
had defeated her. Oh, she'd waded through it, but once
the adrenalin had subsided she'd had to agree with the
shrink that a little breathing space might be a good idea.
The scars were fading already, leaving her skin as sound
as the new front door. Alf had sorted that out as quickly
as he'd promised, and slapped paper and paint all over
the vestibule and hall in less time than it had taken Colin
to run to earth a door with a stained glass panel almost
the twin of the one that had been lost. Colin had also
found details of an antiques fair where he was sure she
could get a dining table and chairs to replace those the
water had damaged. The insurance company had seemed
to think that a good idea. A shop on the High Street

had come up trumps with curtains even better than the originals.

So when Kate looked around her territory this morning, she felt at home in it once more. Content. As if she were a tortoise whose shell had been repaired. She slung her tennis bag on to its new hook, closed the front door behind her and headed for the shower. She flung open windows on the way up. The sun had brought her neighbours out into their gardens already, though it was still only nine o'clock. Next week she'd be back at work and back in the seven o'clock coaching slot: this week she'd allowed herself the luxury of an extra hour in bed.

Alone.

There'd been a change of name for the MITs – to Murder Investigation Units – and a change of structure. Rod would now be in charge of three teams, all led by DCIs. A chance for Graham at last, assuming he'd want to work under Rod. Maybe he'd be more content running the squad with or without a new superintendent. The extra responsibility had meant Rod had been whisked off down to Bramshill. Before he'd gone, he'd done the decent thing with flowers and chocolates and a challenging selection of books. He hadn't mentioned their nights together and neither had she. Some things you wrote off as experience. She'd just chosen a man whose attitude to the law was much more rigid than she'd realised. He'd been shocked to the core by her cavalier approach. Shocked and unforgiving.

She was just sluicing off the shampoo and the shower gel when the front door bell rang. Post? Not that she was expecting anything. So she slung on the unisex bathrobe last worn by Simon – no, by Rod! – wound a towel round her head and ran downstairs.

'Graham!' she said stupidly.

'I've come at a bad time.'

She stood back to let him in. 'Not at all. I've just come back from my tennis lesson.' She closed the door behind him. 'It feels very strange, what with a new coach and everything – only both the physio and the shrink insisted I shouldn't give up.'

'No ill effects?' His sudden smile told her he didn't see anything wrong.

'None.' The shake of her head loosened the towel. 'Have you got time for a coffee? No, you'd rather have tea, wouldn't you? Come on through—'

The kitchen was bright with sunlight, the flooring warm under her bare feet.

'Why don't you make it and take it out into the garden? Such as it is. While I—' She gathered up the towel.

'Alf's been busy?'

'Alf and his army. I never thought Stephen would have worked so fast – yes, it's all documented for posterity, now – but he finished in record time. And then Alf moved in.

OK, I haven't any plants — all I've got out there is earth, till Colin's landscape friend comes on Saturday — but I've got a garden bench.'

'It was plants I came about. There's — we had — well, the squad wanted to give you something to cheer you up. So I suggested something for the garden. I've got some stuff in the boot.'

'Oh, Graham — that's wonderful.'

'Shall I go and get it now — while you—' It was as if he became aware for the first time of the trailing towel, the oversized robe. And of her bare feet. He was staring at her feet. He dropped his eyes still further, biting his lip.

'That'd be great,' she said, too quickly. 'I'll just go and—'

'OK.'

Upstairs, she grabbed bra and briefs from the mess that was her drawer. When she tried to ram it shut, a stocking trailed out. Leave it.

As she stood, briefs in hand, she looked up. Graham's eyes looked into hers through the dressing-table mirror. There was no mistaking what they said.

This must not happen.

She must not let it happen. Not like she feared it would, not with violence.

Another man and she could yell the place down — bring the neighbours running. Another man she could stab with the nail scissors if he touched her. Another man — but this was Graham. She turned to him.

He had his hands on her shoulders. He pulled down the robe, pinioning her arms. She could still fight, still scream.

Wanted to scream, at the sight of his face. Not the tired, anxious face she knew. But the face of a man driven by forces he'd never come to terms with. Normal, human desires.

Holding his gaze, she smiled. To remind him who she was? Or to welcome him?

And she waited.

He lay across her, his sobs shaking her. There was nothing she could do, trapped by his weight. If only — yes, she shifted, so she could put her arm round him. Then the other. He might not have noticed. All he said, over and over, was, 'My God, what have I done? My God, what have I done?'

And until he could listen, she couldn't tell him.

JUDITH CUTLER

POWER ON HER OWN

A KATE POWER CRIME NOVEL

Personal tragedy cut short Kate Power's accelerated-promotion career in the Met. She's lucky, though – Birmingham CID give her a job, and chance to make a new start in the house her great-aunt has given her. Soon Kate discovers that she's trying to fix up the house from hell, with garden to match. Domestic equals professional pressure: though most of her new colleagues are helpful and supportive, some just think she's fresh female meat to harass.

Some seem to think Kate's not pulling her weight in their current case of the abduction and abuse of young boys. Then personal life starts overlapping with the investigation. Should Kate follow the conventional line of enquiry, or strike out on her own?

HODDER AND STOUGHTON PAPERBACKS